THE FUTURE WILL BE BS-FREE

ALSO BY WILL MCINTOSH

Burning Midnight
Watchdog

THE FUTURE WILL BE BS FREE

WILL McINTOSH

Delacorte Press

Text copyright © 2018 by Will McIntosh
Jacket design by Neil Swaab
Jacket illustrations © 2018 by Jacob Thomas

All rights reserved. Published in the United States by Delacorte Press, an imprint of Random House Children's Books, a division of Penguin Random House LLC, New York.

Delacorte Press is a registered trademark and the colophon is a trademark of Penguin Random House LLC.

Visit us on the Web! GetUnderlined.com

Educators and librarians, for a variety of teaching tools, visit us at RHTeachersLibrarians.com

Library of Congress Cataloging-in-Publication Data
Name: McIntosh, Will, author.
Title: The future will be BS-free / Will McIntosh.
Description: First edition. | New York : Delacorte Press, [2018] |
Summary: Seventeen-year-old Sam and his friends find themselves
on the run after exposing their corrupt government using a highly-effective
lie-detector they invented.
Identifiers: LCCN 2017025279 | ISBN 978-0-553-53414-6 (hc) |
ISBN 978-0-553-53415-3 (el)
Subjects: | CYAC: Political corruption—Fiction. | Lie detectors and
detection—Fiction. | Inventions—Fiction. | Friendship—Fiction. |
Single-parent families—Fiction. | Dystopias—Fiction. | Science fiction.
Classification: LCC PZ7.1.M4353 Fut 2018 | DDC [Fic]—dc23

The text of this book is set in 11.25-point Berling LT Std.
Interior design by Jaclyn Whalen

Printed in the United States of America
10 9 8 7 6 5 4 3 2 1
First Edition

Random House Children's Books supports the First Amendment
and celebrates the right to read.

To Joy Marchand Davis, book whisperer, who
made this, and pretty much everything I've written,
much better than it otherwise would have been

1

I stood in the middle of Rebe's garage and took it all in. It was really happening. This wasn't a school project, or a game—this was real. And it. Was. Awesome.

Boob and Basquiat were hunched over a pair of linked PCs propped on the workbench. Rebe was typing frantically as lines of code appeared in the air in front of her. Molly was poring over brain scans. All I could see of Theo were his black hiking shoes and the cuffs of his brown corduroys sticking out of the MRI machine that took up most of one whole bay. Deathblow was blaring from Rebe's portable stereo, the accompanying holographic video flashing above it.

We'd been working on the project for five months, but now that school was out, we were making serious progress.

Boob noticed me watching him. "You going to actually, you know, *do* something?"

"I *am* doing something," I shot back. "I'm supervising." I clenched my brow and folded my arms across my chest, striking a supervisory pose.

"Why don't you go supervise me some lightning juice if you don't have anything better to do."

I tried to think of a witty reply, but nothing came, so I fetched Boob a can of Vitnik Energy Drink from a Styrofoam cooler half-filled with tepid water and a few drowned bugs. Someone had mercifully peeled the labels off the cans, so I didn't have to see President Vitnik's face. The only reason we bought the energy drink was because Vitnik products were the cheapest, and tax-free, to boot.

Rebe raised her hands in the air as Blacklight pulsed in the background. "I'm in. Oh, baby."

I went and looked over her shoulder. "Terrific. In where?"

"The quantum processor at MIT. We still need more processing power, so I'm borrowing a little corner of MIT's processor that they're not using."

I patted her back. "Nice." Okay, *borrow* was probably not the most accurate word for what she was doing, but if we were going to do this, we needed to get creative.

The door to Rebe's kitchen flew open. *"Dinner!"* Rebe's mom screamed at her.

"Okay!" Rebe screamed back.

Rebe's family seemed to communicate solely by screaming at each other. They didn't seem *mad*, they just had issues with volume. No matter how loud she screamed, though, Rebe's mom was one of my all-time favorite people, and not just because she was letting us use her garage as our workshop.

"You guys can keep working," Rebe said as she climbed the concrete steps. "I'll be back in twenty minutes." She didn't need to tell us that. Unless her mom screamed at us to go home, nothing would stop us from working until curfew forced us to stop. It wasn't like we had school tomorrow— school had ended two weeks early due to lack of funds. And it wasn't like we had anywhere else to go, since we were all suffering from a severe lack of funds ourselves.

Theo inched his way out of the MRI tube. It was a struggle for him to navigate the tight space because of his cerebral palsy. He was incredibly self-conscious about it, though its effects weren't as noticeable as he seemed to think. Theo walked with a limp, and his left hand was stiff and tended to curl in when he wasn't using it. That was about the extent of it.

Theo sighed mournfully, perched on the edge of the MRI machine. "We're never going to be able to make it small enough without a SQUID, and access to a 3-D printer."

Superconducting quantum interference devices were supersensitive detectors that could produce brain images using ultralow magnetic fields, which were the only kind you could generate from a distance.

"We'll figure it out," I said.

Theo nodded skeptically.

"I don't want to be the pin in our balloon, but any idea *how* we're going to figure it out?" Basquiat asked.

"'The pin in our balloon'?" Boob said. "Is that a Caribbean saying?"

Basquiat gave him a look. "It's not a saying. I just made it up." He turned back to me. "So?"

Everyone had stopped what they were doing. All eyes were on me. "I mean, once we have the prototype, I'm going to find an investor for us to partner with us. Until then . . ." I hesitated, because I knew they weren't going to like my solution. "We sell everything we own if we have to."

Everyone started talking and howling and whining at once.

"I'm not selling my car," Boob said over the cacophony. "Don't even go there."

Boob's father had passed the Harley Air on to Boob when the lung damage he'd sustained from inhaling vermillion gas during the war finally caught up with him. Selling it could bring in two-thirds of the money we needed.

Good old Mr. Kong. I missed him. When Boob was born, Mr. Kong was so excited and exhausted that when he filled out the birth certificate, he added an extra *o* to *Bob*. Eventually the mistake got fixed, but of course when people at school found out, everyone started calling Boob, Boob. Looking back on it now, it seems mean, but we were all so young the sting's worn out of it.

Boob was laying out reason number six or seven for why he wasn't selling his car when Molly cut him off.

"Do you really believe we can do this?" Molly asked him. "Because if we're just playing at this, I don't want to sell my things, either. In fact, I don't want to waste my time working on this at all." She shook her head. "There are a lot of things I'd rather be doing. But if we're serious? What's a few junkers and skis and stuff compared to the kind of money we're talking about?"

Boob had been shaking his head through Molly's entire speech. "I'm not selling my car."

"When we're up and running, I'll buy you a Tesla seven," I said. It was hard to imagine being able to afford a Tesla in today's tar pit of an economy, but if we could pull this off, I would.

Boob made a chopping gesture with one hand. "Fine, if I sell my car, and all you're selling are some comic books and sweatshirts you don't wear anymore, I get more shares in the company."

"*No.* No one gets more than anyone else. We're even partners," Theo said.

Boob gave an exasperated huff. "Of course *you're* going to say that, you socialist." He turned back to his work. I wasn't sure whether that meant he was agreeing to sell his car or digging in his heels.

"It's probably a good thing we're running into this problem before we sink any more time into this project," Molly said. "This is a good test."

I caught Molly's eye and nodded a silent *thank you* for her backing me. She smiled and turned to the workbench.

Because Molly was smallish and a little mousy-looking, with sparkly brown eyes behind black-rimmed glasses, guys tended to think she was sweet and approachable. But scratch the surface and you discovered a woman who would gladly hand you your nuts, still smiling sweetly, eyes still sparkling, if you pissed her off.

I was so madly in love with her it was ridiculous.

"And if we *are* serious, remember: no talking about the project with anyone but the people we agreed on," Theo said. "And don't discuss it in public places."

"Right," Boob said. "We wouldn't want the employees at Taco Bell stealing our idea."

"You never know who's monitoring a surveillance camera remotely," Theo said as he climbed back into the MRI. Looking at that big, clunky machine always set my heart fluttering with anticipation.

When Mr. Chambliss discovered an old MRI machine that Nyack Hospital had donated to the school, he'd made it our focus. Soon it was more than our focus—it was our obsession. We learned how it worked, how to repair it, how to read the brain and body images it spit out. We wrote programs to make interpreting the output easier. Hell, Theo learned to take it apart and reassemble it in two hours.

When Theo got interested in something, he grabbed onto it like a pit bull latching onto an ankle and didn't let go until he knew *everything* about it. Then he'd insist on telling you every single thing he'd learned in a flat monotone.

I can still remember the rush I got when Theo told us his Big Idea. The first piece came from something Molly had learned in the online neuropsychology class she was taking.

Neuroscientists had identified a part of the brain whose sole purpose was to create and manage lies. You have to *manage* your lies, because once you tell one, you have to keep track of it—who you told it to, how it meshes with the factual details of your life. The key to it all is handling inconsistency, and that, in a nutshell, is what the anterior cingulate cortex does.

The other piece of the puzzle came from Mr. Chambliss, our advisor in the Science and Technology Scholar Program, who told us about a breakthrough in weak magnetic field imagery that made it possible to record someone's brain activity without sticking them in an MRI tube for twenty minutes.

One day in April, Theo came bursting into the cafeteria, red-faced with excitement. He'd put it all together. The magnetic field breakthrough meant you could theoretically measure anterior cingulate cortex activity from a distance. And if you could do that, what do you have?

A lie detector. A cheap, portable lie detector.

And not some garbage heart-rate-based polygraph that is sort of, maybe right some of the time, but a lie detector that peels back your skull and peers directly at your brain. A lie detector that's right all the time.

Eventually someone else would connect the same dots, or come up with a different way to do the same thing. We needed to have a prototype finished before they did. And we were just the people who could pull it off on a shoe-string budget in a garage. At least, *I* thought we were. Yes, we were still in high school, but when we weren't working with Mr. Chambliss, we were working on online graduate courses in our specialty areas.

"I can't wait till we're finished and I get my hands on one of these," Molly said as she fed the latest batch of MRI scans we'd conducted on our own brains into the ever-growing database. "It's going to show that people who have out-of-body experiences, see ghosts, and sense the future aren't *lying*. And if they're not lying, there aren't a whole lot of other explanations for what they experience."

Unless you counted wishful thinking and delusions. It was weird—other people who believed in the paranormal annoyed me, and I tended to avoid them, but I found Molly's belief endearing. Misguided, but endearing.

The Blacklight album ended, and the garage was suddenly quiet.

"My turn," said Theo, who was again buried head to ankles in the MRI tube, his voice muffled. He squeezed out to pick music as Boob and Basquiat groaned in unison.

"Please. Nothing depressing," Basquiat said.

Theo stood at the stereo and scrolled through the esoteric music collection on his phone. He loved old, depressing music. Eighties goth. Country western from the fifties.

"Ah." Theo touched the phone on his wrist to the stereo's port and turned on what sounded like a bunch of musicians tuning their instruments.

"What *is* that?" Boob asked, scowling.

"Jazz fusion," Theo said.

"It *sucks*."

The door opened and Rebe rejoined us. "What did I miss?"

A couple of us laughed.

"What?" Rebe asked, hands on hips.

"Anything you own that's got any value at all?" Basquiat said. "Kiss it goodbye. You're selling it."

Rebe shrugged. "I'm good with that. You gotta spend money to make money."

I held out my fist as Rebe passed. She gave it a bump.

"Hey." Rebe paused. "We could have a garage sale."

2

The sun was setting as the long, smooth concrete wall of Clarkstown Heights came into view. Seventeen minutes until curfew. I would make it home with about ten minutes to spare, but I had cut it close trying to squeeze every minute out of the workday. I turned right on the path around the wall's perimeter. I could remember the time before the wall was built, when Clarkstown Heights was nothing but a little gated neighborhood. Now it was an entire town inside a town, with its own stores, doctors, schools, and police, and the only movie theater within twenty miles. Plus, it didn't have a curfew. I'd only been inside twice, invited by Devon Walsh, a kid I was friends with when we were four. It had been like stepping into the future. Devon watched TV in a seat that turned three hundred sixty degrees as holographic characters moved around in a 3-D background that stretched past the room's walls to a virtual horizon.

No one in Clarkstown Heights had a foolproof lie detector, though.

I slowed as I reached the collapsed overpass that used to cross Route 304. The debris had been cleared away so traffic could flow, but they'd never replaced the overpass. No funds. Same story with the Bear Mountain Bridge, and a thousand other collapsed bridges and overpasses across the country. No funds. Nothing got painted or cleaned or repaired anymore. The world got older and uglier each day.

I walked my bike down the steep bank, under a ten-foot-tall billboard advertising Vitnik Shampoo and featuring our president's grinning face, waited for a gap in traffic to cross Route 304, then walked up the weed-choked bank on the other side, obsessing over Molly the whole time.

She wasn't seeing anyone right now. Until eight months ago she'd been with a guy named Blaze. *Blaze.* What kind of a name was *Blaze?*

I'd seen Molly and Blaze together only once, coming out of the Pathmark supermarket. For no good reason beyond my not wanting to have to look Blaze in the eye and smile and shake his hand, I'd ducked into the olive and pickle aisle before Molly could spot me. I went home without the Rock Chocolate I'd pedaled four miles to buy, feeling like my heart had been run over by a truck. Blaze was tall, one of those bursting-with-testosterone guys who always looks like he could use a shave. I, on the other hand, need to shave only once every three days.

Seriously, I'm not kidding. Every three days.

Molly had since broken up with Blaze, though. She'd turned me down the one time I asked her out, but that had been freshman year. She might have changed her mind since then.

I'll be the first to admit it: I can be immature when it comes to love. At the same time, isn't it mature of me to recognize my own immaturity? How many seventeen-year-olds can own up to their flaws so honestly? I'd like to think I'm quite mature in my immaturity.

I spotted a war veteran as I passed the homeless village in the parking lot of defunct Clarkstown Plaza, which was choked with tents and huts made from kiddie pools, cinder blocks, and a million other salvaged things. She was sitting in a lawn chair, her silvery artificial eyes unseeing. They'd probably stopped working long ago, like Mom's legs. Farther on, a girl raised her hand and waved. I waved back, squinting, trying to make out who she was. I sort of recognized her, but couldn't quite place her.

About a mile later, it hit me: it was Jessie Grady. She had sat next to me in English class freshman year. I didn't know she was living in a homeless camp. Most kids don't go out of their way to advertise that fact.

I swung into the street to get past an old woman walking the other way carrying two plastic bags of groceries. She was clearly trying to hurry, though she wasn't covering much ground with her stiff, short strides. She looked scared. My guess was that she lived in the homeless village; if that was true, there was no way she was going to make it there by curfew.

I cruised to a stop a dozen feet shy of her, not wanting to frighten her further.

"You're cutting it awfully close."

The woman looked up, noticing me for the first time. "I didn't think it would take me this long. My son usually goes, but he's got the flu. I asked him if he thought he could keep down some saltines and he said yes." Panting, she raised one of the bags slightly. Probably the one containing the saltines.

I lifted my hand, checked my phone. "You've only got twelve minutes." And so did I, but I was just five minutes from home.

"Did you pass any police between here and Clarkstown Plaza?"

"I didn't see any." You got ten days in jail for breaking curfew, unless you could afford to pay the fine/bribe; from what I'd heard from a couple of friends who'd made the mistake of getting caught, it was a brutal ten days in a packed cell. And there was no senior citizens' discount—you got ten days whether you were nineteen or ninety.

The old woman shuffled past me, not daring to stop for a second.

"If you like, I can give you a lift."

That made her stop.

"Would you?"

"Sure." I got off my bike, turned it around. "Climb onto the seat and hang on to me. I'll stand and pedal."

"But won't you miss curfew?"

"I don't live far. I can make it."

The problem was, she couldn't get her leg over the bar. After trying a few different maneuvers, I finally had to wrap my arms around her waist from behind and lift her onto the seat. I glanced at my phone as I struggled to climb on in front of her: nine minutes until curfew.

"Hang on."

She slid the handles of the plastic bags up her wrists so she didn't have to hold them, and grasped my sides. "I'm Tamara, by the way."

"Hi, Tamara. I'm Sam." And Sam was going to have to pray that he didn't run into any police on the way home.

"You're an angel, Sam. It gives me hope. This country has gotten so hard and mean. I worked thirty-eight years for Westchester County, and eighteen years into retirement, they canceled my pension. Just like that, they took it away."

"Sorry to hear it." I pedaled as fast as I dared, riding tandem with an elderly woman.

When I dropped Tamara off, she gave me a hug, then pushed me toward my bike. "Go. Hurry."

I took off, pedaling for all I was worth. As soon as I could, I left the road, turned into the Pathmark shopping center, winding around crushed Vitnik Cola cans, milk crates, chips of concrete. This route would take a little longer, but I'd be off the road and out of sight. Around back, I coasted between two dumpsters that had been moved so larger vehicles wouldn't be able to get through.

Beyond the dumpsters, two cops leaned against their jet-black cruiser. Someone had stenciled *Kings of the Road* in yellow under *Police* and mounted a skull wearing a crown above the emergency lights. The skull looked real.

I hit the brakes, planning to turn around, then decided that was a bad idea. It was still four minutes to curfew, so technically I wasn't doing anything wrong. If I turned around I'd look like I had something to hide. So I pedaled on, slow and steady, trying to look inoffensive. Happening upon police was like happening upon a snake: some were completely harmless, some were incredibly dangerous, and it was hard to tell the difference, so you were better off avoiding all of them.

As I drifted to the right, planning to give the two cops as wide a berth as possible, one of them motioned for me to stop.

I cursed under my breath, my heart rate doubling. I hit the brakes and dropped one foot to the pavement.

"Evening." I tried to sound cheerful.

"Damn right it is." The cop was a big guy, with a big gut and a red face. "You're breaking curfew."

"No, I still have three minutes." I turned my wrist to show him the time.

"Not according to my phone." He didn't actually look at the phone, just went on considering me with sleepy, half-lidded red eyes.

I knew it was a bad idea to argue, so I grimaced, squeezed my eyes closed for a second. "I'm sorry. I'm heading home. I live just over there." I gestured vaguely.

"Been drinking?" he asked.

"*No.* I'm only seventeen."

"Get off the bike." He turned and headed back toward the cruiser. There were a half-dozen empty beer bottles on the hood.

As I got off my bike and set it down on the pavement, the second cop, who had long blond hair and sideburns, approached me carrying what looked like a fat Magic Marker.

"Stick out your hand, buddy."

When I held out one hand, he grabbed my wrist and pressed the tip of the thing he was holding against my forearm. I felt a sharp pinch, and jerked my hand away.

"What *is* that?" I asked.

"Drug test." The cop held the object close to his face, then showed it to the other cop. They both looked disappointed.

"It's still ten days for breaking curfew," the red-faced cop said.

A fresh jolt of fear shot down my legs. "Come on, just let me go on my way? If I broke curfew, it was by a minute or two."

"*If* you broke curfew?" The blond cop folded his arms.

I held out my hands, palms up. "Just . . . please."

The cops exchanged a glance.

"You could pay the fine instead," the blond cop said. "Thirty bucks. Cash." He held out his hand.

"I don't have thirty dollars to my name."

He pointed at my pocket. "Let me see your wallet."

I pulled out my wallet. I had six dollars.

He gestured past me. "We'll take the bike. Bring it over."

My bike. I'd be walking ten miles a day without it. "Please, can you give me a break this once?" My mouth was suddenly dry. "I'll watch the time more carefully from now on."

The blond cop shrugged, a big smirk on his surfer-dude face. "Can't do it, cousin. The law's the law."

Except I hadn't broken the law. Not yet, anyway.

"Tell you what," the red-faced cop said, looking around. "Give us the six dollars and twenty laps around the supermarket."

The blond cop burst out laughing. "Make that twenty-four. One for each dollar you owe us."

"Twenty-four," the other cop agreed. He waved toward the supermarket. "Go on."

I started running, relieved beyond belief, their laughter following me.

I could remember a time when you could walk up to a cop, pretty much any cop, and tell them you needed help, and they would help you, no questions asked. Now, with their customized cruisers, they were more like a gang, shaking people down and making them feel small and weak. Yet the town went on paying them. Why?

The police took care of anyone who dared suggest that the mayoral election was rigged, that it seemed fishy people had elected a guy with no political experience and ties to organized crime. I'd read in the micropress that the president sold off towns and cities the way she sold gum and frozen pizza. You paid her, and you owned the town. There hadn't been a local election in six years, and there were none planned for the future.

I jogged around the corner. The blond cop, who was lounging on the cruiser hood and windshield with a beer in his hand, called out, "One!" He set the bottle down and clapped a couple of times.

One day soon, I told myself, my mom and I were going to be free of this. There was no way I'd live in a walled town with dress codes and a thousand-page rule book. No way. We'd go thirty miles out, to the edge of the suburbs, where civilization met the wilds, and build a big compound where we'd live with no curfew.

By the tenth lap I was sweating and my sides ached. I wasn't much of a runner.

Blondie cupped his hands around his mouth and shouted, "Pick it up, Droop-a-Long, or I'll add another ten!"

I picked up my pace until I was safely around the corner and could slow down again.

Each time I rounded the third corner I picked up speed so I was moving fast when in view of the cops, until Blondie finally called out, *"Twenty-four!"* I stopped and bent over, my hands on my knees, trying to catch my breath.

As I headed for my bike, puffing and sweaty, Red Face said, "Aren't you forgetting something?"

I turned, confused.

He held out his hand. "The six bucks."

3

My legs felt rubbery, my sweaty T-shirt clingy as I pulled off Germond Road and onto my street. It looked as if the Pampins had finally given up mowing their lawn. That left only the Zimets' and Schindlers' neat green lawns to break up the otherwise continuous strip of waist-high weeds surrounding the houses on our street. *Who would be the last to give in?* felt like the greatest cliff-hanger in the neighborhood. I'd have to stay tuned to find out.

Mom was in the living room watching News America. President Vitnik was wrapping a young girl's leg with a bandage.

"What's she doing now?" I asked.

"A kid on a tour of the White House fell and cut her leg. Vitnik happened to be there and dropped everything to administer first aid."

"They don't give tours of the White House anymore."

"I know."

I watched for about a minute before I couldn't stand it anymore. "How can you watch that? You know it's not real."

"Yeah." Mom was eating a TV dinner placed on the fold-out tray of her wheelchair, her black-and-silver titanium legs uncovered.

"Then why do you watch?"

She tore off a piece of fried chicken, ate it thoughtfully. "I want to know what that lizard wants me to *think* she's doing."

I burst out laughing. "That's about the only answer that would make sense."

Vitnik, hard-line ex-general that she was, had succeeded in strong-arming Congress into repealing the two-term limit on the presidency, and now she was running for a fourth. She would probably win again, since she owned the only big news channel left and had more money than a lot of nations.

"Besides, what the hell else do I have to do?" Mom added, sounding more outraged than defeated.

I held out one hand to her. She took it, squeezed.

"Once we've got our project off the ground, I'm going to need people I can trust to work on the business end with me. I'm talking a six-figure salary," I told her.

Mom gave me the sort of smile she used to give me when I headed outside with a shovel, planning to dig to China.

"Well, I've got work to do." I gave her hand a final squeeze, then headed to my room, still thinking about her defeated shrug.

Before the Museum of Natural History closed and she lost her job as chief of security, Mom had never watched TV. She hated being idle. She wheeled herself around in a chair because the government had stopped paying for the upkeep on veterans' replacement parts about six months after the Sino-Russian War ended. Otherwise not only would she be able to *walk*, she'd be able to run thirty miles per hour. When I was little I watched her do it all the time. Since losing her job, losing her legs seemed to bother her a lot more. Maybe she had too much time to think about it.

I started going through my dresser drawers, making piles: things I could sell on BidBuy; things I could sell at a garage sale; things I couldn't sell and/or needed for basic subsistence. It hurt to put some things in the "sell" pile. The last of my once-mighty comic collection was especially painful to let go of. All I had left were the books that were important to me in a personal way: Son of Hulk No. 6, my first comic book, which my dad had bought me; the entire run of Sino-Russian Black Ops; Dork Comics No. 1, which Molly had bought me for my birthday.

More than anything, though, I couldn't imagine life without my keyboards. But they were worth decent money, so they had to go. I damned well couldn't expect Boob to sell his car while I held on to my keyboards.

I was working through my closet when Mom wheeled in, frowning at the piles. "What are you doing?"

"Looking for things to sell. We need money for the project."

Mom studied the piles. "Which of these is the stuff you're planning to sell?"

I pointed with forked fingers. "Those two. Everything except the pile on the left."

Mom reached for the pile closest to her. She picked up a book, then dropped it and grabbed a black dress shoe. "I bought these. I bought a *lot* of this. Don't I get a say?"

I rubbed my eyes, trying to muster some patience. "Mom, I'm not selling this stuff to buy video games or cigarettes. I'm starting a *business*. Most parents would see that as a good thing."

"And what if the business doesn't pan out, and at some point we have to attend a wedding? Are you going to wear tennis shoes with your suit? Or are you selling that as well?"

I *was* selling the suit, but now didn't seem the best time to admit that. "So what you're saying is, I should stop pretending my friends and I can actually turn our idea into something real, and go loiter outside Burger King like the other kids."

"I'm saying you need your clothes, and your . . ." She reached toward one of the piles. Her hand froze. "Are you selling your *keyboards*?"

The shock and sadness in her voice made me choke up. "I'm selling everything." I stared down at Mom's legs—the thin titanium rods, the bladed feet, the black steel casing below her thighs that shielded the fragile electronic parts.

She'd always kept her legs polished to a brilliant shine, even after they stopped working, the way someone might care for their vintage Harley. Now they were scuffed and dusty.

I raised my head, but Mom didn't meet my eyes. "There's no such thing as a college scholarship anymore, Mom. Even if there was, there are no jobs. You know that better than I do. If Boob and Rebe and the rest of us are going to make it in this screwed-up world, we have to find another way."

Mom hadn't taken her eyes off my keyboards. Tears were rolling down her cheeks. I put a hand on one cold metal knee.

"Mom, we're *serious*."

She nodded tightly, reached up to wipe her cheeks. "Okay. Fine. Sell it all." She spun her chair and wheeled out, leaving me alone, feeling like crap.

Three years ago when she was working, Mom would have backed me. She would have believed in me. Now everything was negative with her. There was no getting around it: my mother was depressed. I couldn't blame her, trapped in that chair, in this house, with no car and no buses running. It was one more reason my plan had to work.

4

The streets of New City were empty, the black road slick from last night's rain. I'd been up since four worrying about my mom. In those first moments after I woke, it was like the part of my mind that spun out worst-case scenarios and deepest fears was working, but the part that talked me down and told me everything would be okay was still asleep. I could get into a really hopeless place in those few minutes.

I could hear the Cure's gloomy bleating as I rolled up to Rebe's garage door. I rolled the door open to find Theo hunched over a card table, working on the peeled-open cylinder he'd gutted from the MRI the night before. A cable snaked from the cylinder to a laptop.

Theo pushed away from the table, lifting two of the table's legs and almost toppling it. "I got it. Check it out."

"You got it?" I'd been planning to tell Theo the story about my brush with New City's finest, but I rushed over instead. "You mean it's *working*?"

"It's working on me, anyway." Theo rotated the laptop so the screen was facing him. "Leave your phone over there." He pointed at the gutted MRI. I peeled my phone off my wrist. "Any electronic device within twenty feet drowns out the signal because it's so weak. Stand still. Right over there. It still can't track a moving head. And it's still way too big."

I stood across the table from him, arms at my sides, heart pumping.

"How much do you weigh?" Theo asked.

"Um, one sixty." I weighed more like one thirty-eight, with my clothes on after a big meal.

Theo touched the bridge of his wire-rimmed glasses, studying the readout. "That's a lie?"

"Yes! We should be recording this. This is like Thomas Edison's first phone call." I set my phone to record.

Theo rolled his eyes toward the ceiling, thinking. "When is your mother's birthday?"

"June eleventh."

Theo leaned toward the laptop screen. "That one's true."

"That's right." I couldn't believe it was working. I'd believed we *could* do this, but, I realized, I hadn't believed we *would*.

"What about your father?"

"October ninth."

"False." Theo looked up. "But it's close, isn't it? Either October is right, or the ninth?"

"Holy—" My father's birthday was October tenth.

Theo gave me a huge grin. "It's not either-or. It's giving

us a reading of ACC activity. If the ACC really lights up, it's a big lie; if it stays gray, it's the whole truth and nothing but the truth."

"But there's a lot in between," I said. I'd known our lie detector wasn't either-or, but having Theo pluck that detail out of my head felt like magic.

I couldn't stop grinning. Theo was grinning right back at me, which looked kind of strange, because Theo never smiled.

Theo's eyes were red-rimmed; his good hand trembled, his palsied hand cradled against his stomach. Four empty Red Bull cans were scattered on the floor near his chair. "Have you been here all night?" I asked.

"Mm-hmm."

While the rest of us had being getting our beauty sleep. "We really should be dividing up the company fifty-fifty. You get half, and the rest of us split the other half."

Theo shook his head. "Everyone gets an equal share."

I studied the unremarkable-looking laptop on the card table. "It's completely portable now?"

"It is. It's going to have to get a lot smaller, though."

I eyed the metal beast on the card table and laughed. "You think? We *can* do it, though, right?"

Theo nodded. "We just need money to buy the SQUID, to convert to a weak magnetic field. And the readout is too complicated." He pointed at the blob on the laptop screen that represented my brain. "We need Rebe and Basquiat to finish that zero-to-ten meter."

"I'm guessing this will light a fire under them." Not that they'd been lollygagging, but they had been sleeping nights.

"Everything is about to change." Theo had that faraway, ecstatic look in his eyes. "For the first time in history, good people—honest people—are going to have the advantage. It's going to turn the existing power structure on its head. I can't wait to see it." Theo followed politics the way I followed underground music, even though doing so made him furious and miserable. No one hated lies and bullshit more than Theo. I think that's why he came up with the idea for the lie detector before anyone else—to him, it wasn't a way to get rich, it was a dream come true.

I patted Theo's shoulder. When he got going on his "Dawn of a New Age" talk, I just nodded. I wasn't convinced things were going to change *that* much. Besides us becoming incredibly rich, of course.

"We should do something to celebrate."

"Not a party," Theo said, sounding slightly mortified. Theo was not a party person.

I shook my head. I'd been fantasizing about this day for close to a year; I'd had time to come up with the perfect way to mark the occasion.

"Poker game."

5

I fanned out the three cards I'd drawn, holding my hand close to my face. I'd picked up a second pair, giving me tens over twos.

"I'll bet a thousand." Molly tossed a white chip into the pot.

I reached for the laptop, which was currently facing Basquiat. "May I?" I turned the laptop so I could see the screen, the camera pointed at Molly.

"Can you beat a pair of aces?" I asked.

Molly shook her head, then burst out laughing as I watched her ACC glow bright red.

"Liar. What do you have? Two pair?"

"Maybe," she shot back.

"Two pair. You have two pair, don't you?"

Molly's ACC started to glow again, which meant she *didn't* have two pair. I set my two pair on the table, face up. "I'm afraid I'm going to have to fold."

"Me too." Theo set his cards down.

"Hang on." Basquiat shoved all his chips into the pot. "I'm all in."

Molly spun the laptop so its camera pointed at Basquiat. "Can you beat three tens?"

"Nope," Basquiat said, laughing, tears in the corners of his eyes. He'd been laughing almost nonstop through the whole game.

Molly pushed a bunch of chips into the pot to see his bet, then showed her three tens. Not that we needed to see them to know she had them.

At the top of the stairs, Basquiat's Yorkie scratched at the door and whined.

"Go away, Clark, we're not letting you in," Basquiat called. Clark was a relentless moocher, and the basement was already small enough without a dog in it.

"We're going to destroy poker," Rebe said.

"Nah," Boob said. "You'll have to check your lie detector at the door. I mean, you can't bring extra cards, or mirrors on the end of long sticks."

"What are you talking about? I always bring my mirror on a long stick when I play poker," Basquiat said.

I pointed the laptop at Basquiat. "Have you ever cheated at cards?"

"Absolutely." He paused a beat. "With my sister, when I was, like, eleven." The readout said he was telling the truth.

Basquiat spun the laptop around. "What about you?"

"Same," I said. "Only when I was a kid."

"Have you ever cheated on a *test*?" Rebe asked.

The others leaned in to see the screen.

I didn't even have to answer. "Ooh." Rebe waggled one finger at me. "Naughty boy."

"Algebra, right?" Basquiat asked.

"Right." I'd told him about it at the time. "And once in chemistry, when I missed a bunch of classes because of a respiratory infection." I could feel my face burning. Kids cheated on tests all the time in our school. All the time. They bragged about it like it was something to be proud of. We didn't cheat, though. We didn't *have* to cheat. Or maybe it was more than that. Maybe our integrity was supposed to be worth more than a good grade.

I turned the laptop to face Rebe. "How about you? Have you ever cheated on a test?"

"Only like eleven thousand times." Rebe smiled brightly. She was telling the truth. I felt a little better, though I knew Basquiat had never cheated, and not only would Boob roast in his own guilt for years if he ever cheated, he'd be too terrified of getting caught to even try. I'd eat a minivan if Theo had ever cheated on a test, which left Molly. She probably hadn't, but then again, that question wasn't high on my list of things I wanted to ask her.

"I've got one. This one's for everyone." Rebe took control of the laptop and turned it to face Boob. "Are you a virgin?"

Boob folded his arms. "I'm not answering that. That's way too personal."

Theo raised a finger. "The thing is, you don't have

to answer for the machine to work. If I say, 'You are a virgin,' for example, your ACC is going to react to the statement."

Rebe leaned toward the screen. "It stayed mostly blue."

"Get that thing out of my face." Boob reached over and shoved the computer so it wasn't facing him.

"Which means the statement is true," Theo said.

"How about you, Basquiat?" Rebe rotated the laptop to face him.

"Me? I'm afraid I'm no longer chaste."

Rebe moved on to Theo, who reddened as he stammered, "I've never even k-k-kissed a girl."

I was next. "Yep." I tried to sound matter-of-fact, but I could feel myself turning red again. Basquiat and Boob knew I was a virgin, but to admit to it in front of the girls was embarrassing. I don't know why—I was only seventeen, but somehow being a virgin felt too consistent with having to shave only once every three days.

When it was Molly's turn, her answer was just a whisper. "No." Her voice grew louder as she added, "Can we stop with the immature questions? We can test it without this sort of thing."

"We could, but that wouldn't be fun," Rebe said.

I was reeling from Molly's answer. Since I first fell in love with Molly during freshman-year orientation for the science magnet program, I'd always thought she would be my first, and I would be hers. But no, her first had probably been *Blaze*.

"I think Molly's right," Theo said. "This is getting out of hand."

"Yeah. Let's just play cards," Boob chimed in.

Rebe raised her eyebrows at Boob. "What are you afraid of?"

Boob half stood, as if he was going to walk out, then sat again. "It's like you get pleasure out of making people uncomfortable." He gestured toward the door. "You're not going to be happy until we're all screaming at each other the way your family does, are you?"

It was immediately obvious that Boob had hit a nerve. Slowly, deliberately, Rebe turned the laptop to face Boob again. "Is that why you dumped me, because you think I enjoy getting a rise out of people?" Her voice was shaking.

"What?" Boob sounded flabbergasted. "I didn't dump you."

"That's enough," Theo said. "Come on, Rebe."

Ignoring Theo, Rebe gave Boob a flat *Who do you think you're kidding?* look. "We were going out, and you said you wanted to stop. What would you call it?"

Boob sputtered. No actual words came out, as far as I could tell. I'd been under the impression the breakup was mutual. That's what they'd said, at least.

"Was I too boring?" Rebe checked the readout. "Do you think I'm white trash? Am I too fat?"

Rebe was overweight, but in the right places. She didn't have trouble finding guys who were interested, but usually they weren't the guys she *wanted* to be interested.

"Come on." Boob shoved the laptop so it wasn't pointing at him.

Rebe went to repoint the laptop at Boob, but Molly grabbed her wrist. "Rebe, cut it out."

Rebe yanked her hand free. "Let go of me."

"How would you like it if we started interrogating *you?*" Molly asked.

Rebe spun the computer around so the camera was pointing at her. She folded her arms. "Go ahead."

"I don't want to. I want *you* to stop."

"Yeah, come on Rebe," Basquiat said.

Rebe looked from Molly to Basquiat. "Gee, I wonder what the two of you are afraid might come out."

Now I was confused. I had no idea what Rebe was talking about.

Molly eyes were glowing with rage. "You want to see what it feels like? Fine." She leaned toward the laptop screen. "Have you ever made yourself throw up?"

"What?" Rebe looked like she'd been slapped.

"You want to get everyone's secrets out in the open, right?" Molly asked.

"Why would you ask me something like that?"

Molly rolled her eyes. "The stalls in the girls' room at school aren't *soundproof.* I can't *see* what you're doing in there, but I have *ears.*"

I exchanged a wide-eyed glance with Theo. Wow. This was out of control.

"*What?*" Rebe looked from me to Theo. "I saw that look. You have something you want to say?"

"No, I—"

Rebe grabbed the laptop. "Sam, are you in love with Molly?"

I turned my hands palms-up. "That's not exactly a revelation. Although I think 'in love' is an exaggeration."

Rebe studied the readout. "No, it isn't. You love her. But you think all her psychic stuff is crap, don't you?"

Boob stood. "All right, that's enough."

"I never said that." My throat was tight, my voice higher than usual.

"You never said it to *me*, but you said it," Rebe shot back.

Yes, I had. To Boob and Basquiat, in confidence. And one of them had told Rebe. "You're not using the lie detector; you're betraying a confidence. There's a difference."

Rebe ignored me. "So you love Molly, but you think what she believes is silly. So really, you're in love with how she looks."

"Come on—" Theo started to say, but I cut him off.

"Are you saying I'm shallow?"

"No more than most guys. It's just, most guys are more honest about it."

"Where is this coming from?" I nearly shouted. "I'm not the one who heard you sticking your finger down your throat in the bathroom. Are you jealous because I don't like *you*?"

Basquiat turned the laptop to face Rebe. "Are you?"

Rebe glared at Basquiat. "Does he know about you and Molly?"

I laughed.

Only, Basquiat wasn't laughing.

Suddenly I felt sick, like I'd eaten eleven hot dogs.

Boob headed up the steps to the door. "That it. I'm going home." He opened the door, then paused, one hand on the knob. "I think you should cut this out before none of us are friends anymore."

No one moved as the door closed.

Rebe was staring at the table. I was having a hard time looking at anyone, too. My best friend was seeing the one girl I liked behind my back? The other ten girls he'd gone out with hadn't been enough—he had to have Molly, too?

"Maybe we'll be better off because of this." Molly sounded like she was trying to convince herself. "Maybe it's best to get everything out in the open and have nothing left to hide."

"Nothing left to hide?" Basquiat turned the laptop toward Molly. "Is there anything we're not asking that you *really* wouldn't want anyone here to know?"

Molly swallowed. She didn't answer.

Basquiat looked at me without touching the laptop. "How about you?"

I nodded. Oh yes, there was something I most definitely didn't want Molly in particular to know, and as the implication of Basquiat's question sank in, I felt a rising panic. Last winter Molly and I had been talking on the phone, and

Molly failed to disconnect the line. I, honest sport that I was, muted my end of the line and secretly watched Molly for the next two hours. During hour two, Molly took a shower. Awful and guilty and slimy as I felt, I still had to cross my legs just thinking about it.

Basquiat pointed at Theo and Rebe in turn. They both agreed there were things they didn't want anyone to know.

"Me too," Basquiat said. "We're just scratching the surface. What if we knew the right questions to ask?"

Molly shoved the laptop so it wasn't pointed at her. "This is *awful*."

I couldn't argue. I felt awful. Miserable. Ashamed. Betrayed.

"We shouldn't use this anymore," Basquiat said. "It's like juggling sticks of dynamite."

"Why are we making it, if we don't want to use it ourselves?" Molly asked.

"You use it sometimes. Not all the time," I said. The truth was, I was doing it for the money. How people did or didn't use it was their business.

"People won't be able to resist using it all the time," Rebe said. "It's like the most powerful drug ever invented."

"It's not a drug," Theo said. "It's the *truth*."

Basquiat nodded. The armpits of his Jets T-shirt were so damp, there were visible rings.

Molly stood. "I need to get home." She didn't say *I'll see you tomorrow* or anything; she just headed for the door.

Once she was gone, an incredibly awkward silence followed. We all stared at the floor, avoiding eye contact.

Does Sam know about you two? Rebe had asked. Did that imply present tense? Were Molly and Basquiat together *now*?

Theo broke the silence. "It's good that we know what we're dealing with. It's going to change everything. Business, government, friendships; how people talk, how they think. It'll be hard at first, but in the long run it's going to be a better world."

Theo was always talking about paradigm change this and revolution that. For the first time, I felt like I understood what he was talking about. This technology *was* going to change everything.

Rebe walked out without a word to anyone. She'd probably hung around only because she didn't want to walk out at the same time as Boob or Molly.

When Theo stood to leave, I fell into step beside him.

"Sam, can I talk to you for a minute?" Basquiat called.

I didn't want to talk to Basquiat. Honestly, I didn't want to talk to anyone right now. I stopped walking.

"I'm sorry we didn't tell you," Basquiat said when Theo was gone. "I asked Molly if we could keep it to ourselves because I knew you'd be hurt."

Hurt? I was destroyed. Basquiat and I had been friends since second grade.

"When Molly and I were in the same trig class in the fall, we studied together a lot, and one thing led to another. . . ."

An image of the two of them kissing passionately on the bed in Molly's room popped into my head. "Are you still seeing her?"

"Yes."

I managed a nod. "I'm going to go."

"Okay. I really am sorry."

I got out of there as quickly as I could.

Molly wasn't my girlfriend. Basquiat wasn't fooling around with my girlfriend behind my back, and Molly wasn't cheating on me. But it sure felt like they were.

As I headed down Basquiat's driveway, I spotted Molly standing by the big white birch on his front lawn.

"I'm so angry at you," she said without turning.

I stopped in my tracks. "You're angry at *me*?"

She turned to face me. "You talked about me behind my back. I'm used to people thinking what I believe is stupid, but I never thought you'd say mean things about me behind my back."

"It wasn't mean. I just said that I—" I caught myself. No, it had been mean. Not hateful, but snide and petty. I'd said I couldn't understand how someone who understands science could live in a fantasy world filled with mind readers and flying saucers. "You're right. I'm sorry."

Molly looked up at me, tears welling in her eyes. "You know why I think it hurt so much? It used to be *us* talking behind other people's backs." She laughed. "You know?"

"Yeah." I smiled, remembering those late-night phone conversations. Sometimes we'd both be doing other things, not even talking, but the silence was never awkward. Once Molly started seeing Blaze sophomore year, the conversations stopped. For some reason they didn't start up again after she broke up with him.

"Can you talk to Basquiat the way we used to talk?" I knew it was the wrong thing to ask, but I couldn't help myself.

"What do you mean?"

"I'm just curious."

"That's not really your business."

I folded my arms, turned toward the street. "Fine."

Molly rolled her head back and stared up into the tree. "I don't want to argue with you. I know what you're asking me, and in the spirit of the truth machine I'll give you an honest answer. But you might not like what you hear. Okay?"

"Okay."

"I'd be lying if I said I wasn't attracted to you, back when we were having those marathon phone calls. A few times I came close to telling you I'd changed my mind about us."

That revelation left me a little stunned. "Why didn't you?"

"You're sweet and easy to talk to, and I love your energy and the way you can get so excited about something. But you're a boy. Basquiat is a man."

The words stung. They sank into me like acid. "Just because I don't have hair bulging from my armpits doesn't mean I'm not a man. Basquiat *looks* like a man, but he acts as much like a boy as I do. We have the same sense of humor, a lot of the same interests. We're best friends. We used to be, anyway."

Molly grasped my elbow, stopping me. "Let's not do this, okay?" She squinted at me, pleading with her eyes. "You're my friend. I miss talking to you every day. I was hoping we could get back to being like that, now that we're working together. Now that my father isn't living at home, I could really use a friendly voice, you know?"

"Things rough at home?" Molly had always been close to her dad. Her mom suffered from migraines and mood swings, and didn't have much energy for Molly. Her dad had moved out six months ago, after her mom discovered he was having an affair.

"She's worse since my dad moved out. Always has a headache, or claims to, spends most of the time in bed." Molly's nose was bent slightly to one side. More than slightly, actually, although I'd never really noticed before. It might account for the hint of nasal in her voice, as if she was always fighting a cold. "So it's settled? You're my best friend again?"

"I'd love that. Any time you need me, day or night, I'm here." The "boy" comment still stung, and it would be hard to be friends with her, knowing Basquiat was her boyfriend, but I'd do anything for Molly.

"Do you want to keep working on this project, after all this?" Molly asked.

"*I* do. Don't you?"

"Absolutely."

"We were supposed to have the garage sale tomorrow afternoon so we could buy the parts to start miniaturizing."

"Maybe things will calm down by then." She pressed one palm over her eyes, shook her head. "I can't believe I embarrassed Rebe like that. It's just, she was taking such joy in embarrassing *us*."

"She definitely has issues."

Molly laughed through her nose. "Unlike the rest of us."

We hugged; then I headed home, still thinking about what Molly had said. What did that mean, exactly, that I was a boy? Would I be a man when I was twenty? I didn't think that was what she meant. I think in her eyes I'd still be a boy when I was thirty. I had trouble imagining what a "mature" me would look like. Would I stop joking around? Stop liking comic books and indie music? Would I become interested in mutual funds and patio furniture? I mean, I was the driving force behind inventing a new technology. How was *that* boyish?

I suspected a lot of it had to do with how I looked. When I reached puberty and people, relatives especially, still talked about how *cute* I was, I knew I had a problem. The combination of a baby face and a five-foot-five-inch frame is not ideal.

6

When I rode up the next morning, Theo was standing in Rebe's driveway, a bulging paper bag tucked under one arm.

He nodded a greeting, his expression grim, his mouth a tight line. "It's locked. I was going to call you, but I figured you'd be here any minute."

"Have you knocked on the front door?"

"No."

Of course he hadn't. Theo did not do confrontation.

"Why don't we give that a try?"

Theo followed me up the small strip of concrete with weeds on one side and overgrown shrubs on the other.

"What's in the bag?" I asked.

"I baked a loaf of sourdough bread last night. I thought it might help everyone."

The guy who hadn't uttered a harsh word to anyone baked a loaf of bread to smooth things over. And it would be awesome bread—Theo was as serious about baking as he was about microelectronics.

Basquiat rolled up as we reached the stoop, so we waited for him before knocking. Strength in numbers.

Rebe answered, a coffee cup in one hand. "Find somewhere else to work. I'm out."

"Come on, Rebe, don't be that way." Basquiat had this singsong Caribbean accent he used when he wanted something, and he used it now.

Rebe held up one hand. "I can't work with Molly and Boob." She looked at me, her eyes half-lidded. "I can barely work with you."

"I understand you're angry, but this is *business*." Basquiat gestured toward me. "Look at Sam. He's so angry at me he can't even look at me. You don't see him bailing."

Rebe's eyes were smoldering. "Sam can do what he wants."

Basquiat pressed his palms together. "Can we *please* use your garage, at least? That way if you change your mind, we'll be right here, and if you don't, we'll pay you rent once we have cash coming in."

Rebe made a sour face. "I don't want to see their faces every day."

"Just for a week," Basquiat pleaded. "Until we can find somewhere else."

Rebe closed her eyes. "Fine. Just leave me alone."

"Who's going to get us time on quantum computers if she's out?" Theo asked as we headed around to the garage.

Steal us time on quantum computers, he meant, but I got his point. "I don't know." We'd have to bring someone to replace Molly.

"What if the others don't show?" Theo checked the time. "They're twelve minutes late already."

"Molly said she'd come."

"What about Boob?" Theo asked.

"What else is he going to do? It's not like he can get a summer job." No one under eighteen was allowed to work—whatever jobs existed were for those who had families to support, or so the logic went. The law was pointless anyway. Who was going to hire a seventeen-year-old when fifty people with experience were waiting in line?

"I hope he's looking at it that way," Theo said.

Molly's mom's car pulled up, and Molly stepped out. As the car pulled away from the curb I waved to Mrs. Burroughs, but she was looking straight ahead and didn't notice, or pretended not to. I didn't take it personally—Mrs. Burroughs kept her distance from everyone. I'd actually talked to her maybe twice at most.

We filled Molly in on the latest drama before getting to work.

After last night I wasn't as enthusiastic about unleashing the truth machine on the world, but I still needed the money. The only reason the bank hadn't foreclosed on our house was because no one would buy it from them anyway. Maybe that was a crass way to look at it, but I couldn't afford to be all philosophical about the truth machine. Not that Theo could either, really.

Boob showed up a half hour later.

At a little after eleven, the inside door swung open and Rebe stepped out. She went to work without a word.

Theo and I exchanged a smile.

We worked in silence, only speaking when it had to do with the project. At noon I took a break for lunch, cutting off a slice of Theo's bread before reaching for one of the energy drinks lined up on the table. Someone had replenished our supply, but neglected to peel off the labels. Dozens of President Vitniks smiled at me with that wide, plastic grin that didn't reach her eyes. Without a word, I peeled off all the labels.

Her face was everywhere. There were Vitnik steaks and Vitnik champagne, Vitnik resorts, Vitnik bubble gum. All her products were tax-free. Most people had no problem with that. Mom said before the war—before parts of Manhattan and Boston were leveled, and Russian troops controlled the West Coast for almost a year—people questioned their leaders more. It got worse only ten years later, when the Russians got revenge on us for winning the war by tanking our economy by hacking brokerage accounts in huge banks and making intentionally awful financial transactions in the banks' names.

I let the silence stretch on for an hour before finally breaking it.

"Are we doing this garage sale or not?"

No one answered.

Rebe finally noticed I was looking at her. She shrugged. "I told you I would. You have to spend money to make money, and I'm doing this for the money."

She wasn't doing it for the company, in other words.

I put my hands on my hips. "Why are you mad at *me*? I didn't say anything to you. If anything, I should be mad at *you*."

"I'm not mad at you." Right. Rebe could barely look at me, but she wasn't mad at me.

I looked at Boob. "Are you in?"

"Yeah," he huffed.

I didn't ask Basquiat. I still didn't want to speak to him.

Boob agreed to transport the stuff to the shopping center parking lot across from the courthouse, where we figured we'd have the best luck. Mom said the reason garage sales were called that was because people used to have them in their driveways, and people would *drive* to the sale. Back then, even people who were looking to buy someone else's old clothes had a car. Hard to believe.

A familiar beat-up Ford Shockley pulled into Rebe's driveway. I hurried to greet Mr. Chambliss as he stepped out, but Molly beat me to him, hugging him fiercely.

"Whoa! Down, girl." Mr. Chambliss patted Molly's back, looking supremely uncomfortable, until she let him go. The rest of us left it at a handshake.

Mr. Chambliss squinted at us. "Do I detect a little tension

in the air? Usually I can't get a word in because of all the banter."

You couldn't get anything past Mr. Chambliss.

"Artistic differences," Rebe said.

"Yeah, well, cut it out. You're making me uncomfortable." Mr. Chambliss looked into the garage. "So this is where it's happening—the double-top-secret project."

"Once we're finished, you'll be the first person we show it to," Theo promised.

Mr. Chambliss went on peering into the garage, as if seeking clues to what we were working on. "It's a nice setup, but it's missing something."

He stepped to his car, popped the trunk, and lifted out a blocky piece of machinery.

"*A 3 D printer.*" Theo rushed forward as if he was going to hug the printer as hard as Molly had hugged Mr. Chambliss, but he pulled up at the last minute and caressed it with his good hand instead. "Fan-*tastic*."

"I was using it in the lab at school, but it's actually mine. I figured you could use a 3-D printer no matter *what* you're working on."

Theo turned to us. "He gets a share. Mr. Chambliss gets a share."

Boob made a choking sound. "A full share, for a 3-D printer?"

"And an MRI?" I reminded him.

Mr. Chambliss pressed one finger to his chin. "Well, technically that wasn't mine to give. . . ." Not that anyone would miss it, now that the Science and Technology Scholars program was no more. It was amazing it had lasted as long as it did, with President Vitnik's administration canceling every public education program in sight. Maybe it was because the program had the word *technology* in it, and anything *technology* was good.

"Won't you need the 3-D printer for school in the fall?" Molly asked.

"Nah. I got canned."

"They *fired* you?" Rebe shouted.

Mr. Chambliss shrugged. "With your program canceled, I'm expendable."

"You can live off your share of the company," Theo said.

"I appreciate the gesture, but that's okay. You can just name the thing, whatever it is, after me: the Chamblometer."

He had no idea. I could see it in his face—he thought we were working on some silly little variation, some slight improvement on the existing MRI. "Well, if you change your mind, the offer's always good."

Mr. Chambliss nodded thanks. All we needed now was to raise enough money to buy a SQUID.

7

A guy with a bushy beard was trying on my dress shoes. I felt a little sick. Seeing people handle my things, stash them in backpacks, and walk away was much harder than putting them in the "sell" pile had been. I was going to be down to the bare minimum, able to carry everything I owned on my back like the people in the homeless camps.

This better work. We'd better be able to shrink something the size of a car battery to the size of a ring. We'd better be able to track a moving head, and shield the weak signal from interference from people's phones and microwaves. There were still so many obstacles in the way.

"Afternoon, ladies. Welcome to our science project sale." Basquiat smiled at two women in badly worn clothes, probably a mother and daughter from the town plaza homeless camp, which was just down Main. He and Molly were in charge of public relations; Rebe negotiated prices. The rest of us were working security, making sure no one stole anything.

"Did you see Congress passed legislation in the middle of the night making it a felony to ridicule a federally elected official?" Theo asked. "Now you can be jailed for calling Vitnik *names*."

I shook my head. "I didn't see that. I try to avoid the news as much as possible. Following this stuff just makes me miserable."

Theo pointed at me. "But that's exactly what they want! They *want* you to not pay attention."

"I hadn't noticed. I wasn't paying attention." I laughed at my own joke. Theo just shook his head sadly.

I put a hand on his shoulder. "If we can't laugh once in a while, they really *have* won."

"I'll laugh when Vitnik is in prison."

Boob joined us, probably wondering what I was grinning about.

"We need to decide on a name," I said.

"I thought we'd settled on 'the truth machine,'" Boob said.

I made a sour face. "That sounds so lame. What about 'the truth app'?"

"But it's not an app," Theo said. "You can't download it—it comes with hardware. How about 'the truth engine'?"

"'The bullshit detector,'" Boob said, which got me and Theo laughing. He lowered his voice so the others couldn't hear. "I'm still rattled by last night. I didn't sleep."

"I know," I said.

"I'm not sure I could take having people point those things at me all day long."

"It might be good, once we get used to it," I said. "Either that, or it would be complete hell."

That got a laugh.

"Can someone get us more water?" Basquiat called.

"I'll do it." It was the first thing I'd said directly to Basquiat since last night. I was still angry, but it hurt to be angry at him. Sometimes it felt good to be angry at someone—it felt right, and filled me with a hot energy, like fire feeding a steam engine. Being mad at Basquiat felt like the fire was burning *me*.

I grabbed the big thermos and headed for the water station near the homeless camp.

If the rest of us didn't quite fit the stereotype of smart kids (with the possible exception of Theo), Basquiat was the anti-stereotype. He was on the football team. He was good-looking and charming. He could have claimed his place at the lunch table of the social elite of Clarkstown High long ago. Instead, he stuck with us.

When Eddie Reich started spreading a rumor that Rebe stuffed her bra with toilet paper, Basquiat pinned him against a locker and promised to pound him to jelly if he didn't apologize to Rebe. Even though I had arms like pipe cleaners, I'd never been bullied in school, and I was pretty sure that was because Miller Basquiat was my best friend. On top of all that, the poor guy had lost his little sister when he was eight, when she fell off their deck. It was tough to stay mad at him. He deserved a mile of slack. But Molly . . . How could he hook up with Molly behind my back?

"Sam?" someone called.

I looked around. A guy in a suit with a buzz cut was hurrying toward me.

"Got a minute?" he called.

"Sure." I was trying to figure out how he knew me. I didn't recognize him—he was white, in his twenties, dark hair and eyes, a Long Island accent.

As he reached me, he held out his hand. "Xavier Leaf."

"Sam Gregorious."

"I know." He was standing just a little too close. I took a half step back and he closed the space again, plus an additional two inches. I could smell his aftershave. "We're both busy people, so let me get right to the point. You're working on something that intrigues the firm I work for, and they would like to discuss—"

"Where did you hear that?"

He gave me a big smile, clapped my shoulder. "Come on, Sam. No one can keep a secret these days."

I licked my lips, which were suddenly dry. "We haven't talked about it, tweeted about it, or posted selfies of us working on it. I don't understand how some tech firm heard about us working on something in our garage."

He was one of those relatively good-looking, relatively well-built, relatively tall men who ooze confidence, and relish the fact that you don't. "Let's put it this way. The people I work for are in the business of knowing other people's business. The important thing is, they want to buy the rights to your technology, and they're willing to pay above fair market." He leaned in even closer, and this time I pulled back emphatically. "We're talking seven figures here, Sam. And the number does not begin with a one. In exchange, you turn over your research, forswear all rights to develop this technology, and agree never to speak about it to anyone."

I mentally laid out a number with a tail of six zeros. Millions. He was talking about millions.

We'd talked about this possibility, and agreed we wanted to own the truth app. If it was ours, the sky was the limit. One day we'd be on TV, telling the story of how we started TruthCorp in our garage. Assuming the offer was legit, it meant we were on the right track.

"I can take an offer to my partners, but I'm telling you right now, they won't be interested."

Xavier Leaf looked at the ground, shook his head like he was disappointed. "Sammy, you really want to take this offer."

A woman pushing a baby carriage passed us. As we waited, I looked up and down the trash-strewn sidewalk, wondering why this guy had approached me *here*. Why hadn't he set up a meeting with the five of us in his company's swanky office? Come to think of it—

"How did you find me here?"

Xavier Leaf shrugged. "My employers can find you anywhere, Sam. Your friends, too. Theo. Molly. Rebe. Basquiat."

He rolled his eyes toward the sky. "Who am I forgetting? Oh, right—Boob! How could I forget a guy named Boob? Where I went to school, they'd have kicked his ass every day until either he changed it or moved away."

The way he had ticked through our names gave me a chill. And here we'd thought Theo was being paranoid.

"Unless they keep you kids in the genius program completely separate from the rank and file so they can't pick on you?" He spread his hands. "I'm not sure how it works."

"I'd like to watch someone pick on Miller Basquiat."

Leaf pointed at me. "That's true. I forgot he was a running back. You're right, no one would screw with that guy."

"Give me your number. I'll let you know."

Leaf handed me a card. I shoved it in my pocket.

"I really hope you take the offer, because you seem like a nice kid. These are serious people, Sam."

"So are we."

He smiled. "You think you are, but you're not. It's tough to be serious when you're seventeen." He turned, raised one hand. "Good luck with your garage sale." The way he said it made it clear just how pathetic he thought a garage sale was.

8

"How did he know where to find you?" Boob asked for the tenth time.

"I think that was the point," Molly said. "To show us he could find us anywhere. It's shock and awe, to make us feel weak so we'll sell."

"We *should* sell," Boob said.

"*No.*" Theo put a protective hand on the laptop. "They'll probably keep the technology secret and use it to their own advantage. Or sell it to the government. I want to disrupt the status quo, not *empower* it."

"We talked about this," Basquiat said. "We're not going to let some corporation steal this from us."

"I say we take it," Rebe said. "Millions of dollars, guaranteed?"

I was happy to hear Theo was on my side. It was four to two against selling, but in fairness, even if Theo's was the only no vote, he should have gotten his way.

Boob dragged one hand through his close-cropped hair. "Who told them we were working on it?" He looked around. "One of us leaked this, after Theo warned us a thousand times not to say anything to anyone." He pointed at the ground. "Right here, right now, everyone needs to say who they told." He pointed at me. "Who have you told?"

"My mother. Period. Just like we agreed."

"No one else? You swear?"

"You want me to cross my heart and hope to die?" I huffed in frustration. "You know what? If we're going to do this, let's do it right, so there's no lingering suspicion."

"Good," Theo said. "I want to test the new modifications anyway."

I turned the laptop toward Rebe. "Who have you told about our project?"

"The pope," Rebe said. "And Santa." She ticked the names off with her fingers as the true/false meter rose toward ten, also known as *Pants on Fire*. "God, Luke Skywalker, the president—"

"Cut it out, Rebe," Boob said. "Who have you told?"

Rebe looked at Boob, resting her chin on the backs of her fingers like a cutesy model. "No one. I told my parents it was a science project. I told my sister it was none of her damned business."

The virtual needle didn't budge. It sat at zero. Rebe was telling the truth.

Boob consulted the list he'd created. "So we know there are seven people besides us who know." Boob neglected to mention that he was responsible for *three* of them. "We need to interrogate those people."

9

Boob, who was slouched on the beanbag chair in the corner of Basquiat's basement, muttered to himself. Molly was looking up something on her phone. Basquiat was sitting on the floor hugging his knees, staring off into space.

"How can they know?" Rebe asked. "If nobody told them, how can they know?"

"One of us must have said something to someone, but doesn't remember," I suggested. "If you don't remember, it wouldn't register as a lie."

"That seems like a stretch," Basquiat said. "Theo reminds us about six times a day that this needs to stay secret. I can't imagine one of us telling someone and then *forgetting*."

I threw my hands in the air. "Then how did they find out?"

"I don't know." Basquiat bumped his forehead with his fist. "I don't know. I don't know. I don't know."

My phone rang.

"Sam? Xavier Leaf."

"Hi there, Xavier. We were just talking about you."

Everyone moved closer.

"Have you had a chance to discuss our proposition with your partners? I know we never actually talked figures."

"I'm not sure we've discussed anything *but* your proposition."

"Let me fill you in on the details. The offer is eight point five million. You turn over all documents and hardware relating to the project and sign a nondisclosure and noncompete agreement."

I almost asked him to repeat the number. *Eight?* Had he said *eight?* "Hold a minute." I muted the phone. "They're offering eight point five million."

"What?" Boob clapped a palm to his forehead. "Oh my God."

"Two, eight—the principle's the same," Basquiat said. "They're offering it because the truth app is worth ten times that."

"He's waiting. Thumbs-up or thumbs-down?" I said.

Rebe's was the only thumbs-up vote. I looked at Boob, eyebrows raised.

"Screw them," Boob said.

I looked at Rebe, who was still giving a thumbs-up.

"Okay, fine." She turned her thumb down. "Screw them. Let's go for the big bucks."

Basquiat leaped to his feet, raced over, and hugged Rebe.

I unmuted my phone. "We took a vote, and I'm afraid it's a unanimous no."

"Wow. I'm shocked. I don't think that was the right move."

"Excuse me, but this is our project. We developed it. If we don't want to sell it, that's our business."

Leaf heaved a sigh. "I don't really think it's that simple."

"What's that supposed to mean?" From the start, there'd been an undertone when Leaf spoke, like a bully blocking me from getting to my locker.

"I already told you, Sam. I represent serious people."

"And I told *you*, we're serious, too."

Rebe held out her hand. "Let me talk to him."

"Take another vote, Sam. Get it right this time. Call me back." The line went dead.

"What did he say?" Rebe asked.

"He said we should take another vote and get it right this time, because he works for serious people."

Theo peeled his phone off his wrist, turned it around, and popped the tiny door off the back. He pried the lithium-ion battery out with his fingernail. He gestured at Boob's phone. "Take out your batteries. *Everybody*. This has to be how they tracked Sam to the flea market. They hacked into a GPS satellite."

When we'd all complied, Theo looked around and retrieved his backpack from the couch. "We have to get to work. We have to finish this project and get the truth machine into the world as soon as possible. Whenever we're together, we have to take our batteries out of our phones. We make sure nothing is connected to the net in the workshop."

"Give me those." Rebe snatched up the phones. "I'll disable the interactive functions so we can at least use them to lurk."

Watching Rebe work a phone was like watching a concert pianist play Mozart. She whispered commands that I didn't understand while simultaneously tapping nonstop as subscreens opened inside subscreens. It was hard to believe the phone was the same device as mine. I couldn't help wondering what Rebe might be able to do if she had a state-of-the-art system instead of the ten-year-old crap we could afford.

She handed me my phone. I strapped it back on my wrist.

"How are we going to communicate with people if we can't do anything with these but lurk?" I asked.

"Face to face," Rebe said.

"Night and day. We have to work night and day until we're done." Theo pushed the bridge of his glasses, looked at me. "Do we have enough money to buy the SQUID?"

I looked at Boob. "As soon as he sells his car, we do."

Boob cursed under his breath.

"Please. Sell the car," Theo implored. "If the project fails, I'll find a way to pay you back. You've got my word. We have an opportunity to make that mean something again, when someone gives their word. We can't lose it. We just can't."

10

It was dark, and raining, when I left Rebe's, my rear tire spraying water up the back of my shirt.

The door of a shiny black Lexus parked along Scher Drive opened. A black umbrella unfolded as a man stepped out.

I slowed, pulled to stop alongside Xavier Leaf.

"Not a very nice evening for a bike ride."

I didn't answer.

He gestured toward the rear door of the Lexus. "Get in. Let's talk."

I remained straddling my bike. Ms. Holbrook, our social studies teacher, once told us part of winning a negotiation was to take control of the situation—who sits where, who talks when—because it makes your adversary feel like a child. Maybe Leaf just wanted to stay warm and dry, but I wasn't going to let him tell me where to sit. "What do you want?"

Leaf looked into the dark sky from under his umbrella. "The offer is seven point five million. It drops a million a day."

"So in eight days it'll be zero, and you'll stop bothering us."

Raindrops pattered on Leaf's umbrella. "Man. I'm trying to help you, and you're just not getting it."

I stood still, rain pouring down my face, shocked by his words. There was no mistaking it this time—it was a threat. "What are you saying?"

He tilted his head. His brown eyes were cold and flat, like a lizard's. "You know, when I was in high school there was this kid named Arthur Modell. Skinny kid. He had a mouth on him, and ended up getting into an argument with this girl, clueless to the fact that her boyfriend was Ralph Shapiro, whose nickname was Conan the Barbarian. Conan leveled Arthur with one punch." Leaf demonstrated the knockout punch in slow motion. "But he didn't stop there. He lifted Arthur off the floor *by his hair* and was about to punch him again when guess what idiot stepped in to stop him?"

He waited for me to guess. I waited for him to make his point. Since I didn't know where Leaf had gone to high school, or when, the answer seemed pretty damned obvious.

He pointed to a thin scar running through his right eyebrow. "I'd like to think I put up a better fight than Arthur, but Conan gave me this, along with a lot of bruises. My point is, I'm one of the good guys. I'm trying to step in before you guys get creamed." He got into his Lexus. "Tomorrow the offer is six point five."

I clutched my bike's handlebars, too shaken to ride.

11

Mom leaned so far forward, her hands gripping the wheel-chair's armrests, that I was sure she was going to topple out of it.

"Seven and a half *million* dollars? Is he serious?"

"I think so." *These are serious people,* Xavier Leaf had told me, although he'd clearly meant it in a different way, as a threat.

She pressed one finger to her lower lip. "Both times he approached you in the street, though. That sounds like a scam." She held out her hand. "Let me see the card."

Mom studied it, turned it over, held it up to the light. "We have to contact a lawyer. A lawyer's going to want ten percent, but it's the only way to be sure they don't cheat you."

"I told you, we don't want to sell."

"Sam, it's *seven point five* million *dollars.* Do your friends' parents know about this?"

"It's none of their business. *We* did this, not our parents. You gave me grief about selling my *dress* shoes to fund the project, now you're going to jump in and tell me what to do?"

Suddenly I wasn't so sure about this plan. Mom had been in a Special Ops unit after being outfitted with bionic legs. She understood threats and intimidation. I figured she could help me figure out whether the threat was real, and if it was, help us deal with it. Instead, she was latching on to the damned money.

"You can't take a chance with this much money on the table. Your invention might not work, or someone could beat you to it." She threw her hands in the air. "How are you going to manufacture it? Who's going to distribute it?"

"We have ideas. We'll sort it out once we have a working prototype."

Mom swept Leaf's business card from the coffee table. "I'm calling him."

I lunged, ripped the card from her fingers. "Did you hear what I said? They're *criminals*. They probably surveilled our phones. They threatened us."

"*Everyone's* a criminal," Mom said through her teeth. She tossed her hair out of her face. "I lost *one* leg in that firefight in Portland." She slapped her right leg. "They cut *this* one off because you can't run thirty miles an hour if one of your legs is mechanical and the other isn't."

I nodded impatiently—she'd told me this a dozen times.

"If they'd left that leg, I wouldn't be in *this*." She slapped one arm of her wheelchair. "Of *course* they're criminals. That's why we hire a criminal of our own to make sure you're not cheated."

She was so cynical. She had no faith in anyone, and that included me.

"Even if I wanted to, it's not my decision," I said. "There are six of us. Theo's done half the work, and he doesn't even care about the money."

Mom jerked her head back in surprise. "What does he want, then?"

"He wants the future to be bullshit-free."

The answer threw her. It wasn't what she'd expected. I don't think she'd really considered the full implications of the truth machine until that moment.

"It's tough to be a criminal if everyone knows you're a criminal. Theo thinks whoever Leaf works for will keep the truth app for themselves. They'll use it to rig the stock market, or sell it to the government for billions."

Her eyes went soft, unfocused. "Theo sounds paranoid," Mom said, but she was staring off into space, distracted, as she said it.

12

Molly had skinny bird legs, and sort of walked like a bird, her head bobbing from side to side. I liked noticing her flaws. It gave me hope. And that was kind of pathetic, really. I thought a lot of pathetic things when I was tired, and right now I was exhausted.

I sat on the grass beside Molly and grabbed a slice of the pizza that had just been delivered by a guy on a motorized bicycle. No one wanted to eat in the garage. We were sick of the garage.

Theo had a slice in his good hand, the package containing the newly arrived SQUID nestled in his lap like a beloved pet as he double-checked Rebe and Basquiat's work.

I learned how hard-core Theo was on the second day of the science magnet program, when I went into the men's room carrying a comic and spotted Theo's ratty tan loafers through the gap at the bottom of the stall. Data printouts were spread on the floor around him. I read comics on the toilet; Theo pored over data.

Boob had opened a screen the size of a candy bar, and was taking advantage of the break to catch up on his favorite microchannel stars.

"Who are you watching?" I asked.

"Silhouette Lark, baby." Boob grabbed a slice of pizza without taking his eyes off the screen. "That's who we need to get this guy off our backs. Silhouette Lark."

"I like her," Rebe said. "She's like two feet tall, but she takes absolutely no crap."

I watched Silhouette over Boob's shoulder. She couldn't have been more than five foot one, had a gold Afro the size of a small moon, and wore matching gold lipstick. She was grocery shopping. A swarm of penny-sized screens, each with a tiny face in it, swirled in the air behind her. Silhouette had one of those state-of-the-art phone systems that allowed her followers to open screens in the air so she could see them (except Boob, whose phone was no longer interactive). It was a bizarre, amazing sight.

Anyone could post a plea for a bully bust on her wall, but while taking down bullies as millions looked on was Silhouette Lark's brand, her success was as much about her high-energy, take-no-prisoners personality. Every moment of her life was a performance. You could watch her pretty much 24-7. I'd often suspected her channel was computer generated, but she insisted she was, as she put it, "all natural."

The front door opened, and one of Rebe's relatives

came out, a guy in his thirties who rose up on his toes as he walked, like he was a bad dude. There were seventeen relatives living in Rebe's house. Maybe more—Rebe hadn't given us an update in a while. The guy was heading toward the street but paused to look us over.

"What do you all *do* in there all day long?"

"We're building a time machine," Rebe said.

"Can I have a slice?" Rebe's uncle, or cousin, asked.

"No."

The guy snapped his fingers to express his disappointment, then headed for the street.

"That sandbag and I share twenty-five percent of the same genetic material." Rebe took a bite of her slice, wiped away a string of cheese that swung across her chin. "I was stunned when I found out I was smart. My whole family was stunned."

"My mother's disappointed I'm not *smarter*," Boob said.

"That's not true." Basquiat waved at Boob dismissively. "She just thinks you're wasting your vast intellectual potential watching Silhouette Lark every waking hour."

"Hoo-ha. That's hilarious."

Boob's mom *hated* that he spent so much time watching microchannel stars. She referred to the microchannels as "mind rot."

I couldn't say my parents had been surprised when I turned out to be smart (although maybe not as smart as my friends). Both of my parents were relatively smart, although no one suspected Dad was smart, because he was one of those fun, happy-go-lucky alcoholics. A guy who never quite grew up. A boy, you might say. Last I'd heard he was living in Florida.

Boob's mom pulled into the driveway. Boob stood. "Who needs a ride?"

"Oh, come on." Theo looked pained. "I thought we were going to pull an all-nighter."

Boob shook his head. "It's a miracle she lets me come over here during the *day*, after what Xavier Leaf said."

"If I'm not home to make dinner, my mom won't eat." Molly rose to her feet.

When Basquiat got up as well, I stood. Mom hadn't forbidden me from staying overnight, but I was so tired. The opportunity to throw my bike in the back and catch a ride home was just too enticing.

Theo looked at Rebe. "Do you mind if I stay and work awhile?"

Rebe shrugged. "Hell, no. But there's no room inside for you to sleep."

"Don't worry about it. I'll walk home right before curfew." He shot us a disappointed glance.

"I'll be back first thing," I said.

13

It was still dark outside as I pulled on the same jeans I'd worn yesterday, and the day before. I smiled grimly as it occurred to me that we'd lost another million dollars. Tomorrow we'd be below a million dollars each.

Leaf's threats didn't seem as serious now that they were a day old. He was just trying to intimidate us into selling. What had they done, really? Hacked our phones like a bunch of immature trolls. The next time Leaf showed up I was going to tell him to give us a year and we'd make an offer to buy out *their* company.

I went out through the garage, hopped on my bike, and headed down the driveway.

"*Sam!*" Mom rolled out the front door.

I hopped off my bike. When I saw her face, my heart started thumping. She was wide-eyed, her mouth a tight line.

"What is it?"

Mom swallowed hard. "It's Theo. He was hit by a car on his way home."

I let my bike clatter to the ground and sprinted up the driveway. "Is he all right? Where is he?"

"He's gone, Sam."

I stopped in my tracks. "Gone?" The word came out as a strangled whisper, like I was trapped in a nightmare and couldn't get my lungs to work.

Gone? That couldn't be. It just couldn't be.

My knees gave out and I dropped to all fours, my palms slapping the asphalt. That just couldn't be.

"I'm sorry, Sam. God. Poor Theo." Mom was slumped forward in her chair.

"Who runs into someone walking on the side of the road?" A tear dropped from the end of my nose, onto the driveway. "How does that even *happen*?"

"Some drunk, probably. Whoever it was just kept going."

Of course they didn't stop. Theo would have stopped, but these days there seemed to be a hundred Xavier Leafs for every Theo.

Out of the corner of my eye, I saw a shiny black Lexus pull away from the corner, up the block.

These are serious people. I heard the words in Xavier Leaf's voice. *I'm trying to step in before you guys get creamed.*

"*Leaf.* It was that bastard Leaf."

14

We huddled together, in our sneakers, at the cemetery like a tiny herd of gazelle, wide-eyed and shell-shocked. Mom had been right about my dress shoes. Sneakers were not appropriate for a funeral, but that was all we had.

The truth kept slipping away from me. It couldn't possibly be real, that my friend was dead, maybe murdered over new technology, so I kept falling back into thinking it was something I'd seen on TV, or dreamed, or imagined. Theo couldn't be dead.

Only he was. Each time I wrapped my mind around it, it was like a shot of acid sliding down my throat and blooming in my stomach.

Theo's mom staggered by us, a forty-year-old woman who suddenly looked sixty, the rings under her eyes like bruises. People went up to her, whispered condolences. Everyone seemed to want any excuse not to look at Theo's coffin hanging from a winch, hovering over a freshly excavated grave.

"This is the one place he knows we'll be." Boob looked like he'd lost ten pounds in the past two days, his cheekbones sharp. "Leaf could be pointing a rifle at one of us right now."

"We don't even know for sure that it was him," Basquiat repeated for the tenth time.

I glanced toward Mom, who was parked in the grass ten yards away, scanning the tree line, my late grandfather's .22 hunting rifle across her titanium legs. It was the only firearm we owned, and all but useless against someone with a real gun.

"Rebe!" Rebe's mom screamed, although she was only ten feet away and closing. "You've paid your respects. It's time to go."

"He was my friend. I'm staying for the service!" Rebe shouted back.

"We're going." Rebe's mom turned to me. It looked like she hadn't brushed her hair that morning. "I want all that stuff out of my garage by tomorrow, or I'm throwing it away."

I nodded. My friend was dead. I didn't want to talk about the stuff in her garage.

"Every day that stuff is still there, we're at risk." She made a chopping gesture. "I want it out."

"All *right*. I *heard* you."

"Don't speak to me in that tone," Rebe's mom said.

Basquiat got between Rebe's mom and me. "Mrs. Walsh, if you don't mind, we're mourning our friend. We'll move the equipment."

Basquiat's parents appeared, heads down, walking slowly over the rise. For a moment I couldn't understand why they would have taken a stroll in the cemetery just before Theo's funeral, and then I realized: Basquiat's little sister, Trina, was buried in the same cemetery. They must have gone to visit her grave. Sometimes I forgot Basquiat had had a sister. He almost never talked about her.

Looking at him standing beside Molly, suddenly I felt so petty for being angry at them for getting together. I went over to them, wrapped them both in a hug.

"I love you guys. I wish you the best together."

Basquiat squeezed me tighter as we stayed with our heads close, crying quietly for Theo.

My phone rang. I reached for my pocket, then remembered Mom had my phone on her wrist. As she answered, her other hand went for the rifle in her lap.

"Stop talking," she said into the phone, her voice low and threatening. "Stop talking and listen. If I catch you anywhere near these kids again, I'll kill you, you sack of shit."

She listened, her fingers tightening on the rifle's muzzle.

"Oh, you just watch how much damage I can do with it." Leaf was watching. Just like he must have been watching Rebe's garage when Theo started walking home. It *had* been him.

I turned in a circle, scanning the landscape for a figure lurking behind a tree or something. Nothing.

"You think you scare me?" Pause. *"I will end you!"* she screamed into the phone. *"I will hunt you down and slice your fingers off and cut your balls off and* end *you."* Her eyes went wide. *"You think that's funny? I've seen the sky on fire. We took on ten thousand walking guns and lived to—"* Mom turned her face toward the sky and screamed in rage and frustration. Leaf had disconnected.

Everyone at the funeral had stopped talking. They were all staring at her like she was an escaped mental patient. Most of them still believed this had been an accident, like the police report said.

Mom scanned the landscape, rifle half raised. Her eyes scared me. She was looking through the people around her like they weren't there, like she was somewhere else.

"We're in way over our heads," Boob said.

Rebe swept back her long hair. "We should have taken the damned money."

Boob turned to me. "We have to give him everything and walk away."

My head was spinning. I didn't want to give in to these bastards, but how could we stand against them? We were six kids and a mom with one .22-caliber rifle. Five kids. Who couldn't even afford dress shoes for our friend's funeral.

Basquiat put his hand on my shoulder. "I don't think we have a choice."

I looked to Molly. Her cheeks were tearstained, fresh

ones tracing new tracks. "I want to *hurt* them. I want to hurt them so bad for what they did."

"I do, too," Basquiat said. "But that's a fantasy."

Over by Mom, I heard Basquiat's father say, "The police won't help us." He spit the word *police*.

People moved out of the way as Mom spun her wheelchair and headed toward us. "We have to go. We're too exposed here."

"No, Mom, I'm not leaving until the funeral is over."

Mom closed her eyes for a second. "Fine. Then let's get this service over with." She swung her wheelchair and raised her voice. *"Let's get going."*

This was not my mom's voice. This shrill, panicked voice was not Mom's. As far as I knew she'd never had flashbacks from the war, but if this wasn't a flashback, it was something close.

"Call Leaf," Boob said. "Tell him we give up. I'm not going to sleep until this is settled."

I looked from one face to another. I didn't want to do this, but what if I refused and tomorrow I found Molly's body by my mailbox?

"All right." It hurt to say it. The thought of calling Xavier Leaf and hearing him gloat made me want to pull my ears off. Everything we'd worked for, none of us harder than Theo, would go into the greedy claws of Leaf's employer, whoever the hell that was. I guess I'd find out when the truth app hit the market, if it ever did. "Does anyone know where Theo's safe drives are?"

Everyone looked at each other.

"I hadn't thought of that," Basquiat said. "They must be in the garage, or in Theo's room. We'll need time to locate them. You have to tell Leaf that."

Someone called for everyone to circle round for the service. We headed over to say goodbye to Theo.

15

Mom pulled my phone off her wrist and handed it to me. "Do it."

Xavier Leaf answered in a subdued voice. "Hey, Sam. I'm sorry about your friend."

I squeezed my eyes shut. "Can I ask you something?"

"Sure. Shoot."

"How did you find out about our project? When no one else was even taking us seriously, how did you figure out what we were doing?" I was so angry I had a headache. My head was pounding in time with my heart.

Leaf sighed. "Let me give you some advice for your next project—and I have no doubt there will be many more. If you tap into other organizations' computers for your processing power, those organizations can see what you're utilizing that processing power *for*."

Someone had noticed Rebe borrowing processing power from their system, and figured out what we were doing based on the data being processed. It was so obvious, now that I knew.

"Theo kept everything on a safe drive. It's going to take us time to locate it and figure out how to open it."

"Not a problem," Leaf said. "Take a day. Two if you need it. Keep me in the loop."

"I don't know if two days will be enough."

"I'll tell you where to bring everything once you've got it together," Leaf said, ignoring me. "Good call. And, Sam?"

"What?"

"Get your mother some help." He disconnected.

Head pounding, I called the others to tell them it was done.

I don't know why I was playing Theo's music. Maybe I was a masochist, or maybe it fit my mood. For the first time in my life, music that oozed despair fit my mood. I had to get out of my head. I'd never felt so miserable, so hopeless.

The only thing I could think to do was call Molly.

"It's so good to hear your voice." She was still crying, or maybe she'd started up again. "I can't sleep. It's like I forget what it would even *feel* like to sleep."

"Me too."

She took a long, ragged breath. "I can't believe it really happened. Over a thing, a product, a bunch of wires and code."

"I keep thinking about what Theo's last seconds must

have been like. I don't *want* to think about it, but I can't help it. I hope it was instant."

"I've been going through Theo's public pages. Music links, photos, blog. There's so much of it—I had no idea."

"He was always writing. Mostly about politics and philosophy."

"Listen to this." Molly paused, then began to read. "'Lying is how you get power in this world. Powerful people aren't smarter or more capable than the rest of us; they're just more willing to lie, cheat, steal, even kill. The true currency of our economy is deception. If deception ever becomes impossible, the wealthy and powerful will fall, and the honest will rise.'"

Powerful people aren't smarter or more capable than the rest of us; they're just more willing to lie, cheat, steal, even kill. It was true. Xavier Leaf's people hadn't been smart enough to come up with the idea for the truth app. They hadn't developed it. The only reason they were taking it was because they were willing to kill for it.

"Theo said he didn't think the company Xavier Leaf worked for would release the truth app to the public. He thought they'd use it *on* the public," Molly said. "In that case we'll never know if they were successful."

"I know." I hated them so much. I was going to be haunted by this for the rest of my life; I couldn't imagine sitting in class when school started, and caring about anything my teachers had to say. Not because of the money I'd lost, but because of Theo. If they got the truth app, they not only killed Theo, they killed his vision as well. Everything that mattered to him would die with him. But we were still five seventeen-year-olds and a disabled veteran.

"Mr. Chambliss didn't show up for Theo's funeral. Did you notice that?" Molly said.

"Well, he did say he didn't want us bringing our personal problems to him."

"His best student *died*. That's not a personal problem."

I didn't know what to tell her. I liked Mr. Chambliss, but I didn't think I'd ever understand him. "He probably had a reason. It might not make sense to anyone but him, but he probably had one."

Suddenly, I missed Mr. Chambliss. He had a strange, refreshing way of looking at things. He also never treated us like kids, although there were pluses and minuses to that. He wouldn't hesitate to laugh right in your face in class if you said something stupid.

"I'm going to go talk to him."

"To Mr. Chambliss?" Molly asked.

"Yeah. Maybe he can think of another way out of this."

"That would be so good. I don't want to hand it all over to them, Sam."

I didn't, either, but it was hard to imagine Mr. Chambliss saying anything that could get us out of the corner we were backed into.

16

Turned out Mr. Chambliss lived in Pearl River, which was an eight-mile ride. I had no idea how he would react when he saw me on his stoop.

You know that teacher in the movies who'll do anything for his students? The one who'll come over and talk you to sleep at three in the morning because your heart is broken? I'm not him, Mr. Chambliss had said. Don't bother me after hours, not for any reason. Don't bother me with your personal life. Don't whine about your grade. You never knew with Mr. Chambliss, though. He always had this half smirk, like everything he said (and everything you said) was a joke.

He lived in a cut-up—one of those suburban streets where the houses had been divided into three or four apartments with a shared kitchen. His apartment was in the rear right. There was a rusting latticed patio table with one chair tucked under the eave.

I knocked, waited. Then I knocked harder.

I heard a door close inside, then footsteps. Locks clicked, and Mr. Chambliss appeared. His gray Afro was sticking out in places, like he'd been asleep. He was wearing a white T-shirt, white boxer shorts, and red socks.

"Can I help you?" he asked, no hint of recognition on his face.

"It's me. Sam Gregorious."

He tilted his head and squinted, like he was trying to place me. Then he broke into a grin. "How you holding up, Sam?"

I shrugged. "I'm not."

Mr. Chambliss nodded, his smile fading. "I'm sorry about Theo."

He opened the door wider, then went and plopped on the couch in his living room. I took that as an invitation to follow him inside.

"We were hoping we'd see you at the funeral," I said.

He waved dismissively. "Oh, I don't go to funerals. I wouldn't attend my own if I could avoid it. There were two or three a day during the war. You get tired of them." He glanced at a framed photo on his desk: a dozen soldiers in white winter fatigues posed in front of a portable building. It took me a moment to recognize Mr. Chambliss standing in the back, his head shaved.

"What unit were you?"

"The cybernetics unit at the Siberian front. We called ourselves the Hero Builders," Mr. Chambliss said.

"My mom is a disabled cybervet."

Mr. Chambliss nodded. "That's right, you told me." He lifted a bottle of ginger ale from the coffee table and took a drink. "So what are you doing here, Sam?"

I told him everything. His eyebrows flew up when I told him Theo's death hadn't been an accident. They rose even higher when I told him about the truth app.

He loved the idea; he seemed downright giddy talking about it. The rest of it—Xavier Leaf, the threats—didn't surprise him. I turned on my phone and projected what Theo had written onto the wall.

Mr. Chambliss grunted when he finished reading. "He was a perceptive kid. He didn't have time to learn that this isn't just an observation about the present, though. It's always been this way. We've never been noble creatures. The noble ones, like Theo, tend to be killed."

"He thought the truth app could change things."

"It would sure make things interesting." Staring off into space, Mr. Chambliss grinned, like he was imagining what that world could be like.

"If we give up, Theo died for nothing."

His eyes snapped into focus. "Is that why you're here, because you thought I could help you figure out a way to beat them?"

When I didn't answer, he nodded. "I'm sorry you came all this way. You're doing the right thing. Turn it over to this guy and walk away." He spread his hands. "It's possible he's working alone, trying to rip you off. In that case, you could take him. But he also could be working for a major corporation with its own militarized mafia. A lot of companies have them these days. The thing is, you don't know, and this guy is obviously not going to let up until he's got what he wants." Mr. Chambliss pointed at me. "They'll kill you next. Theo was the brains. Now they'll go for the heart."

A truck rumbled by outside. It set a half-dozen neighborhood dogs barking.

"Can you even finish the thing without Theo?" Mr. Chambliss asked.

It was a fair question. The rest of us were smart, but Theo had been Einstein. Einstein, Nikola Tesla, and Eva Kosmanov all rolled into one.

"If we can find his safe drive with all his notes, I think so," I said. "He was almost done, since we'd gotten the SQUID."

"Then all you need now is a well-armed private security force to protect you twenty-four seven, and you're all set." Mr. Chambliss took another swig of ginger ale. I was pretty damned thirsty after the bike ride, and I'd left my water bottle out on my bike.

Mr. Chambliss grunted as he rose from the couch. He went to his desk, tapped the glass on the framed photo of the shiny, new bionic soldiers. "What you need is a time machine. A platoon of bionicos would do the trick." He shrugged, the tips of his fingers still on the frame. "Hell, two or three good ones would do you."

A time machine. I'd pedaled to Pearl River to be told I needed a time machine. If it was twenty-five years earlier,

Mom and an automatic weapon could have protected us. Hell, if her legs still worked, she could protect us now.

I looked at the photo, then at Mr. Chambliss, an idea taking shape.

"Couldn't you repair my mother's legs? If that's what you did in the war . . ."

Mr. Chambliss threw back his head and laughed. "Sure, Sam. You just need to come up with eighty thousand dollars for the parts. I'll throw in the labor gratis."

For a second, for one single second, our problem had been solved. We needed protection. Who better to protect us than a war-tested veteran?

"You could always visit the bionics junkyard and get used parts. That would be cheaper," Mr. Chambliss said, sounding completely serious.

"Right." I knew better than to fall for it. "They sell eyeballs by the pound."

He raised his eyebrows. "You've been there, then?"

I wasn't in the mood for Mr. Chambliss's joking. "So where do used parts go when their owners don't need them anymore?"

Mr. Chambliss pointed at the floor. "Into the ground with their owner. Can you imagine Uncle Sam showing up at the morgue to pull the legs off a dead vet?" He inhaled to say something else, but held it. We stared at each other across his living room.

Mr. Chambliss pointed at me. "You're thinking what I think you're thinking, aren't you? Forget it."

The parts I needed were buried in the ground. I could search obituaries for enhanced vets who'd died soon after the war, before their legs had had time to wear out and break down.

Would the others go along? Molly would. She was reading Theo's writings; she believed in his vision. Boob wouldn't. Rebe and Basquiat, I wasn't sure about. Could I persuade Mom to go along? Would she alone be enough to protect us? She'd have to sleep at some point, so I needed to find another disabled vet somewhere who would be willing to throw in with us in exchange for working parts. All before Xavier Leaf figured out what we were doing.

"You already own a share in the company," I told Mr. Chambliss. "If I can get the parts, will you help us?"

He turned away from me, toward the photo of him and his unit. "Absolutely not. I'd just end up getting you killed."

"Think of how many lives are going to be lost. If everyone had a truth app, it would be nearly impossible to get away with murder."

Mr. Chambliss kept his back to me. "In theory. How would you even arm these people?"

"I don't know. Do you?"

Mr. Chambliss turned, his hands palms-up. "Do I look like I know where to find automatic weapons? That's what you'd need, you know."

"I'll figure it out. Will you do it?"

Mr. Chambliss squeezed his eyes closed. "I'm sorry. I

don't want to get you kids killed. More important, I don't want to get myself killed."

"You said the world has always been like this, that the honest people like Theo get killed while the liars thrive. I mean, the money aside—what's worth risking your life for, if not changing that?"

Mr. Chambliss didn't have a snappy answer for that.

I held out my hand.

He looked at it a little uneasily. "God, I hope I don't regret this."

17

Before I could even finish, Boob stood, brushed toast crumbs off his jeans. "You're out of your mind."

"Boob, sit down. Let him finish," Molly said.

Boob paced to the door of the diner and back again, both of his hands pressed to his head. He squatted at the end of the booth, pointedly not returning to his seat. "I can't believe you. You want to go up against these people with your mom and a couple of other fifty-year-olds who fought in a war twenty-five years ago?"

"My mom was a warrior. With her legs back, she'd rip Xavier Leaf's head off. And for all we know, Xavier Leaf is working alone. That's what Mr. Chambliss said."

"He also said Leaf could be part of a well-armed corporate mafia." There was no one eating in the next two booths on either side of us, but Boob still whispered.

"He also said *I'd* be their next target," I said. "So if my body ends up in a ditch, I was wrong, and you can hand everything over to Leaf. I'm willing to take that chance. Otherwise Theo died for nothing."

"Mr. Chambliss doesn't know for sure who'll be next. It could be any of us. Or all of us at once." Boob closed his eyes and sighed. "No. It's not worth it."

I stared off into the diner's open kitchen, where a graying cook who needed a shave was cracking eggs onto the grill one-handed while flipping a line of pancakes with the other hand. He spun and buttered four slices of toast, dropped two on each loaded plate, and delivered the plates to the pickup counter before turning back to the grill. His movements were odd—quick but simultaneously careful and deliberate.

"When we started this project, I admit, all I cared about was making a lot of money. Now I don't care if I make a dime. I'm sick of being rolled by the cops, of trying to buy one pair of shoes online and having my credit card charged for fifty. I'm sick of being lied to. So was Theo. He was right—what really matters, what's worth risking our lives for, is creating a bullshit-free world."

"A bullshit-free world," Boob said. "*Sounds* nice until you think about that poker game. Ten minutes with that thing and we're at each other's throats."

I watched the cook, marveling at his efficiency. It was my idea to meet here. It had been months since any of us had eaten out, and it might be the last time we'd be safe being out in public if I got my way.

"Even if we agreed to do this—and I don't think that's a

smart idea—how would we finish the prototype?" Basquiat asked. "We don't know where Theo's safe drive is."

"I know where it is," Rebe said matter-of-factly.

Everyone turned. Rebe was staring at her plate, her face hidden by her long, straight hair.

"How?" Molly asked.

Rebe shrugged. "He told me. I think it was Theo's idea of a romantic gesture. He had a crush on me."

"Why didn't you tell us?" Basquiat asked.

Rebe pushed her hair out of her eyes. "That Theo had a crush on me?"

"About the *drive*." Basquiat didn't even crack a smile.

She thought for a moment. "I guess I wasn't ready to give up hope. I would've told you in a day or two."

I had my doubts about Rebe's crush theory, but whatever Theo's reason, we had the drive. That was one obstacle out of the way.

Rebe looked around. "What do we do? Do we vote?"

"*No*. You can't put our lives up to a majority vote." Boob raised a hand. "And don't tell me I can quit if I want. It's not like you can call this guy and tell him who's in and who's out."

"Well, *you* don't get to decide for the rest of us, that's for sure," Rebe said. "Voting is the fairest thing."

"If we do this, we're going to have to stay together, out of sight, day and night," I said.

"Sounds kinky," Rebe said.

"I'm serious. Until the truth app is on the market."

"What about my mom? I'm not sure she's okay on her own," Molly said.

"She can stay with us," I suggested.

Molly shook her head. "She wouldn't leave our house. Maybe our next-door neighbors could look in on her."

The vote was three in favor, one against. We looked to Basquiat, who hadn't voted.

"I think this is a risky idea. But if this is what most of you want to do, I'll get behind it."

"Speaking of which"—I pulled the cemetery map I'd printed out of my back pocket—"I need someone to help me get the parts for Mr. Chambliss to repair my mother." The cook was delivering three more plates to the pickup counter as I unfolded the map. As he turned, his eyes caught the light, and I glimpsed a flash of silver. Suddenly I understood why his movements were so deliberate: he was blind. He was a war vet like Mom, except his eyes were broken instead of his legs.

With the gang on board, it was time to approach my mom. I practiced my speech, nervous and uncertain whether her protective side would curl in or lash out. I tried to imagine her interruptions and questions. But when I gave my speech, she heard me out without uttering a word. When I finished, she said exactly six.

"Go get me some damned legs."

18

In the movies, graveyards are secluded places, which makes grave robbing a simple matter. Saint Peter's Cemetery sat on a grassy slope along Route 9W, right in Haverstraw.

Basquiat and I ducked from one headstone to another like soldiers under fire, until we reached a maintenance shed a hundred feet from the road. Vehicles rumbled by every minute or so, even at two a.m. The curfew didn't apply to people heading to or from work.

"Which one is it?" Basquiat asked. I hadn't expected him to be the one to volunteer to help, but in retrospect, Molly, who believed in ghosts, wasn't going to, and Boob certainly wasn't going to. That left Rebe and Basquiat.

I flicked on the little flashlight and consulted the map. Emma Marshall's grave was to the right of us. Carefully, I counted headstones.

I pointed. "Third row in from the path, fifth headstone from the left."

Basquiat motioned. "After you."

I waited for a truck to pass, then sprinted to the head-stone, shovel in hand, and dropped behind it. Basquiat joined me a moment later.

"How do we do this?" he asked.

"One of us digs, the other watches the road. As soon as the watcher sees headlights, he calls 'down,' and we both drop until the vehicle passes. When the digger gets tired, we switch places."

Basquiat pulled the crowbar out of his pants and dropped it in the grass. He picked up the shovel. "All right, then. Let's get your mom some legs."

Behind me, the shovel hit the ground, and Basquiat cursed. "The ground is like concrete."

"Lovely." We'd biked and walked for two hours to get here, most of it through dark woods to minimize our chances of being picked up by the police for breaking curfew.

Basquiat handed off the shovel after digging down about six inches. It wasn't so much digging as chopping the ground with the shovel blade, then scooping away what we'd man-aged to chop loose. After about twenty minutes of this, blisters were forming on my palms. I handed the shovel back to Basquiat. It was still awkward between us, but not as bad as it had been. He and Molly never acted like a couple around me, and that helped me ignore the truth of the situation somewhat.

Basquiat tossed a shovelful of dirt from inside the hole

and paused. "This is creeping me out much more than I thought it would. Will she be just a skeleton?"

"After twenty years? I think so. A skeleton in a dress."

Basquiat covered his eyes. "A dress. I don't want to see this."

I couldn't agree more. It was one thing to imagine digging up a grave, another to actually stand in a hole that kept getting deeper, knowing that any time now, you were going to hear the *thunk* of the shovel hitting a coffin.

Basquiat stopped digging. "This makes me think of Trina."

The words would have been disturbing in the light of day, let alone while digging in a graveyard at night. "I hadn't thought of that. Rebe should have come instead of you."

Basquiat never talked about Trina. I still remembered the day he came back to school after the accident, climbing onto the bus and dropping into the seat beside me. He turned and asked me about assignments he'd missed. We were eight; Trina had been four. At her funeral, Basquiat had been like a zombie, sitting on a bench near the grave, wide-eyed and absolutely still, hands in his lap where his mother had placed them.

Basquiat went back to digging. Even from where I was squatting, I heard the *thunk*.

"Your turn." He held the shovel toward me.

"Oh, gee, thanks." I accepted the shovel and slid into the hole, taking a small avalanche of dirt with me.

It looked like a nice coffin. It was reddish in the light of the flashlight, and might have been cherry, although I wasn't much on identifying woods. I didn't know why Basquiat had brought the crowbar. I'd pictured wooden slats like in old westerns. We dug footholds and clung to the sides of the hole—which sloped outward rather than straight up and down—because we couldn't open the casket while standing on it. I reached down to open it, and realized I was on the wrong side.

"It opens on your side," I said.

"Great." Basquiat took a huffing, anxious breath. "I so don't want to do this." He reached down and lifted, groaning with exertion. The lid rose slowly.

I reached across and grasped it. My fingertips brushed the soft material on the lid's underside.

Basquiat's front foot slipped loose from its toehold. Shouting in alarm, he lunged with both arms outstretched, looking for something to grab onto. There was nothing but loose dirt. He tumbled backward, into the coffin. A second later, he was back on his feet, shrieking, trying to climb out of the coffin, but all he managed was to pull down an avalanche of dirt.

I was laughing. I couldn't help it.

"It's not funny. I'm *standing* on her."

"We're going to have to stand in there to get the legs anyway."

"Not *on* her." His eyes were bulging. "Stop laughing. Show some respect."

"I'm sorry." I stopped laughing, but somehow I couldn't stop smiling. "I think I'm in a bit of shock." I handed him the flashlight. "Find a spot where you're not standing on her."

His chest rising and falling, Basquiat turned the flashlight on and pointed it into the coffin.

I stopped smiling. Emma Marshall's hands were still clasped across her chest. She'd been buried in her uniform. All that was left of it were patches of rotting material.

Basquiat was standing on her shoulder and upper arm. Grimacing, he repositioned his feet slowly, gently, on either side of the skull. There wasn't much space for standing.

"Come on down, Mr. Chuckles."

I inched around, toward the foot of the coffin, until I was clear of the lid. It felt like spiders were crawling down my spine as I stepped between Emma Marshall's metallic legs.

Her legs were bolted to what was left of her femurs.

"We left the hacksaw by the headstone," I said.

"I'll get it." Moving carefully, Basquiat found the footholds and climbed out of the hole. He handed down the hacksaw, then held the flashlight from above, pointing it into the coffin.

I looked up into blinding white light. "You coming back down?"

"For what?"

"Moral support."

"I can provide that from here. You have my full support."

Squatting, I grasped one metal knee and lifted until the femur was elevated. Then I sawed. It only took about thirty seconds, but it felt like much longer with Emma Marshall's eyeless skull glaring at me. I passed the leg up to Basquiat, then got to work on the other one.

I clambered out of the hole as soon as I'd finished. As we stood silently over the open grave, my fear subsided, and I was left feeling a cocktail of hope and guilt. What we'd just done was very wrong, but at the same time, right. "We'll put these to good use, Lieutenant Marshall. Thank you for your service. In the war, and now."

I'd read that before the Sino-Russian War, you had to go all the way back to World War II to find a war where there weren't protesters and questions about whether or not the war was necessary. If you could find anyone who had a shred of doubt about the Sino-Russian War, all you had to do was take them on a tour of the bombed-out sections of lower Manhattan; or the Boston waterfront; or Savannah, Georgia; and their doubts would vanish.

Basquiat reached down and closed the lid. I picked up the shovel.

19

The smell of Mrs. Kong's *jajangmyeon* wafted from the kitchen as the drum-heavy opening theme song of *Harley's Shares* blared from the TV. With Mrs. Kong here much of the day to watch over Boob, our little house was absurdly crowded. I wasn't complaining, though, what with the abundance of home-cooked Korean food and getting to see Molly all day. Plus, there was something about the chaos and commotion that signaled forward momentum, life. Too often these past few years this house had felt too quiet.

Rebe was organizing Theo's files from the safe drive she'd retrieved from the hole in the tree in her side yard. There wasn't much more we could do until we had recovered our materials from her garage, and we were afraid to move them without protection. Speaking of which.

I checked on Mom. She was still sitting on the kitchen table surrounded by parts, her bladed feet leaned up against the refrigerator. I knew better than to ask Mr. Chambliss how it was coming, but the fire in Mom's eyes told me everything I needed to know.

"Bend it," Mr. Chambliss said.

Mom flexed her left knee. She laughed, the sound bubbling up from her belly like a kid on Christmas morning about to turn the corner and see what Santa had left under the tree. She *laughed*. I hadn't heard that sound in a long time.

"Those pistons have almost no wear on them." Mr. Chambliss reached for a tiny tool that looked like a dentist's mirror.

I retreated into the living room, where Molly and Basquiat were sitting on the carpet facing each other, a deck of cards between them, their knees almost touching. It looked as though they were playing hearts or something to pass the time, except they both had their eyes closed.

I fought to squash a surge of jealousy. I *would* be mature about this. They were two wonderful people who had fallen for each other, and damn it, I *would* be happy for them. Or at the very least not angry and resentful.

Molly opened her eyes. "Jack of clubs?"

Basquiat showed her the card he was holding: the king of spades.

Molly slapped her thigh. "Damn it." She noticed me and smiled. "There's the problem right there. Skeptics block the flow of energy."

"I'm not blocking. I'm rooting for you."

"You don't believe in paranormal phenomena. That makes you a skeptic, and an energy blocker."

I burst out laughing. "An energy blocker. Man, that's harsh. Next time I want to insult someone, I'm going to use that."

"Damned energy blocker!" Basquiat nodded approval. "That's good."

Mr. Chambliss appeared in the doorway to the kitchen. "Ladies and gentlemen, I'd like to introduce the new and improved"—he swept a hand into the kitchen—"Melissa Gregorious."

Mom walked into the living room. Everyone burst into cheers and applause, and Mom took a bow.

"Let's test them out." Mom sprang onto the kitchen table effortlessly. She barely had to bend her knees. She jumped down, crossed the room in a hop and a skip, and threw a kick.

Her foot went through the wall.

She turned to me. "What do you need from Rebe's garage?"

"Don't we need to figure out how to get you a weapon first?" I asked.

"I'll take care of that on the way."

"How are you going to take care of it? Do you have a pile of cash lying around I don't know about?"

Mom looked me in the eye and said, "No. I'm going to steal one."

I laughed, because I thought she was joking.

"This is war. I'll do whatever it takes to keep you kids safe."

She went out the back. The mechanical legs gave her a weird, slightly jerky gait. I watched from our patio as she leaped the chest-high cyclone fence that separated our yard from the Luccas' and took off, moving about as fast as a Doberman at full speed, even though she was just loping along.

20

Boob's hands were pressed against the sides of his head as if he was afraid it was going to explode. "We can't fit the magnet and receiving coil in a ring. Even a really big one. We just can't."

"Two rings?" Basquiat suggested.

I pointed at Basquiat. "Two rings. Why not?"

Without Theo, we were having to learn to do all the things we'd been counting on him to do. From his notes we understood how to create a working model of the truth app, and we had the SQUID and the 3-D printer, but actually *doing* it was different. Moving the operation to my house hadn't helped. There was no garage, so we had workstations spread around the house. There were electronics scattered all over the floor.

I was worried about Boob. He'd always been tightly wound—the kid chugging Pepto-Bismol before an exam—but now he looked headed for a nervous breakdown.

Besides the fact that he was my friend and I cared about him, with Theo gone, Boob was the closest thing we had to an engineer. It was up to him to figure out Theo's notes on how to use a weak magnetic field to perform the brain scan, and how to shield the signal from interference from nearby electronics. I understood in theory, but I had no idea how to actually create the necessary technology.

I rubbed my eyes. We were out of energy drink, so I'd have to settle for coffee. I hated coffee.

"Sam?" Rebe was holding up my phone. She was monitoring my calls while keeping the phone in zombie mode. "Message from Leaf: 'Give me a status update.'"

I cursed under my breath. "How about 'Still searching for the safe drive. You'll be the first to know when we find it.'"

"Good." Rebe typed it in.

"Where's your mom?" Molly asked.

I shrugged. "Outside. She stays out of sight and watches the house. Don't order pizza—she'd probably riddle the delivery guy with bullets."

"She's trying not to let it show, but her hips and abs are killing her from the run to Rebe's house and back," Mr. Chambliss said from the kitchen, where he'd set up shop. "It's going to take a while for her body to readjust to this level of exertion. And she's going to have to sleep at some point. You need to find me another vet. It's not like you can post an ad in the paper."

"I know." I'd been waiting for everything to be up and running. Now it was. "Can you give me a ride?"

"Sure. Where to?" Mr. Chambliss patted his rib cage, double-checking the holstered handgun Mom had given him.

"Clarkstown Diner." I pictured that flash of silver I'd seen when the cook turned.

When I told Mr. Chambliss who we were going to see, he looked at me like I was out of my mind, taking his eyes off the road much longer than I was comfortable with. "You don't know him at all? What's to stop him from selling us out?"

"Gee, I don't know. Let me think." I put one finger to my lips, relishing a rare moment when I had one on Mr. Chambliss. "If only we had some way to know for sure when people are lying . . ."

Mr. Chambliss threw his head back and laughed. "That would come in handy."

"Before we tell him much, we can bring him back to the house and check him out."

We pulled into the diner parking lot.

"Maybe I should talk?" Mr. Chambliss said. "This might sound less strange coming from another vet."

"Sure. Go for it."

We sat at the counter, six feet from the vet, and ordered two coffees. It was three in the afternoon, so the place was nearly empty. The vet finished cooking a cheeseburger, scooped fries onto the plate, and delivered it to the pickup counter.

"That's some damned fancy platework. You learn that in the army?" Mr. Chambliss asked.

"Only thing I cooked in the army was Ruskies." He had a narrow, squinty-eyed face, slicked-back hair, and a goatee. The last time I saw someone wearing a goatee, I was about four.

"Ben Chambliss, Twenty-Third Tech Brigade, Siberian front."

The guy stepped over, extended a hand. "Kelsey Cook. Do not attempt a joke unless it's truly original, 'cause I've heard 'em all."

Mr. Chambliss shook his head. "No one ever accused me of being original."

"You local?"

"Stone's throw. I'm here with this young man, Sam Gregorious. He's a regular. He was in here admiring your work a couple of days ago, and suggested we come and see you."

The vet turned his sightless silver eyes on me, stuck out his hand. "Come see me about what?"

"We have a job offer for you. If you pass the interview," Mr. Chambliss said.

A door thumped closed nearby. A gray-haired woman limped away from the restroom, a toilet brush in hand.

Kelsey barked a laugh. "Hey, A.J., you hear that? They're

going to steal me away to cook at their five-star nouveau restaurant."

A.J., the woman who'd been cleaning the bathroom, pointed at us. "Don't you dare."

"Or let me guess," Kelsey said, "not a head chef. Umpire? School bus driver?"

"Private security force."

I expected Kelsey to laugh, but he scowled, his eyebrows pinched. "That's not even a little funny."

"It's not a joke. I mentioned I was in the Twenty-Third. I was a cybertech."

"Come on." Kelsey waved a hand dismissively. "You're gonna pony up forty grand? Or even better: you want me to come up with the money. Take your con somewhere else."

"It's not a con. The job is protecting five kids from an operation that wants something they have. We don't know how big an operation we're up against, or when they're going to strike. You interested?"

Kelsey pinched his goateed chin. "You know, when I was a kid, I used to have dreams where I could fly. Every night I went to sleep hoping I'd have a flying dream." He pointed at his face. "When my eyes stopped working, I stopped having dreams where I could fly and started having dreams where I could see. I felt the same sort of rush as when I dreamt about flying, I'd just lowered my ambitions a little. The thing is, now I don't dream about either, and I'd just as soon keep it that way."

Mr. Chambliss lowered his voice. "What if I told you this was as important as the war so many of our friends died in?"

Kelsey raised his head and stared off into space, considering. "I'd say that's not a comparison you should make lightly, and I shouldn't have to tell you that."

"I'm not making it lightly. The war is the only thing I never make light of."

Kelsey paused at that, his face turned toward Mr. Chambliss's voice, thinking. He reached back and untied his apron. "A.J., I'm going to take my dinner break early."

"Have you ever done anything illegal, Mr. Cook?" I asked, eyes on the readout.

Kelsey laughed like he'd never heard something so funny. "Are there still laws? Could've fooled me." He cleared his throat. "I never killed or hurt nobody except in the war. I stole before, but never from a friend. Fair enough?" The needle had barely budged.

I nodded, then remembered he couldn't see. "Fair enough."

"Can we trust you?" Basquiat asked.

Kelsey nodded. "If you're straight with me, I'll be straight with you. I like a drink now and then, but I'm never drunk on duty, whether the job is combat or cooking omelets."

Kelsey's comment about liking a drink didn't surprise me. He had a wiry build, his arms still showing some muscle and veins bulging, but he had the weathered face of a seventy-year-old man. His face reminded me of my uncle Ron's, and he'd died of cirrhosis at forty-five.

I looked around at the others. "We good?"

"Sign him up," Mom said.

Nods all around.

"Mr. Cook, we'd like to offer you a job. The pay is three meals a day, repair and maintenance for your vision, and a one percent share in TruthCorp."

He squinted. "What the heck is TruthCorp?"

"I'll show you," I said. "I'm going to ask you some more questions, but this time I want you to lie some of the time."

The demo got Kelsey's attention in a hurry. When it was over, Basquiat and I prepared to retrieve Kelsey's eyes from their current owner, Anders Seifreid, who was interred in Mount Moor Cemetery in Nyack. I wrapped both my hands in a thick layer of medical tape. The blisters from our last dig hadn't healed yet.

21

A shout of pain from the kitchen made me jump. Kelsey had insisted Mr. Chambliss didn't need to locate anesthetic to replace his eyes, that "three knocks of Jim Beam" was all the painkiller he required. I wondered if he was regretting that bravado.

Maybe it wasn't bravado. Maybe Kelsey was so eager to see that he'd rather suffer the pain than wait another day. I glanced at Mom, wolfing down a turkey sandwich so she could get back to her post, her shoulders squared, eyes bright. She'd been sore as hell yesterday, her muscles unused to running and jumping, but she looked twenty years younger, like a werewolf who'd finally gotten the full moon it had been waiting for.

Yeah, maybe Kelsey was willing to put up with a little pain to get under his own full moon.

I went back to work helping Molly, who was trying to

get the head-tracking app within a photo app to communicate with the ring that created the weak magnetic field.

"We're getting close," I said as we worked. Everyone else was so focused on their specific pieces of the project that I wasn't sure any of them realized how close we really were.

"How much longer, do you think?"

"There are still some problems we haven't figured out, but assuming we figure them out, less than a month. Maybe two weeks."

In the kitchen, Kelsey called out, "Oh, *hell* yes! That's what I'm talking about. Hey, I didn't realize!"

"That I was black?" Mr. Chambliss asked.

"No, that you were such a handsome guy." Kelsey breezed into the living room, grinning like a jack-o'-lantern. "Now who's who?"

22

Rebe was in the dining area, bleary-eyed. She let her head drop, buried her face in her hands.

"You need anything?" I asked.

"I need you to shoot me in the head. All these Fourier transform calculations, the conceptual modeling, pattern recognition, interpretations—I have to write all those programs, make all the formats, and encode and encrypt all that crap because it has to function like Internet traffic. And it is *not* normal Internet traffic." She dropped her hands. One eyelid was twitching, as if it was planning to rebel, to shut whether Rebe wanted it to or not.

I grabbed a lawn chair and dragged it over next to her. "Can I help?"

Rebe squeezed her eyes closed for a second. "Sure. Thanks."

"We're so close."

Molly got up from her station in the living room, headed

for the hallway. She glanced at me, glanced again, and stopped in her tracks. "Stop *looking* at me! Every time I get up, you're watching me."

Suddenly feeling like a creepy stalker, I dropped my gaze. "Sorry."

Molly stormed out of the room.

"What's *her* problem?" Rebe asked.

"Cabin fever." Basquiat was standing in the entrance to the kitchen. "We've been cooped up in here for too long."

That was probably true. When people are ground down by stress or exhaustion, they say things they normally wouldn't, but I'd also found those things are sometimes legitimately *bugging* them.

I stepped toward the bathroom to wait outside the door for Molly, but Basquiat waved me over. "Just give her some time. It's the pressure, it's not you."

He was probably right. I was definitely feeling it myself. "I'd do anything to get out of here for a while. Just to toss a Frisbee in the park, go hear a good band. At least you and I got to get out for the spare parts. Soon, though. A week."

Basquiat didn't look particularly enthusiastic about the prospect of finishing.

"What?" I asked.

He stretched his neck from side to side. "When we first talked about building a foolproof lie detector, I pictured people getting caught in ugly lies. Murderers and rapists, people embezzling millions of dollars, corrupt politicians, heroin dealers."

"And the truth app is going to expose all of them."

"Yes. But I wasn't thinking about all the lies we tell to protect people's feelings. And to be honest . . ." Basquiat paused, laughed harshly. "'To be honest.' There's an irony. I might as well be honest now, before I have no choice. To be honest, I'm not sure I'm comfortable feeling exposed like that."

A brief flashback of Molly in the shower lathering her body as I watched from my electronic hiding place sent a stab of guilt and panic through me. Would she ever speak to me again if she found out?

I didn't want to talk about it. That type of thinking sapped our resolve, and with everything that had happened, everything we were facing, we needed to stay positive, or the whole enterprise would collapse, and Theo would have died for nothing. Boob was barely functioning. We couldn't afford to lose Basquiat. If we were ever going to give birth to this device, we couldn't be afraid of it. And we were definitely afraid of it.

"We want to release this on the world," Basquiat went on, "and I'm not sure *I* want one." He raised a hand. "I'm not backing out—I agreed to help, and I'll keep that promise. But I wonder if I have any business creating something I don't want to use myself."

He waited for an answer. He was right—we couldn't be afraid of our own technology.

I shrugged. "I still think we're better off with the truth. We just have to learn not to be afraid of it."

Basquiat gave me a skeptical look. "And how are we going to do *that*?"

I had no idea. I thought of my own secret. How could I not be afraid of Molly finding out?

There was only one way: pull the splinter. Get it out. Confess. Maybe Molly would never speak to me again, but once the truth was out, one way or the other, I wouldn't be afraid of it coming out. Once all my secrets were out, what would I have to fear from the truth app? Not a damned thing.

"What if we confess it all?" I said.

Basquiat's eyes got wide. "All of what?"

"Everything we don't want people to know about us. Rip the Band-Aid off. Get it all out in the open."

He looked at me like I'd lost my mind.

I hadn't grown up particularly religious, but my grandfather had been Catholic. He'd gone to confession every week without fail.

Down the hall, the bathroom door opened. Molly headed toward us.

"Sam thinks we should have another poker game," Basquiat said. "Only this time we drag it *all* out into the open."

"I didn't say that. The poker game was angry and confrontational. This time we would be kind about it." At least, I hoped we would.

"Like a confession," Molly said.

I pointed at her. "Exactly."

Her hair was matted and oily, her glasses smudged and crooked, and as she stepped closer, I caught a whiff of a musky, old-sweat odor, but she was still so beautiful to me. I hoped Basquiat appreciated her.

"I'm willing to try it," Molly said.

23

My mouth was so dry, my upper lip kept sticking to my teeth, and my tongue made a clicking sound. I didn't want to do this. No one else looked particularly eager. "This is not an interrogation, it's a confession," I said. "The idea is, if we have no secrets, we have no reason to be afraid of the truth app."

"Cast no shadow," Basquiat said softly, staring at the grass.

Rebe frowned. "What?"

"It's a line from a Bungees song: 'When you cast no shadow, you can walk where you will.' I always took it to mean if you have nothing to hide, you have nothing to fear."

I nodded emphatically. "Exactly. We take turns. When it's your turn, give us the worst thing you're hiding."

"We don't judge. This is a healing process." Molly looked around our little circle, her eyes pleading. "Be kind. The worse the secret, the more courageous you are for confessing it."

"I like that way of looking at it," Basquiat said, his voice shaking.

Rebe tossed a stick into the little bonfire we'd built in the far corner of the yard, as private a spot as we could find under the circumstances. "What about Boob?"

I shrugged. "It's his loss." I caught a glimpse of Mom, up on the roof. I still hadn't gotten used to seeing her out of her wheelchair.

"I'll go first. I want to get this over with." Basquiat blew out a breath, puffing his cheeks. "All right. Here we go." He looked upward, avoiding eye contact with us, which was so not Basquiat. "When I was eight years old, my sister, Trina, died, and I've been lying about how it happened ever since. Trina didn't fall from our deck when my father was supposed to be watching her; she fell trying to climb the ladder to the tree fort in the woods behind our house."

All the air rushed out of my lungs. Basquiat was talking about the ladder he'd built on a huge tree. I could still picture those rickety boards rising up the trunk to form a makeshift ladder that reached so, so high. That was the point of the ladder—climbing it had been a way to prove you had guts. We never stayed at the top very long, because it wasn't comfortable to sit up there on boards nailed between branches, your feet dangling. Trina would have fallen at the very top of the ladder, trying to stretch her little legs to reach the seats. It had happened nine years ago, but for a moment it felt as if she was falling right now, and I couldn't stand it.

"I egged her on. 'You can do it. Be brave.' And when she fell . . ." Basquiat struggled for control, his chest hitching. "When she fell . . ." He covered his face with his hands and burst into tears. "I ran away. I *ran away*."

Molly wrapped her arms around him, pressed her cheek to his shoulder.

"I went to my room, and I heard our dad calling our names as he walked into the woods looking for us, and then I heard him scream Trina's name—" Basquiat wailed, hands still covering his eyes, rocking back and forth like he wanted to run even now. Molly hugged him fiercely. She was crying as well.

Basquiat took a deep, hitching breath, tried to finish. "I never told my parents I was there with Trina. They still don't know."

I don't know what I had expected, but it wasn't this. He'd been carrying that secret for nine years.

"You were eight years old," I said. "Just a kid. It's time to forgive yourself."

"What I did is unforgivable." Eyes still squeezed shut, Basquiat gestured with one hand. "Move on. Someone else."

"I'll go," Rebe said.

The back door opened. Boob came down the steps, head lowered. We watched him cross the lawn and flop between Rebe and me without a word.

I clapped him on the shoulder. "Good man."

"You already know one of mine," Rebe said.

"Rebe, I'm *so* sorry," Molly said.

"No big deal. It would've come out now if it hadn't then. I've been bingeing and purging on and off for two years." She looked down at herself. "Not that it's done much good."

"You have a beautiful body," I said.

Rebe gave me her best sarcastic glare. "We're being honest here. I'm fat." She held up her hand before I could argue. I was going to tell her to go get the truth app, because I honestly thought Rebe had a pretty damned nice body. "Since that one's already out there, it doesn't count. Fortunately, I have another. Well, I've got a million, but my biggest one is that I steal." She waited a beat for the words to sink in. "I run Internet scams. Nothing big enough to get the attention of the big boys—they don't appreciate competition, so that's a good way to get yourself killed—just enough to help feed my family. You may have noticed I have a big family."

"Does your mother know where the money comes from?" Molly asked.

Rebe considered. "Yes and no. I transfer it right to her account, and she doesn't ask about it. A few years ago, it was just little bits here and there, but by this point I'm one of our primary sources of income."

I wanted to ask if she was stealing the money from corporations and people who wouldn't notice it was gone, or from people like us, but I thought that might sound judgmental, so I kept my mouth shut.

"Thanks for trusting us," Molly said. "Who's next?"

It was either my turn or Boob's, and Boob was staring at his heavily taped Nikes.

"I guess I am." I so didn't want to do this. I turned to Molly. "Last winter, we were on the phone and you accidentally left the link open." I swallowed. "I cloaked the line and secretly watched you for about an hour."

Molly's eyes went wide. I'd expected her to be angry, but she didn't look angry. She looked disappointed. Somehow that was worse.

"What was I doing?" she asked.

I looked into the fire. "You took a shower." I didn't need to see her face to know I was now a different person in her eyes. I wasn't a trusted friend; I was a creepy stalker.

"Thank you for telling me." Her voice was tight.

There was a long, awkward silence. I wasn't sure if Basquiat had even followed what I'd said. He looked like he was still baking in his own private hell.

"Hey, Boob?" Rebe said. "I see your body's here. Is your brain planning to make an appearance?"

Boob folded his arms across his chest. "What do you want me to say?"

"What do you want, an instruction manual?" Rebe said. "Come clean. Whatever you don't want people to know about you, spill it."

Boob stared into the fire. He refolded his arms, with the opposite arm on top.

The seconds stretched out. I wanted him to say something,

anything, to move us on from my confession. My face was burning like I had a terrible sunburn. Why had Boob bothered to come out if he wasn't going to say anything?

Finally, Boob inhaled like he was going to speak. Instead, he held the breath. I was about to tell him to say something, when he finally spoke.

"I have no self-esteem whatsoever. Zero. I'm scared all the time. I doubt myself every day. My mother does most of my homework, including writing papers for me, because she's afraid I'll screw it up." He kept his gaze glued to the fire. "She tells me how disappointed she is in me on a daily basis. She thinks I'm wasting my life watching Silhouette Lark, or one of the other microchannel stars, and she may be right, but their lives are way more interesting than mine." He squeezed his eyes shut. "Can I stop now? Because if this is supposed to make me feel better, it's not."

"It's like pulling splinters. They hurt on the way out." I wasn't sure if I actually believed what I'd just said. The idea was that this would make us stronger and bring us closer together. For all I knew it was tearing us apart.

"I wish Theo was here spilling his guts with us. I miss him," Rebe said.

"He's the only one of us who would have actually liked this," I said.

Molly leaned in toward the fire, elbows on her knees. "I guess it's my turn. Okay, I can do this." She was pressed close to Basquiat. "You all know my mom and dad separated six months ago. What you don't know is, this all happened because Mom found the corner of a condom wrapper in their bed. She confronted Dad, and he admitted he'd had an affair with a coworker a few months before." Molly paused, whispered something under her breath. "The thing is? It wasn't his condom wrapper. It was mine."

Basquiat stared into the fire. He didn't look surprised.

"I never told my parents the wrapper was mine, because by the time I found out, it was too late. Dad had already confessed. I didn't want him to hate me for breaking up their marriage." Behind her glasses, Molly's eyes glistened, welling with tears. "A lot of kids wonder if it's their fault their parents got divorced. I know for a fact it is mine."

"Why were you doing it in your parents' bed?" Rebe asked.

"Mine is too small."

Basquiat was six foot three. An image of the two of them in Molly's little bed conjured itself in my head. I pushed it away.

A *thump-thump-thump* startled us—the sound of muffled rifle fire. I caught movement out of the corner of my eye: Mom, jumping from the roof, landing on the lawn, still firing her rifle.

"Inside." She hurdled the back fence, into the Spanoses' yard. As the others ran for the door, I glanced back, then slowed. Mom was kneeling beside an especially dark spot on the dark lawn. Two weeks ago I might have mistaken it for a couple of trash bags.

Mom looked up, saw me alone on the lawn, watching. *"Get inside."*

Kelsey ran past me, pistol in hand, looking all around, a glint of gold coming off his eyes. *"Clear to three hundred yards.* Inside, Sam."

I went inside. Whoever that was on the ground in the Spanoses' backyard, I had no doubt he'd come to kill us. He might have been taking aim when Mom got him. I hoped like hell it was Xavier Leaf, that this was all him, a one-man intimidation campaign.

"Get away from the windows," Mr. Chambliss said as I slipped inside the house.

We ducked down on the floor, beside the couch.

"I guess they're done being patient," Rebe said.

The screen door flew open. Mom backed inside, holding black-booted feet. Kelsey was carrying the body's front end. It was a woman, African American, maybe twenty-five, in a bulletproof jumpsuit. There was a bloody hole above her left eye.

"That's it for the element of surprise." Mom set her end of the body down on the carpet. "Now they know about me and Kelsey. Next time they'll send more people, and they'll be careful. I don't think anybody in the neighborhood even peeped out their windows, fortunately."

"They didn't," Kelsey confirmed.

I couldn't take my eyes off the woman. She was really dead. My mother had shot her.

"We need more soldiers," Mr. Chambliss said.

"I know somebody. Beltane." Kelsey shook his head. "Beltane is badass. She was Black Ops. She's a quad now."

It took me a minute to realize he meant quadriplegic. She'd lost her arms and legs, which meant she'd be both fast and strong once she was repaired.

"Do you know where to find her?" I asked Kelsey.

"Sure. She lives with her mother and brother. She'd be thrilled to get out of there; she hates them. And, full disclosure, she hates me, too." Kelsey grinned. "We had a thing a few years back. Didn't work out."

Mom was going through the dead woman's pockets. She pulled a second handgun from her jacket. "No ID." She set the handgun on the carpet. "I would have been surprised if there was."

Rube snapped a photo of the dead woman's face. "If we raise some cash, I can run a facial recognition search and see where she's been lately."

"What do we do with her body?" Basquiat asked. He looked like he was about to be sick.

"I'll take care of it," Kelsey said. He made it sound as simple as taking out the trash. I didn't want to know how you took care of a body.

24

Beltane considered the truth app like it was a dog turd she'd stepped in. Or maybe that sneer, her lip curled in disgust, was her resting face. "What is this thing?"

"I'll tell you in a minute. First we do the interview."

"*You're* doing the interview?" The notion seemed to amuse and disgust her in equal measure. She was wearing a low-cut sweatshirt, no bra; rows of ribs jutted below her collarbone. With her original arms and legs, she probably tipped the scales at about eighty-five pounds.

"Have you ever committed a crime?" I asked.

She tilted her head. "Sure. Bank robbery. Mom stuck a gun in my hand and wheeled me into the bank. I can't *feed myself.* How the hell am I going to commit a crime?"

Mr. Chambliss laughed, the laugh quickly turning into a cough.

I glanced at Basquiat, who was standing at my right shoulder. He gave me a look that suggested he found Beltane about as charming as I did.

"Can we trust you?" I asked Beltane. "If we fixed you up, can we count on you?"

"You fix me up and keep my limbs working, you feed me, give me a bed with no one else in it"—she looked pointedly at Kelsey—"I'll take good care of you."

The readout stayed in the green.

"Sam, can I talk to you in private?" Basquiat asked.

I stood. "Excuse us a minute."

Beltane shrugged. "Take your time."

We headed into my bedroom. Molly, Rebe, Boob, and Mom filed in behind us.

"She makes me uneasy," Basquiat said. "She's not our kind of person."

"She's a total bitch," Rebe said.

"That's exactly why we need her," I said. "If you need protection, you don't get a sweet, old golden retriever. You get a crazy pit bull."

"I agree," Mom said. "If someone points a gun at her, it's just going to piss her off. I'd take her over Kelsey, to be honest."

Basquiat held up both hands. "In that case, I'm all for her. I'm certainly not going to question your judgment, Mrs. Gregorious."

I gritted my teeth, forcing a smile. My judgment, it went without saying, didn't carry the same weight.

We paraded back into the living room and I welcomed Beltane to TruthCorp.

"I'm honored," she said. "Now can you get me the hell out of this chair?"

25

"Oh *yeah*," Beltane cooed from the kitchen. "Oh God, do me. That's it."

I pressed one hand to my forehead, shook my head.

Boob looked up from the computer screen. "Is he done with her arms yet?"

I glanced into the kitchen. Beltane had both arms raised over her head as Mr. Chambliss worked on attaching the salvaged left leg. She threw her head back. "God, that feels good."

"Yep. He's on the legs."

"Good. Maybe she'll shut up soon," Boob said.

"I *heard* that!" Beltane called.

Boob flinched. He put his head down and dove back into his work. I didn't blame him—Beltane was scary.

Mom put a hand on my shoulder as she passed through the alcove and into the kitchen. "Beltane? Once you're up and running, are you up for joining me on an errand?"

Beltane's eyes lit up. "Once I'm standing I don't plan to sit for about a month."

"Great. We need cash. I want Rebe to run that facial recognition search, see if we can figure out who that woman was working for." Access to all the private surveillance video out there was not cheap.

"Where are you going to get cash?" I asked.

Mom looked me in the eye. "We'll get it. That's all you need to know."

I could tell Mom expected me to protest, but the truth was, if stealing could save our lives, I was okay with stealing.

Molly passed between us, carrying a plate of french fries. Then she disappeared into my room. With all that had happened, I hadn't had a chance to talk to her alone, to tell her how sorry I was about the shower incident.

I waited a minute or two, then followed her. I knocked on the open door. "Can I talk to you?"

Molly shrugged, chewing. "If you can find a place to sit."

I cleared someone's clothes off the bed. "I haven't had a chance to apologize to you."

Molly studied her plate, rearranged the fries.

"I've always thought apologies were lame—you do something awful to someone, then say some words and expect that to somehow absolve you for what you did. Except I don't know what to do besides say the words. I'm so sorry."

Molly's eyes had filled with tears while I was giving my little speech. "You know, if it had been any other guy, I wouldn't be surprised. I'd be furious, but I wouldn't be surprised. But you . . . you're my friend. You're the person I trusted more than almost anyone. I never would have thought you were capable of doing that to me."

Even while I was doing it, I'd felt guilty, but I figured Molly would never find out, and I would never tell another soul, so where was the harm?

"I'm sorry. I don't know how to make things right."

Molly didn't reply. I took that as my cue to leave.

"Wait." Molly set the plate down and walked up to me. I thought she was going to give me a hug, but instead, she slapped me across the face. Hard. It felt more like a punch than a slap.

I doubled over, clutching my cheek.

With some effort, I straightened up, still holding my cheek.

"You better go put some ice on that."

Cheek throbbing, I left.

The bathroom door opened and Beltane was suddenly blocking the hall. It seemed like half of her was made of glistening tungsten.

"You have no idea what a pleasure it is to be able to wipe my own butt." She raised her arms toward the ceiling. "*Melissa?* I'm ready. Let's roll."

26

I leaned back in my chair, turned my head side to side to stretch my tense neck muscles. My head ached constantly. When was the last time I'd gotten more than two or three hours' sleep in a day? A month ago?

Rebe was working on the facial recognition search. Boob was sitting at his monitor, head down, doing nothing. I was about to get on him for slacking when I took a good look at his face. He was pale and sweaty.

"Are you okay?" I went over to his little station in the dining area.

Boob shook his head. "I can't do this. I can't concentrate. I can't sleep, can't eat."

"Why?"

"What do you mean, 'why'?" He gestured toward the backyard. "Someone tried to kill us, and they'll try again. I'm *scared*." He blew out a big breath. "I forgot to mention it during enhanced truth or dare, but I'm also a coward."

Mr. Chambliss appeared in the kitchen doorway. "You're suffering from an anxiety disorder. I could see that in class, but it didn't seem appropriate to bring it up then."

"Fine," Boob said. "I have an anxiety disorder. I can't take this. I need my life to be boring and predictable."

The walkie-talkie crackled to life. "Chambliss?" You can't hack a good old-fashioned walkie-talkie and spy on people through it.

Mr. Chambliss lifted the device to his face. "Yep?"

"I'm getting hungry up here. Can you send up a ham sandwich and a Coke?" Kelsey asked.

"I got it." I went into the kitchen, pulled the ham out of the fridge, piled half of it on a slice of white bread, and squirted mustard on it. I was guessing on the mustard part.

There was an extension ladder leaning against the side of the house. I managed to climb it with one hand. When I reached the roof, Kelsey was there to take the plate.

"How well can you see with those eyes?" I asked.

Kelsey turned and looked off down the street. "Nothing's gonna get within a thousand yards without me seeing it. And I mean *nothing*. I can see *ants* ten blocks away. At night."

"Damn." I knew the artificial eyes were superior to the real thing, but I had no idea how superior. I felt a little safer. I'd have to pass that information on to Boob. Maybe it would calm him.

I made a bathroom stop before heading back to work. Voices drifted from the bedroom as I passed. I poked my head in.

Basquiat and Molly were sitting on the bed close enough that their shoulders were touching. They were speaking in low tones, heads down. The jolt of jealousy was immediate and overwhelming. I thought I'd gotten past that, but no.

Molly noticed me. "Hey. Any word from Rebe?"

"She's still working on it," I managed. My heart was racing. I swallowed, trying to shrug it off.

"Here we go," Rebe said from the living room. Then, louder, *"I got something."* I hurried away.

We gathered around Rebe, who was playing a video clip of a woman walking down a street, then walking up the steps of a brownstone.

"That's got to be New York City," Mr. Chambliss said. "Brooklyn."

"That'd be a bingo," Rebe said. "Thirty-two Livingston Street, Brooklyn Heights. Picked up by a surveillance camera on a traffic light a block away."

"Wow," Mom said. "I'm impressed."

"Nah, this is easy if you've got the bank," Rebe said.

Gingerly, Beltane pulled on a jacket Mom had lent her, wincing from the pain in her atrophied muscles. Mom was only slightly better. I'd never seen two people consume so much ibuprofen.

"Let's see if I can boost the body count a little," Beltane said.

"What?" Molly and I said almost in unison.

"We're after bodies? I thought we wanted information," I said.

Beltane held up a handgun, popped out the clip. "You think they're going to sit still and answer questions? No. Let me explain this to you. This isn't a freaking action movie. If someone points an assault rifle at you and pulls the trigger, the bullets don't ricochet off handrails and catwalks while you run away. You die. Unless you happen to have eighteen grand for a bulletproof jumpsuit." She slapped the clip back into place. "We get them when they're in their pajamas, while they're taking a leak and their hands are holding their privates instead of assault rifles."

I looked at Mom, who raised her eyebrows and nodded. I hadn't pictured our people going off in the middle of the night to crawl in other people's windows and shoot them.

"Sweetie, things are going to get ugly," Beltane said. "If you don't have the stomach for ugly, give that jackass your invention now and just walk away. At least this way, we're stopping them before they stop you." She turned to Mr. Chambliss. "Can I borrow your car?"

"Mi car es su car." He fished the keys out of his pocket.

"Are you going?" I asked Mom.

"Only me," Beltane said. "That leaves you two and a half soldiers if there's an attack."

Rebe looked around. "Who's the half?"

"Chambliss there is the half." Beltane pointed. "He

was trained, but he has no combat experience and no enhancements."

Mr. Chambliss gave Beltane a little salute. "My ex-wife always said I wasn't half the man her father was. She was wrong—I *am* half a man."

27

I gazed at the rings lying in my palm, feeling an awe bordering on religious ecstasy. They were brass, not much to look at, definitely no one's idea of fashion. We'd linked them to Beltane's phone, because the phone had to be activated to interface with the quantum computer at MIT. We risked being located the same way they'd located us last time, but we were hoping Leaf's people didn't know about Beltane, and we'd masked the data better this time. You wore the VR glasses or contacts that came with your phone, locked onto someone's face with the photo feature, and the read-out appeared in the bottom left corner of your lenses.

They worked. We had our prototype.

"Now we focus on finding a partner," I said. "Someone who can provide start-up cash and distribution." It killed me that Theo wasn't here to see this.

"I've been working on that," Rebe said. "There's a woman named Mott. She owns a distribution business."

"Does she distribute electronics?" Basquiat asked.

Rebe shrugged. "She distributes pretty much everything. She's black market."

"She's a criminal?" Molly said.

Everyone's a criminal, Mom had told me a few weeks earlier. *That's why we hire a criminal of our own to make sure we aren't cheated.* She'd been referring to a lawyer, but the principle was the same. "If she distributes black market goods, she knows how to do it quietly, through underground channels," I said. "And she must have security protecting her operation. That's *exactly* what we need."

"I don't actually know her, but I know of her. You want me to try to make contact?" Rebe asked.

I looked around. "Let's at least talk to her. If we can't trust her, we'll know soon enough."

I flinched when someone rapped on the window. Boob jumped about a foot.

"A little help here," Beltane said through the glass.

She had a body in the trunk. A guy wearing nothing but boxer shorts, with two bullet wounds in his big belly. A lot of blood.

"You could have put down some trash bags first," Mr. Chambliss said.

"I wounded another," Beltane said, ignoring him.

Rebe held up her wrist, snapped a photo of the dead man's face.

Beltane ducked into the backseat of Mr. Chambliss's car

and came out with an assault rifle and a handgun. "Who wants one?"

"Hang on," Mom said. "They're not trained."

Beltane shrugged. "So we train them."

"I'd like to learn," Basquiat said.

"Dibs on the rifle," Rebe said.

"Fine, but run the facial recognition on this dude first. He was sleeping with a forty-four under his pillow." Beltane closed the trunk. "I'm going to dump him. I'll be back in twenty minutes."

"Oh, baby." Rebe looked over at me. "Hey, is this Xavier Leaf?"

I jumped out of my chair to take a look. Leaf was pushing a shopping cart through the cereal aisle of a grocery store, the dead man in the trunk of Mr. Chambliss's car walking beside him. The dead man grabbed a box of Cap'n Crunch and put it in the half-filled cart.

"He shouldn't be eating that," Mr. Chambliss said. "That crap will kill you."

Rebe isolated Leaf's face. "Let's see if we can find out more about him." She ran his face through the database. Hits began to pop up quickly. Xavier Leaf walking past cameras on the street, sometimes alone, sometimes with others.

Mr. Chambliss leaned closer to the screen. "Where are these? That's not New York."

Rebe tapped the air. "Washington, DC. Almost all of them."

"Washington?" Mr. Chambliss muttered. "Could their company be based in Washington?" He lunged at the screen, his elbow bumping my ear. "Wait. What the hell is *that*?"

"Hang on." Rebe called up a video.

President Vitnik was giving a speech on the White House lawn. Leaf was in the video for only a few seconds. He wearing a dark suit, and his hair was shorter, but there was no mistaking his face as he passed behind a crowd of dignitaries.

"Rebe, what's the date on that?" Mr. Chambliss asked.

Rebe brought it up. "February. Eight months ago."

"He's Secret Service." Mr. Chambliss put one hand on top of his head. "We're not fighting a tech company, we're fighting Vitnik."

That didn't make sense. The president of the United States was trying to get control of the truth app? *She* had killed Theo?

"*Pack up!*" Mom shouted. "We're getting out of here. Now."

Beltane pulled a backpack off the dining room table and headed into the kitchen. "I got food." Packages and cans clattered as she swept them into the pack.

Mr. Chambliss grabbed my arm and squeezed. "Pack everything you need for the project. We're not coming back."

"Why are we rushing?" Basquiat asked. "Why would they be coming any minute?"

"They sent one assassin because that's all they thought they needed to take out five kids, and they didn't want their fingerprints on this," Mr. Chambliss said. "Now they'll fly in an elite platoon. As soon as it shows up, we're dead."

"Where are we going?" Boob asked.

"Far away."

There were way too many of us to fit in Mr. Chambliss's car, so we went on foot, staying inside the narrow strip of trees between our street and the one behind it until we crossed Old Route 304 into denser forest. It was dark in there, and we had exactly one flashlight.

"Are we going to walk all the way out of the suburbs?" Boob asked. "That's got to be twenty miles."

"Right now we're just getting away. . . ." Mom trailed off.

We all heard it. the *thump-thump* of a low-flying helicopter. Kelsey took off running, back the way we'd come.

Thirty seconds later, he had returned, puffing from the exertion, clutching his lower back. "It's a V-280. Room for twelve. They set down at the house. Must have searched it and then torched it."

"They'll consult satellite footage to figure out which way we went," Mom said. "We have to move fast. Stay under trees as much as we can."

Kelsey led the way, choosing the easiest path, which still involved pushing through heavy brush. Branches snapped back into my face as I half walked, half jogged and tried to stay on my feet.

The president. I couldn't believe it.

We were all wheezing by the time we reached Zukor Road. We were probably going to circle around the wall of Clarkstown Heights and head to the heavier forest out past South Mountain Road. From there, we could climb the hiking trail over High Tor mountain.

"Who's slowing us down?" Beltane asked from near the front of the line.

"Sorry," Rebe said. "If I had known I was going to have to run for my life, I would have kept in better shape."

Beltane let people pass until Rebe caught up with her. "Get on my back," she commanded. When Rebe hesitated, Beltane shouted, *"Do it!"*

"Okay. Don't *shout* at me."

Beltane wrapped her arms around Rebe's calves and took off. "Now, let's *move*." She was so damned fast. I picked up my pace. Molly, who had been on the track team for a while, was jogging at a steady pace; Basquiat the stud athlete was gliding along behind her looking like he could keep up that pace for a week. Boob and Kelsey were the weak links now, but I wasn't exactly fleet-footed.

We crossed Zukor Road at a canopied spot past the parks office. When we reached the wall, we headed counterclockwise, toward South Mountain Road.

"Melissa? Can you get me up there?" Kelsey pointed to a hill on our right. "I want to get eyes on our pursuit."

Mom went flying up the hill with Kelsey riding piggyback as we circled the wall. My lungs were burning, my legs and back aching. I was carrying maybe thirty pounds of stuff in a backpack, which isn't much until you take my body weight into account. I hoped we had all the things we needed for the truth app. We'd left so quickly, we could have forgotten something crucial.

Mom and Kelsey broke through the foliage.

"Soldiers ahead," Kelsey said. "And closing behind. We're pinned. Either we surrender or try to shoot our way out."

Beltane cursed and punched a tree, which shook like a T. rex had hit it.

"If we surrender and give them everything, what will they do with us?" Molly asked.

The vets looked at each other. Finally, Mr. Chambliss answered. "Likely kill us."

I guess that answer shouldn't have surprised me, but it did. It felt as if a giant hand was squeezing my chest.

Boob sank to his hands and knees, gasping. "I can't breathe."

Rebe knelt beside him. "I think he's having a heart attack."

"Panic attack," Mr. Chambliss said.

"Come on, we need a plan. What's it gonna be?" Beltane said.

Beltane's titanium fingers were still pressed to the tree she'd punched. She was so strong, I pictured her tearing the tree out of the ground, throwing it at the soldiers. That wouldn't help us against rifles.

I looked at the wall rising up, pinning us down. . . . "The tree. Push the tree onto the wall and we can climb over."

Beltane broke into a grin. She moved behind the tree. "Out of the way." As soon as I was out of the way, Beltane bent at the waist and pushed against the trunk, her feet digging for purchase. The top branches shuddered, sending a flurry of leaves raining down.

A sharp *crack* split the air, followed by a series of smaller ones. The tree plunged toward the wall of Clarkstown Heights, then slammed into it with a crash.

"On me, on me!" Beltane shouted.

Mom pulled Boob to his feet and set him behind Beltane, who hiked him onto her back.

"Hold on." Mom motioned for Rebe to climb on Boob's back.

Beltane scaled the tree like a monkey. As soon as she cleared the wall, she swung out onto a sturdy branch until she was hanging over the roof of a house. Then she let go.

Seconds later, she was back in the tree. As soon as she was past the wall, she dropped to the ground and picked up more passengers.

When everyone was over the wall, Beltane shoved the tree off it.

"Stay here." Mom jumped off the roof like it was no big deal.

"You okay?" I asked Boob, who was sitting, clutching his stomach. He nodded.

"It's not going to take them long to figure out where we went." Rebe was studying the dark treetops beyond the wall.

"No, it won't," Mr. Chambliss said. "We need to disappear. Quickly."

I went to the edge of the roof. We were on a neighborhood street, the houses as big as department stores. The street was brightly lit by spotless white luminescent sidewalks. How were we going to disappear in this place? We would stand out so badly with our taped-up sneakers and bionic bodyguards that we might as well have been a herd of purple buffalo.

Mom returned with an extension ladder under one arm. She leaned it, as quietly as possible, against the eaves of the roof. We scurried down to join her on a lawn like a golf course green.

"Excuse me." Mr. Chambliss jogged over to a bald guy walking a white dog that resembled a cotton ball. I'm not sure what Mr. Chambliss said to the guy, but thirty seconds later, the guy was making a call for him.

The call lasted less than a minute, then Mr. Chambliss jogged back over. "The cavalry's on the way."

"Who's the cavalry?" Beltane asked.

"My ex-wife."

Until he'd cracked that joke about his ex-wife saying he wasn't half the man her father had been, Mr. Chambliss had never mentioned he was divorced, but I guess that wasn't something you shared with your students. It was nice to hear we had a friend inside these walls.

"Don't anyone forget: once we're in a vehicle, they can

listen in on our conversations," Rebe said. "No names, no mention of the truth app or anything else that could trigger a live human listening in."

A green van rolled to a stop in the street.

"How are ten people going to fit in there?" Boob asked as we hurried toward it.

"We're going to squeeze like hell," Mr. Chambliss said.

And that's what we did. Five people, including me, jammed into the back with cans of paint, brushes, and other art supplies. Rebe was pretty much in my lap.

Mr. Chambliss's ex-wife turned to study us as the auto-pilot pulled a U-turn. "This has got to be an interesting story. You all have to spill it the moment we get home." She had pretty fingernails, splotches of red and green paint on her knuckles and fingertips, long silver hair.

As soon as we were in her house, she didn't even wait for us to sit down. "Who's going to tell it?"

"Well," I began when no one else jumped in, "we invented a portable remote lie detector, and now the president is trying to kill us, so we got Mr. Chambliss to repair some disabled vets to be our bodyguards."

Mr. Chambliss barked a laugh. "Sam, that was spectacularly succinct."

"The president of the United States?" Mr. Chambliss's ex asked.

"That's right." I was still trying to wrap my head around that.

"That fascist," she hissed. "I'm Lilo, by the way." She

looked at Mr. Chambliss. "You still have the social skills of a mushroom."

Mr. Chambliss winced. "That's a bit harsh. I'd say I have the social skills of a stoat at the very least."

"What the hell's a stoat?" Beltane asked.

"A very large rodent." Lilo leaned over, grabbed Mr. Chambliss's shoulders, and kissed him on the mouth. "It's good to see you, Ben. How can I help?"

"We need a place to hide out tonight, supplies, and help getting out of the county in the morning."

"You got it."

28

I pushed open the bathroom door. Molly was standing in front of the mirror wrapped in a towel.

I yanked the door closed. "Oh God. I'm sorry."

"Nothing you haven't seen before, right?" Molly said through the door.

"Why didn't you lock it?" I asked, my face burning.

"I couldn't figure out *how*. There's no lock on the knob."

"It's voice activated. Just say 'door lock' and 'door unlock.' Don't you watch TV?"

"Door lock." The knob made a faint click. "Thank you," Molly said brightly. "Now go away."

I hurried down the hall, still embarrassed.

Lilo's house was truly like something out of a TV show. Not only did the doors lock when you told them to, but you could move the walls, making rooms larger or smaller in seconds. The ceilings expanded upward, like someone was blowing a giant bubble, when you stepped into a room.

There was a little cleaning robot constantly working, and the furniture adjusted via voice commands.

The vets were congregated in a sitting room, Mom lying on the floor, her knees pulled up to her chest, while Mr. Chambliss massaged Beltane's neck and shoulder blades.

"Who's got the Advil?" Mom asked.

"Oh. My. God. *Ben!*" Lilo was in the living room watching News America. We were on the news.

"No names," I reminded her.

"Sorry," she said as Mr. Chambliss rushed in after me. Everyone followed except Molly.

". . . links to the pro-Russia anarchist group Seela," Roshanna Lupe, the News America anchor, was saying. "The band of teens and army veterans have developed a weapon of psychological terror, shown in this footage captured by a butterfly camera inserted by the FBI after they were tipped off by one of the group's own members, Theodore Harlow."

We gasped as the footage rolled, showing me, Molly, Basquiat, Rebe, and Boob standing over Theo in Rebe's garage. Theo's hands were strapped to the arms of a steel chair that would have looked right at home in a horror movie.

"Don't do this," Theo said. "Please, guys. I had to tell them. What we're doing is wrong."

In the video, Basquiat raised a silver device the size of a coin, or a ring. Theo struggled frantically to get out of the chair, then every muscle in his body tensed. His jaw clenched, yet somehow he still managed to let out an earsplitting shriek. Then his head drooped like he'd been knocked unconscious.

Slowly, Theo opened his eyes and raised his head. "Who are you?" He looked around. "What is this place?"

This was so typical of News America. They murdered Theo because he believed in truth so staunchly they couldn't buy him off, and now they were twisting him into a martyr for their side.

In the video, none of us answered Theo. We watched him, sneering, as Theo looked from one of us to the next, his eyes pleading.

"Who am I? Where do I live?"

Whoever wrote News America's dialogue needed to find a new career.

The image switched back to Roshanna Lupe, who was the spitting image of a young Vitnik: the same pointy nose and too-small mouth, the same bobbed black hair. That was not a coincidence—she'd had extensive plastic surgery to resemble Vitnik. "The device, which they call the Blackout App, can permanently wipe someone's entire memory from a distance of up to twenty feet. If you see these people, call the authorities." Lupe folded her hands, leaned toward the camera. "Or better yet? Round up some friends and neighbors and take them out yourself."

Lilo turned off the feed.

Molly looked absolutely distraught. "My mother is

going to be losing it right now. And I can't call and set her straight."

Basquiat wrapped his arm around Molly and whispered something to her.

I didn't know why I was surprised. This was what Vitnik did. She lied. What I didn't get was why so many people *believed* her lies. It wasn't like people didn't know video footage could be computer generated. Last year, when Dwayne Singeon created a TV show on his computer, in his bedroom, starring students and teachers from our high school, everyone watched it, but no one thought it was real. When Singeon showed our admittedly hot English teacher Ms. Evans having flings with students on the show, people didn't think she really *had*. Yet people believed the footage on News America. One day our sixty-nine-year-old president is running in a half marathon, and the next day a child just *happens* to fall while taking a nonexistent tour of the White House so the president can stop the bleeding and apply bandages? It was all fake.

That must be why Vitnik wanted the truth app so badly. If average people had them, they'd learn how much Vitnik lied.

"Visitors are approaching your house, Lilo," the house's electronic voice announced. "One U.S. Army lieutenant and one private first class."

"Everyone in the basement," Lilo said.

We scrambled for the door to the basement.

"You have no obligation to allow U.S. military personnel into your private residence," Mr. Chambliss called over his shoulder. "They have no jurisdiction in a privately funded community."

"I know," Lilo said.

We huddled in the basement with the lights off. I could hear the murmur of voices—Lilo's and a male voice—but couldn't make out what they were saying.

Moments later, the door opened.

"Clear," Lilo called. "They're going house to house, looking for you."

It wouldn't take long for them to figure out we went over the wall. What they wouldn't know was whether we'd gone into hiding or kept running.

"We have to get moving," I said.

"You think?" Beltane said, her voice dripping sarcasm.

Lilo was rushing around, grabbing packs and shoving them at my stunned friends. "There's an emergency escape route that comes out near the river—"

"You're kidding me," Mr. Chambliss said.

Lilo glanced at him. "In case the poor rise up, I guess. I'm so ashamed that I live in this place. But it's so damned *nice.*"

It was definitely nice. I still wouldn't want to live there.

"Do you have clothes Beltane and I can use to cover our bionics?" Mom tapped her leg.

Lilo pointed at her. "Good point." She disappeared into her bedroom. I could hear her telling her closet what she wanted from it; a moment later, she was back, handing Mom and Beltane shiny tracksuits.

Beltane muttered something about wearing "old-lady clothes" as she pulled them on.

Inside the garage, we piled into the van. Lilo covered the five of us in the back with a paint-spotted drop cloth. Ten people packed into a van was as big a giveaway as vets with working parts.

Ten minutes later, the van rolled to a stop, and Mr. Chambliss slid the drop cloth off us.

We were parked along the side of the road in a heavily wooded area. Lilo led us down a path, over a little bridge, and to a clearing with a windowless blue steel building in the center. She used her ID to open the door. Inside was an elevator that took us to a dimly lit tunnel. It was nothing fancy—concrete walls and floor. There was an electric cart that must have been for maintenance people, but it only seated two, so we walked.

"I didn't know you'd been married, Mr. Chambliss," Basquiat said as we headed down the tunnel.

"Since you've lured me into a situation that'll probably result in my painful, premature death, I think you can call me Ben."

"So what went wrong between you and Lilo, Mr. Chambliss?" Rebe asked. Yeah, he was always going to be Mr. Chambliss to me as well.

"Nothing. We signed a five-year marriage contract and divorced when the contract expired."

"Seriously?" Rebe said.

"No, Rebe. You can't get married with an expiration date. Maybe that's the problem."

"Has anyone noticed that whenever Mr. Chambliss doesn't want to answer a question, he turns it into a joke?" I asked.

"*I* hadn't noticed," Mr. Chambliss said.

"Let's stay focused," Mom said. "When we get out there, everyone is going to be watching for us. There'll be a universal facial recognition alert in place, so don't go anywhere there might be surveillance cameras."

"That pretty much leaves us in the wilderness," Boob said.

"And that's where we're headed," Mom said.

"I *hate* camping," Rebe muttered under her breath.

"Well, you better get used to it." Beltane was walking right behind us.

Rebe glanced back at her. "I wasn't talking to you. Do you mind?"

Beltane gave her a withering look before moving around us and picking up her pace. If not for the leathery skin and the scowl, she'd be pretty, I realized. You had to squint to see it, though.

The tunnel came out in an abandoned quarry sitting on the edge of the Hudson River. We were surrounded by rusting chutes and squat buildings. Behind us, the hills were cut open, the tan rock center, shaped like a giant staircase, exposed.

We waited in the shade of a huge pile of gravel while Beltane jogged off to check on the situation.

"She's not growing on me," Rebe said.

"If she hadn't pushed that tree over, we'd be dead by now."

"That doesn't make her any less annoying."

Boob nudged me. "Silhouette Lark is talking about us!" He was watching Lark's channel on a tiny screen.

"What's she saying?"

"She has her doubts about the video. It's going viral. Everyone's talking about it."

Beltane appeared on the gravel road, her face glistening with sweat. She took a few seconds to catch her breath, then said, "Roadblock."

Mom pointed at the mountain behind us. "We'll have to go over High Tor mountain." I'd been afraid of that. I'd hiked the trail up High Tor a dozen times. It was steep. I wasn't enthralled by the idea of doing it with a pack on my back.

"Or we could steal a boat." Rebe jerked her chin toward a gray dock, where a couple of recreational fishing boats were moored.

"Do you know how to hot-wire a boat?" Mr. Chambliss asked.

Rebe shrugged. "How hard could it be?"

"I don't know, I've never tried."

Ten minutes later, the boat rumbled to life. Mr. Chambliss unmoored it from the dock and cruised down the shore to the quarry, where we were waiting. Quietly, we waded into the river, up to our armpits. Rebe and Mr. Chambliss helped us over the railing.

The boat had a canopied area at the bow, while the stern was open. Most of us sat in the stern with our backs to the railing, so anyone watching from shore wouldn't see ten of us packed onto a boat meant to hold maybe five.

Boob was on my left, our shoulders pressed together. "Is there a bathroom on this thing?"

I leaned forward and looked into the open cabin. Mr. Chambliss was steering, with Kelsey at the bow scanning the banks, and Mom and Beltane sitting with rifles in their laps. "I doubt it."

Boob squeezed his eyes shut. "So what are we supposed to do if we have to go?"

"Hold it, I guess."

Boob didn't look happy. "I'm not built for this. My guts turn to water when I'm scared."

"We just need to hang on. They won't be able to touch us once we release the app."

"I don't care about the app. I just want my safe, boring life back."

"Quit your whining," Rebe called from farther back. She was squatting by an open circuit box, working to disable the GPS signal without setting off the alarm.

"Look," I said, ignoring Rebe, "nothing is going to stop us. Just say that over and over."

Boob huffed, annoyed. "Come on. It's the *president*."

"I don't care. I don't know what they've got to hide, but Mr. Chambliss said it: this thing scares the hell out of them."

"You don't know what they've got to hide?" Rebe said. "Vitnik's network just broadcast a video of us testing a memory-wipe weapon. Vitnik claims all the profits from her products go to charity. Everything she says is a lie."

"But everyone knows politicians are crooks," Basquiat said. "There must be more to it if Vitnik is this desperate."

"It's an election year," Rebe said. "She doesn't want any surprises."

"The important thing is, this world is messed up and we have the power to fix it," I said. "Theo saw it. All I could think about was how much money we were going to make, but Theo understood from the start. We can change this."

Boob shook his head. "Be careful what you wish for, Gregorious the Great. Changing the world doesn't necessarily make it better."

"Come on, Boob. We told each other our worst secrets." Basquiat spread his hands. "Has it really ruined your life? I feel *better*. Sam's right. It would be a good thing for the whole world to cast no shadow."

Boob didn't look convinced. Or maybe he just looked like a guy who had to go to the bathroom and had nowhere to go. "Just wait until you have to tell the truth every second of your life. Do you realize it will be impossible to throw someone a surprise party?"

"Maybe it's time to find out what it's really like." I unzipped my pack and pulled out the Tupperware container where I'd stashed the prototype for safekeeping. I handed it to Boob. "Keep us honest."

"Patrol, twelve o'clock, twenty-four hundred yards," Kelsey called.

"Everybody *down*," Mom said. "As down as you can get." She took Beltane's rifle. "You and Chambliss are a happy couple out for a little jaunt. They shouldn't have your faces logged yet. If it goes to shit, signal to me and I'll come up shooting. Kelsey, too."

Beltane put her arm across Mr. Chambliss's shoulders and leaned in close to him.

A few minutes later, the boat slowed to a stop. The rumble of another, bigger boat filled the air. Beltane raised her hand and waved enthusiastically. "We're on our honeymoon." She held up her left hand, inviting the patrol to admire a nonexistent engagement ring.

Beltane waved a second time. Our boat began to move again.

When we were safely on our way, Beltane came to the back of the boat. "Let me see your packs."

"No." Rebe clutched hers.

I handed mine to Beltane. She knelt, unzipped it, and began tossing stuff overboard. I opened my mouth to protest, but Beltane cut me off. "We're behind enemy lines now, so listen up while I explain how we avoid detection in hostile territory. We travel light and move at night. During the day we crawl into the thickest brush we can find and remain silent until sunset. We move slowly and deliberately.

The team leader will raise her hand every few minutes. When she does, stand still and listen. Avoid breaking or disturbing vegetation."

Beltane moved on to Molly's pack as she continued reciting the rules for avoiding detection in hostile territory. It did not sound like fun.

29

The sun was below the horizon, the clouds pink, as I slipped over the railing into the tepid, waist-deep water and followed Boob toward the shore, which was forest as far as I could see in either direction. I scrunched my toes to hold on to my sneakers as mud tugged, threatening to pull them off.

There was a splash behind me. Kelsey had vaulted over the railing, the last one off. The boat, set on autopilot, pulled a U-turn and rumbled toward deeper water. It was listing noticeably to one side.

"There you go." Kelsey stood watching the boat as the back left corner sank farther, until water poured over the rail.

The weight of the water made the boat suddenly corkscrew. It spun back toward shore.

"No. No, no!" Kelsey called as the back end sank completely underwater and the nose turned up toward the sky.

The engine gurgled and died; the front end slipped slowly into the water.

And then it stopped.

Kelsey slapped the water. "Damn it." Two feet of the boat's nose jutted out of the water.

"Let's go," Mom said. "Hopefully they won't see it."

Kelsey jogged out of the water, still cursing. "It's like a road sign, pointing the way we went."

There wasn't much we could do about it. It wasn't like we were going to swim out and try to push the boat into deeper water.

We stopped on the bank and rubbed mud on our clothes and faces under Beltane's watchful eye, then headed into the woods until we were invisible to anyone who might happen to cruise past on the river.

"Which way?" I whispered.

"Northwest," Kelsey answered. "Into the Catskills. Nothing but wilderness."

"What's the *plan*?" I asked. "We can't manufacture in the wilderness."

Mom stuck her face close to mine. "Right now the plan is to get so far off the feds' radar they have no way to find us. Then we think about next steps."

"Fine, but as soon as we're clear, we have to find a way to get truth apps out there. That's the whole point of this, and it's the only way we're going to be safe for long."

Kelsey hefted his pack. "This way."

Beltane led the way. We walked like we were in a

minefield, choosing each step carefully to avoid stepping on dry twigs or disturbing foliage. When we'd gone no more than a hundred yards, Mom raised one hand and we all stopped and listened.

All I heard was peeping birds getting a last meal before bedding down for the night. We moved on.

30

A beetle was crawling near my face. I flicked it away as quietly as possible. Dried mud was caked in the corners of my eyes, but I couldn't wipe it out because my fingers and clothes were filthy, too. I had dozens of mosquito bites. I was no longer exhausted, because as soon as we'd crawled into the thick brush we were lying in, I'd passed out and slept for probably eight hours. Now I was just uncomfortable and bored out of my mind. We had to lie here—not talking, not moving—until dark, which wouldn't be for another six or seven hours.

I passed the time playing songs, sometimes entire albums, in my head, and trying to figure out how we were going to manufacture the truth apps. I had identified four electronics factories within thirty miles of New City that were sitting idle. My plan had been to approach one of them and cut a deal, but that was out now that we were wanted terrorists. We'd have to build them ourselves, one at a time at first, like we'd built the prototype. For that we needed materials, which meant we needed start-up funds. Our only hope was Rebe's person in the black market distribution business. If we ever got out of this, we'd have to contact her, hope she was interested in a deal, and have cash.

Molly touched my arm. When I raised my head to look at her, she was wide-eyed with panic. She looked out through the brush emphatically.

I followed her gaze, but I didn't see anything.

And then I did. A pair of Army green boots, gently lifting and coming back down. As dread washed through me, a second pair appeared, no more than ten feet away from us. There seemed no chance they could miss all nine of us, split into three clusters. As the soldier passed through a clearing, I caught a glimpse of his bearded face ringed by bulletproof fabric.

The soldier raised his right arm, looked left and right, then pointed. For a second I thought he'd discovered one of our clusters, but he picked up his pace and disappeared through the foliage.

I let out a breath. My racing heart began to slow.

Rebe grabbed my arm, stopping me. "Wait a minute."

Beltane spun, pressed a fingers to her lips, livid. She'd made it clear that just because we'd reached the deep wilderness of the Adirondacks, we shouldn't relax. And I had to admit, so far her strategy had worked. We'd tiptoed our way past neighborhoods, right through a few backyards, and made it here without being discovered.

Rebe cupped her hands around my ear and whispered, "That News America video made us celebrities. Celebrity *villains*, but still, celebrities. We should record the truth and post it on BuckyHead. Vitnik will take it down, but by then it will be all over the place."

I nodded. That might help. If anyone would believe our message over News America's, it was the droves of teens who hung out at BuckyHead. At least there'd be something out there to combat the lies News America was broadcasting.

We stopped the others and laid out the idea.

"Is this worth the risk?" Beltane asked Mom.

"We need allies. Of course it is," I said.

Beltane ignored me, waited until Mom gave her a tight nod.

Mom, Kelsey, Beltane, and Mr. Chambliss spread out, forming a perimeter to ensure no one was close enough to overhear us. For the first time in two days, we spoke in normal voices.

"We'll need to connect to the net for only a millisecond to upload the message," Rebe said. "For a blip like that, I can rig a baffle so it looks like we're sending it from New Jersey, or wherever."

"It's also a way to let our parents know we're still alive," Molly said.

We sat on the ground and planned out what we wanted to say.

"You should read the message, Molly," I said as we put the finishing touches on it. "No offense to the rest of you, but Molly has this quality, this sincerity. People will trust her."

Molly seemed startled. "Thanks."

"I agree," Boob said. "And for the record, Sam was speaking the truth just then." I'd forgotten about giving Boob the prototype.

Molly laughed. "Good to know."

"Needless to say, I agree," Basquiat said.

"Okay. I'll do it," Molly said.

"Here we go, then." Rebe activated the recorder on her phone and pointed it at Molly.

"So here we are"—Molly spread her arms—"the evil terrorists News America told you about. Except, it's a lie. That video they're broadcasting is fake. We did invent new technology, but it doesn't wipe your mind, it tells you when people are lying to you. That's the real reason President Vitnik is trying to kill us. She doesn't want people to know the truth, especially in an election year. Here—I'll show you how it works." Rebe nodded to signal the video had been switched to Molly's POV. She slid on the app glasses. "Sam? If you'd give me a hand?"

"Sure." I stepped out to face Molly.

"This is Sam Gregorious, one of the other terrorists in our vicious gang. Sam, how tall are you?"

"I'm six foot nine," I said.

"See how the readout jumped into the red? That's because Sam was lying. How old are you, Sam?"

"Seventeen."

"That time Sam was telling the truth, so the needle barely moved. Are you a member of the pro-Russia anarchist group, Seela?"

"Hell, no."

As we'd planned, Molly turned to Basquiat. "How about you, Basquiat? Are you a member of the pro-Russia anarchist group, Seela?"

"Yes, I am."

"Notice how the needle jumped into the red?" Molly said. "Basquiat was lying." She turned to face Boob. "How about you, Boob? Are you a member of Seela?"

Boob shook his head. "No, I'm not."

"Rebe, how about you?"

"I am a member of Seela."

Molly nodded to Rebe. Rebe shifted the POV back.

"We want everyone to have this technology. That way we'll all know who the liars are, and together we can create a future that's one hundred percent bullshit-free. Please, help us get the word out. Spread this message. And if someone out there could please make sure my mom sees this, I'd be grateful."

Rebe lowered her phone. "And, cut."

Basquiat threw his hands in the air. He ran to Molly and lifted her off the ground. "That was vascular!"

When he finally set Molly down, I was waiting to hug her. "Nice." I tried not to notice how incredibly good it felt to be in her arms.

"And"—Rebe worked her phone—"it's live."

31

There was a little town nestled in the valley we were skirting. The main street was five or six blocks long. Church bell towers poked above the trees. Chances were not many people lived there. When the Depression hit, small towns emptied. People stampeded toward the cities, because that was where the few remaining jobs were.

I was eleven when it happened, old enough to know something awful was going on, but too young to understand it. I didn't understand economics well enough to grasp the specifics, but I knew that Russia had tanked our economy through a cyberattack on our banks. Something having to do with derivative swaps, which I understood only in the most general way. They're like bets. You place a bet on how the dollar is going to perform against another currency, or whether the price of gold is going to go up or down, without buying the dollars or the gold. Russia bought a ton of these swaps, or sold them, or both, while pretending to be U.S. banks, and they purposely made really bad bets.

Molly fell into step beside me. She looked exhausted, and her hair was damp and matted.

"How you doing?" I whispered.

"My father is dying right now. And for all I know our neighbors abandoned my mother when that first News America video was released, and she's shut inside alone, starving."

I didn't know what to say. There was nothing we could do about it. Hopefully her parents had seen our video and at least knew Molly wasn't part of Seela.

Just ahead of us, Rebe was talking to Mr. Chambliss in hushed tones.

"What I don't understand is, why didn't they just show up at my garage and say, 'Hey, DHS here, what you're doing is a threat to national security,' and confiscate it all?" Rebe said.

Mr. Chambliss tapped his temple. "Because the technology isn't just in the hardware, it's in your heads. Even if they took everything, you could start over. And you'd know you were being monitored, so you'd go underground. Plus, there are *five* of you to keep track of. It's more complicated than it seems."

"So why not just kill us, right off the bat?"

"Killing kids is risky, even for Vitnik. Safer and easier to throw a few dollars at you and get you to walk away. If *that* doesn't work, then take the risk and kill you."

Up ahead, Mom stopped in her tracks and cursed.

I looked around, trying to figure out what she was upset about. Then I saw it. A drone, round, the size of a wren, mottled green and brown for camouflage.

Kelsey raised his rifle and fired, the report no louder than a bottle of champagne being uncorked. He hit the drone with his third shot, and it burst into fragments that dropped to the ground.

Kelsey lowered his rifle. "Not that it matters."

"We have to get far away from here in a hurry." Mom consulted her map, then pointed at Beltane. "On point. Head west. Four miles to Denning Road. Highjack the first good-sized vehicle that passes."

Beltane darted off into the brush, quick as a startled deer.

Mom spun toward us. "I need you to give me everything you have left. You can rest once we're on the road."

We ran.

I had no idea how fast soldiers might get here. Unless a platoon happened to be close by, it seemed like they'd have to send a helicopter after us.

By the time we'd run maybe two miles, I was pretty sure I was going to vomit. My mouth felt thick and phlegmy; my lungs were burning so badly they felt scraped raw. Mom was carrying Rebe. I glanced back: Boob was forty feet behind me, visible as flashes of color through the foliage. Kelsey was somewhere behind him.

"*There!*" A woman's voice, to our left. Her shrill tone startled me.

A heavyset man with a graying beard burst out of the brush, pointing a big automatic pistol. *"Freeze!"*

Three other men and one woman followed him out of the brush. They wore jeans, boots, T-shirts. These weren't soldiers or federal agents.

"We got 'em. We got 'em," a guy about my age said.

"Drop your weapon. *Immediately!*" the heavyset man shouted at Mom, who was pointing her rifle at him.

Mom held her ground. "You don't really want to die for them, do you? Because you're dying if this goes down."

News America must have aired an alert, calling on citizens to go after us.

"They're lying about us," I said. "We don't—"

The kid my age pointed his gun at my chest. "Hands at your sides. You move your hands, I *will* shoot you."

He thought I had a gadget that could wipe his memory. I could see the fear in his eyes.

"We're gonna be heroes." The kid's hands were shaking. "We'll probably get to meet the president and everything."

"Be quiet, Porter," the woman said.

"Put down the weapon," the heavyset guy repeated.

"We're no threat to you," Mom said. "We just want to go on our way."

"You're a threat to *everyone*," the woman said. She was wearing a Snoopy T-shirt.

"They're *lying* about us," Molly said. "Can't you see that?"

The heavyset guy's eyes flew open. He jerked violently as muffled pops filled the air. The others jolted as well, like a thousand volts were being shot through them. It wasn't until they were on the ground that I saw the blood.

Beltane stepped out of the brush, her eyebrows pinched. "Get their guns."

Molly was sobbing. Mom was squatting, head down, eyes glazed. Kelsey was turning around and around, scanning the terrain for threats.

Beltane gestured toward the bodies. "*Get their guns*. I told you this would get ugly. Take a good look. This is what ugly looks like."

The kid who was excited about being a hero was lying across his mother. A face-sized bloom of blood blotted out most of Snoopy on her shirt. The big guy was the worst; he'd been hit at least a dozen times.

Rebe helped me retrieve the guns. I tried not to look at their faces. They'd thought they were doing the right thing. In their eyes, we were the bad guys.

32

Even when lying across a stack of cardboard boxes, I could feel the vibration running up from the floor of the semi's trailer.

"Is that it? Are we done switching?" Rebe asked. We'd switched vehicles twice in twenty minutes, in case we were being tracked via satellite.

"I think that's it for now," Mr. Chambliss said, his mouth full of Oat-N-Honey Crisp cereal. That's what was in the cardboard boxes. Cereal.

I tried to rub the dried mud from the corner of one eye with my dirty fingertip. My entire body was throbbing, my head aching from exhaustion. I couldn't sleep, though; I kept seeing that guy jerking as the bullets hit him.

"Those people. I feel so guilty," I said.

"Lie," Boob muttered, almost to himself. I'd thought he was asleep.

"What?" I asked.

"That's a lie."

"I'm not *lying*. How could I be lying about a thing like that?"

Boob huffed in frustration. "You're right. This thing that people are dying over must not work."

It wasn't true that I felt guilty about the people who'd died? I stared at the boxes of cereal stacked deep inside the truck. *Was* it guilt? I felt sick about it, sad about it, but did I feel guilty?

"I feel bad for those people, but I'm relieved Beltane showed up when she did," I said. "I'm glad it was them and not us."

Boob nodded. "That's the truth."

"Damn." Mr. Chambliss was lying on top of cardboard boxes stacked three high, his face dimly lit by the glow of his phone. "Don't you dare point that thing my way."

"Why's that, Mr. Chambliss?" Boob asked.

"Because I don't want to know how big a lying son of a bitch I am."

"Lie," Boob said.

Mr. Chambliss looked startled. "See? I'm even lying about why I don't want you to know when I'm lying."

"Cast no shadow, Mr. Chambliss," Basquiat said. "It'll do you good."

Mr. Chambliss grunted and went back to his book.

"I don't feel bad for those people in the least," Rebe said. "They're the ones—"

"*Lie*," Boob said, interrupting her.

"What's a lie?" Rebe asked.

"'I don't feel bad for those people.'"

Looking flustered, Rebe pulled her knees up to her chin.

"Whoa." Molly was looking at her phone. "That video we made is actually helping. Vitnik's people released a virus that replaced every copy of it with a version where we're back to being terrorists, but lots and lots of people saw the video before then, and they're talking about it. Sixty-one percent of the people talking about it believe our version. Silhouette Lark is talking about us constantly."

"We should make another," Rebe said. "Keep the conversation going."

So we did.

"I still don't understand how they found out about our project in the first place." Rebe flicked a Cheerio at Boob's head.

Boob clutched the spot where it hit, then muttered, "Cut it out."

I knew how they'd found out, but I doubted telling Rebe did anyone any good. Then again, cast no shadow.

"Did you hack into any government computers when you were finding us free processing capacity?" I asked.

Rebe nodded. "Like six. Why?"

"One of them noticed. They must have contacted the FBI, who analyzed what sort of data was being processed, and figured out what we were doing from the data."

Rebe covered her eyes. "Crap. So this is my fault."

"No, it's not. You were doing your job, and we were all aware of what that meant. We all missed it. Even Theo."

Mr. Chambliss sat up, laughing, his legs dangling off the boxes. "Talk about a small world. We're going to pass within thirty miles of our esteemed president. She's doing a campaign appearance in Belvidere. Maybe we should stop by and ask her why she's trying to kill us."

"You think the Secret Service agents would shoot us on the spot, or take us around back first?" Rebe asked.

"The crowd would beat us to death before Secret Service got the chance," Boob said. "By now our faces are as familiar as Elvis's."

It was strange, knowing the person who wanted us dead would be so close. *Why* did Vitnik want us dead, though? That question was driving me crazy. What sort of secret was so awful she would kill to keep it quiet? Maybe she killed people routinely, and that was what she was trying to keep hidden by killing us. Maybe it was something worse.

"Lie," Boob said to Rebe.

I hadn't heard what Rebe had said, but she smacked Boob in the shoulder. "That's getting annoying really fast."

"That's what I've been saying."

What I wouldn't give to have ten minutes with President Vitnik while wearing that prototype. I wouldn't even have to ask questions; I could just let her talk.

"Wait a minute." *I could just let her talk.* "If I could get close to Vitnik without being recognized, maybe we could get something juicy on her and post it on BuckyHead. That would prove the truth app really does what we claim, and simultaneously put Vitnik on the defensive."

I looked at Boob. "Did I get through that without telling any lies?"

He shrugged. "It was all opinion. How could you lie?"

"You'd be taking our only prototype into the lion's den," Basquiat said. "Is that wise?"

"It's a risk, but I think we're desperate enough that a risk is warranted."

Basquiat didn't argue.

Mr. Chambliss was typing in the air.

"What are you doing?" I asked.

"Locating the nearest party supply store. We need to get some liquid skin."

33

Mr. Chambliss studied my face, his nose a foot from my fake one. He reached out and smoothed the seam on one side, then nodded. "Looks good." He turned his attention to Molly.

My upper lip felt strange; the fake teeth made it bulge slightly. I could actually see my upper lip when I looked down. I'd never been able to see any part of my face besides my nose before.

Rebe nudged in beside Mr. Chambliss. "There's going to be automated surveillance all over the place, designed to pick up suspicious behavior. Don't just stare straight ahead. Look around. Make eye contact with people. Also, don't seem nervous. Don't touch or rub your face. Don't blink rapidly. Don't pace or shift from foot to foot. Keep your heart rate under one thirty."

"So it's okay if I vomit, or wet myself?" I asked.

Rebe rolled her eyes, raised one hand like she was going

to smack me upside the head, then patted my shoulder instead. "Just grin like an idiot and you'll fit right in."

They dropped Molly and me off in front of an abandoned strip mall. We headed down a broken sidewalk, toward the packed Walmart parking lot.

I looked around as I walked, just as Rebe had advised, my hands stuffed in the pockets of my jeans. Most of the stores and businesses along the road were empty.

"I dreamed this," Molly said.

"Just this walk, or going to Vitnik's rally?"

"The whole rally. I'm remembering only now because this walk is giving me a déjà vu–ish feeling."

"Does it all turn out okay?"

"We'll be fine."

We breezed through the plastic and metal detector.

"Heads up, hats and headwear off," a recording repeated on loop as we waited to pass through a long, narrow channel single file. A bank of cameras running automated facial recognition checks lined the channel.

A Secret Service agent watching from outside the channel aimed a steel pointer at me. "Step out, please."

Heart pounding, I stepped through the steel half door he held open. Molly kept walking.

"Raise your arms." The agent patted me down, starting at my neck and working his way down. We'd done our research. I was fairly sure this was a random check, which shouldn't involve ID. If he asked for ID, I was dead.

As he patted my legs, he looked up, studied my face. "Where are you from?"

"Pittsburgh."

He stood, gave me a long look, then pointed at the door. "Enjoy the rally."

Feeling a wash of relief, I hurried through the run and found Molly waiting at the end. There were thousands of people jamming the parking lot, tailgating, drinking beer, munching Vitnik-brand weenies the president's people were handing out at a Vitnik weenies truck. Some rally-goers were wearing Vitnik T-shirts, or had painted their faces red, white, and blue. Molly and I headed toward the stage. The truth app usually worked up to a distance of twenty-eight feet, but with all these people wearing phones, the signal interference might shrink the effective range.

As we reached the edge of the crowd, Molly took my hand and threaded us forward. It felt good to have her cool, small hand in mine. Whenever someone gave us a look, Molly smiled brightly and gestured ahead, giving the impression we were trying to reach friends. She even looked sincere when she was totally lying. We got within twenty feet of the podium before the crowd became too tight for us to move any closer. We stood there holding hands until Molly finally gave mine a squeeze and let it go.

I studied faces in the crowd, curious to understand who these people were who actually supported this woman. There weren't many young faces, but other than that, they looked like any random crowd. There were black people and white, Latino and Asian. They didn't *look* stupid, but if they liked Vitnik enough to be here, they were. Unless they were here for the free food. That was a definite possibility.

The town's mayor, a little guy with a big head, introduced Vitnik. He went on for a long time. People around us huffed impatiently.

When Vitnik finally strode onto the stage, my skin crawled. With her dyed-black bobbed hair and her features blurred from too much plastic surgery, she reminded me of an old actress who couldn't stand the thought of looking her age. I locked the truth app onto her and turned on the record function.

"Hello, Belvidere!" Vitnik cried, raising her hands as background music swelled. "I'm glad to be here."

Lie. It was working—I was close enough.

"Now, before I get to happier news, I have to talk about the blues, those kiddie commies who should be home with their mommies."

The crowd erupted in boos so loud I felt them in the pit of my stomach. The music fell to an ominous bass. It was unnerving, knowing the reaction was for us.

"I know. They're sick. They're rabid clowns who need to go down." Vitnik pointed at the ground as the crowd cheered. "That's right. Put 'em down." The music rose, and her words—*Put 'em down*—echoed robotically through the speakers.

She worked the crowd. The economy had turned around,

and rapid growth was just around the corner. I didn't need the truth app to tell me that was a lie.

It was a combination concert, high school pep rally, and doomsday cult meeting. We were a special people; a magical, powerful people. Russia was the devil. Those things, at least in her mind, were true.

"I don't know what I was expecting," I said, my voice low.

There was nothing here we could use against Vitnik. It was nothing but platitudes chanted at high volume and set to music.

"We're rising, rising! But that's not surprising."

The crowd loved it. Molly and I hooted and clapped so we wouldn't stand out, but I was barely listening.

"It was worth a try," Molly said.

". . . the Russians hit us with a cyberattack—"

I snapped alert as the needle jumped. *Lie.*

"We couldn't stop them, but it's time for payback—"

Lie. When she chanted, *We couldn't stop them,* the needle went off the charts. I didn't understand. How could that be a lie? What, she *didn't* try to stop Russia from wrecking the U.S. economy?

My skin began to tingle, like a shiver that kept going. The truth app was never wrong, though. Vitnik was lying. She *didn't* try to stop the Russians. Why would the president of the United States want to wreck the U.S. economy? Why would she want half the people in the country—in the world—to lose their jobs and go hungry?

I was eleven when it happened. I'd been more interested

in the Incredible Hulk than politics back then, but I remembered Ms. Moreno, my fourth-grade teacher, talking about the crash right after it happened. That had also been an election year, and Vitnik, running for reelection, had been trailing up to that point.

Up to that point. When the crash came, people rallied to the known quantity, the former general.

Could anyone be so cold-blooded?

Yes. I was pretty sure Vitnik could.

When the rally ended, we moved with the flow of the crowd. I waited until we were almost to the rendezvous point before I cued up the recording and handed the glasses to Molly.

"Did you get something?" she asked.

"Just watch it."

"Oh my—" I steadied Molly as she stumbled on the broken pavement. She pulled off the glasses. "Do you understand this?"

"I think I do. Let's get to the truck first."

The truck rumbled up beside us and the back door rolled up. Basquiat gave us both a hand inside. Rebe closed the door as soon as we were in.

"Anything?" Mr. Chambliss asked.

"Maybe." I expanded the screen. The president sprang to life on the wall, the truth meter displayed in the top left corner.

"*. . . the Russians hit us with a cyberattack—*"

Murmurs and exclamations filled the tiny space as the needle jumped.

"Listen to this next one," I said.

"Too late to stop them—"

The cab went silent.

"I don't understand," Basquiat said. "She *didn't* try to stop them? That makes no sense."

I looked at Mr. Chambliss, who was perfectly still except for his eyes, which were tracking left to right and back again, like he was watching something the rest of us couldn't see.

"Mr. Chambliss?" I said. "Am I reading this right?"

"Home run, Sam, Molly. Grand slam." He patted my shoulder. "Holy crap."

"What?" Rebe said. "What's so amazing?"

Mr. Chambliss looked around, spotted his water bottle, and took a long drink. "Sam?"

"The Black Monday cyberattack happened a month before the election. Vitnik was behind in the polls. When Russia attacked and the economy crashed, voters rallied around Vitnik, the ex-general, even though she'd had a crap first term. They figured she'd keep us safe."

Mr. Chambliss shook his head. "Hard to believe. She purposely left us open to that attack. She threw the whole country under the bus to get reelected."

"No wonder she's trying to kill us," Basquiat said.

Rebe stared down at her phone, like she was dying to put it to good use. "We have to get this out there."

"We have to get the *truth app* out there. No one's going to believe this without one." I turned to Mr. Chambliss. "We have to get production under way." All this suffering because Vitnik had wanted to get reelected? Because she wanted to keep her theme park running and her applesauce selling? That was just sick.

"I don't see how we do that while we're running for our lives," Mr. Chambliss said.

I picked up the walkie-talkie sitting beside an empty box of Cocoa Puffs. "Mom?"

"What's up?" she answered.

"I want everyone to hear this. I understand it's risky, but we need to get production under way now. Today." I caught Basquiat's eye. He nodded.

"We'll talk about this once we're safe."

"*No*, Mom. I'm sorry, but no. We need to find a place where we can set up production. Then we need to get in touch with this distributor and convince her to bankroll us. We need magnets, coil—"

"Sam, if I have to, I'll die to make this happen, but I won't watch *you* die. We have Vitnik, the entire U.S. Army, and a few hundred million gun-toting citizens after us."

"They're after us because Vitnik doesn't want truth apps out there. We need to get tons of them out there, and for that we need a factory, and an army to protect that factory, so Mr. Chambliss is going to need to crank out supervets while we crank out truth apps—"

"If I could make a suggestion." Mr. Chambliss was looking

at a 3-D map of the East Coast on his phone. He tapped a point on the map. "Mineral Point, Pennsylvania. Home of the Mineral Point Home for Disabled Veterans." Mr. Chambliss closed the map. "I'll have to work quietly. Identify a few anti-Vitnik types from their social media posts and peel them away, then snowball from there."

"Fine. *Fine,*" Mom said over the walkie-talkie.

"Thanks, Mom. Love you." I set the walkie down.

Boob was taking notes on his phone. "I'm putting together a list of materials. Most of it we can order by mail if we set up a PO box. We can buy the neodymium magnets from an electronics recycler."

We couldn't get any of it until we had money, though.

"There's a ghost town twenty-eight miles from Mineral Point." Busquiut was studying the readout on his phone. "Vintondale."

34

I hopped off the back of the trailer onto broken blacktop. Waist-high weeds jutted through the cracks. We were in the parking lot of Vintondale High School, a squat, two-story redbrick building surrounded by forest on three sides and backed up to a steep hillside. Some of the building's windows were broken, but otherwise it looked to be in decent shape, considering it had been empty for six years.

As soon as the truck's back door was lowered, Kelsey pulled out of the parking lot, off to get supplies.

Beltane broke out the window of a classroom and, one by one, we climbed into what we hoped would become our production facility.

Desks were stacked against the inner wall. In the hallway, lockers stood open, some with chewed papers and twigs at the bottom—probably rats' nests. The place was filthy, the walls covered in graffiti.

Mom and Beltane went out to make sure there was no one else in the vicinity, while the rest of us explored.

Tables still lined the cafeteria, and light streamed in through the tall windows.

"We should set up in here." Rebe pointed. "We could build stations at the tables, create a half-assed assembly line."

"Or even a full-assed one," Basquiat said.

"Are we going to sleep here, too, or what?" Molly asked, surveying the cafeteria.

"Much as I love you guys, I think I'm ready to have my own room again," Boob said.

"Ditto," Basquiat said. "Let's go pick out rooms."

"Dibs on the teachers' lounge!" Rebe called.

We all groaned. The teachers' lounge was bound to be the most comfortable room in the building. It might even have a couch.

"We should probably let Beltane and Mrs. Gregorious have it," Basquiat suggested. "Their old bones can't handle the floor."

"Better not let Beltane hear you say that," Boob said.

We found a stack of wrestling mats in the gym to sleep on. I chose the chemistry classroom because it felt familiar and comforting, plus I figured I could sleep on one of the big lab tables in case those rats showed up.

"Hey, we're neighbors." Molly was coming out of the classroom next to mine as I stepped into the hallway.

I was feeling good, feeling hopeful. I put an arm around

Molly's shoulders as we headed back toward the cafeteria. For just a second, Molly rested her head on my shoulder, and my day was made.

In the cafeteria, everyone was huddled around Boob's phone. Basquiat, who was standing, looked at us crossing the cafeteria. I let my arm slide off Molly's shoulder.

"You guys need to see this." Boob gestured at the video that was playing. "I'll start again from the beginning."

It was another News America video. A van pulled into a parking space on the main street of a quaint town. We piled out, the vets pointing rifles. We spread out in groups, with me and Mom heading for a hair salon. As I burst through the door, I said, "I think you forgot something." I raised my hand, two truth app rings prominent on my fingers.

Everyone in the salon clapped their hands to their ears and doubled over, screaming.

"Actually, I think you forgot *everything*." I raised a fist. "For Mother Russia!"

The scene switched to Rebe and Beltane in a grocery store, approaching dozens of trapped shoppers from opposite ends of the cereal aisle. The shoppers pleaded as Rebe raised her rings and wiped their minds.

"What happened?" a woman cried over the screams of others as Rebe and Beltane turned away. "I don't understand."

Eventually we set our nefarious weapons for "wide band" and drove up and down streets, wiping memories remotely. I'm not sure why we didn't do that in the first place and skip the stores. By the video's end, the town was in chaos.

People stumbled through the streets screaming, calling for help. The final shot was a little girl standing under a traffic light clutching a teddy bear and crying.

The newscaster helpfully told viewers they could protect themselves with a special cap developed by President Vitnik. The caps were available at Walmart, Universes, Costco, and other leading retailers.

I turned to Rebe. "How do we get in touch with this distributor?"

"She's on her way."

"She's coming to us?" I asked.

"I offered to sell her twenty thousand T-eleven phones, cheap, and I got some black hat friends to vouch for my authenticity."

"Was that a good idea?" I said. At twelve hundred apiece that was over twenty million dollars' worth.

"The T-elevens haven't even been released yet," Boob said.

Rebe gave us her best gremlin smile. "Yeah. Imagine how fast she's gonna get here."

35

A white van pulled into the parking lot just before sunset. Eight people piled out, seven carrying automatic rifles. The eighth was a big African American woman wearing jeans and running shoes.

"I guess that's Mott," I said, basing my guess on the fact that she was the only one without a gun. The five of us were standing in the doorway, in all likelihood looking less impressive than Mott's entourage. Beltane and Mom were monitoring the situation from the roof. They had not been happy with Rebe's strategy, although I had to admit, she'd gotten Mott here in a hurry.

Rebe raised a hand in greeting. Mott raised hers in return.

"Be back soon. I sincerely hope." Rebe headed toward the van. The problem, of course, was to convince Mott that we were not in fact terrorists with a memory-wipe weapon before her people recognized us and started shooting, which would leave Mom and Beltane no choice but to return fire.

"You've *got* to be kidding me," Mott said loud enough for us to hear as Rebe got close enough to be recognized. Seven rifles were suddenly pointing at Rebe. "Stop walking. *Now.*"

Rebe stopped walking, raised her hands in the air, and talked really fast. "I'm unarmed. And we did *not* invent a damned memory-wipe device. Vitnik made that up because she wants us dead."

"Yeah? And why does she want you dead?" Mott shot back.

"Because what we did invent will take her down."

"What *did* you invent?"

"Come inside, and we'll show you. I think you'll like it."

Mott put her hands on her wide hips. "You don't have any T-elevens, do you?"

"No."

Mott cursed, turned partway as if to leave.

"We have something way better than any damned phone. We're going to make billions, Ms. Mott, but we need a partner."

"You bring me out to an abandoned school in the ass-end of nowhere with a story about T-elevens, then tell me you've got a deal that'll make me billions. I've got to tell you, this stinks right up to the penthouse." Mott gestured to her people. "Let's go."

"Then why does Vitnik want us dead?" Rebe asked. "You tell me. If we had a memory-wipe weapon, we could have wiped your memories before you even recognized us, and stole the cash you brought to buy the phones."

Mott paused. "One more chance. What did you invent?"

"A lie detector. Portable. Foolproof."

Mott froze for a second. "I could like that. I could definitely like that. If it works."

"Come on in and check it out."

Three of Mott's people stayed with the van. The remaining four followed us.

Mott looked around as we led her into the cafeteria. "Nice place you've got here."

Once introductions were out of the way, Mott settled into a chair. "So show me this lie detector."

I took the seat across from her, held up my hand to show her the rings. She reached over and grasped my wrist, brought the rings closer to her face. "They're portable, all right." She let go of my wrist. "Show me that they work."

"How old are you?" I asked.

Mott folded her arms. "None of your damned business."

"Okay," I said. "How many brothers and sisters do you have?"

"Two."

The needle jumped. "That's not true."

Startled, Mott leaned forward. "None."

"That's true. Are both your parents still alive?"

"Yes."

"That's not true."

Mott leaned forward a little more.

"Do you have a hundred thousand dollars you could front us, if we made a deal?" I figured we might as well cut to the chase.

"Not a problem."

I looked at my friends and nodded. "True."

"Ask me something hard," Mott said. "Something you couldn't find out from anyone who knows me."

I tried to think of something that would convince her beyond a doubt. Then it came to me.

"We need a hundred thousand in start-up money and someone to distribute our product. What's the lowest percentage you'd accept to go into business with us, if we're on the level?"

"Fifty percent," Mott said.

"Is that your best offer?" I asked.

"It sure is."

The truth app said otherwise. "You have a different number in your head that's your real bottom line. Is it forty percent?"

"No." That was true. "Fifty percent." False.

"Would you take thirty percent?"

"No."

I leaned back. "So thirty percent is your bottom line."

Mott smiled. "Damn. All right, I'm convinced."

"Can we trust you?" I asked.

She tilted her head to one side and laughed. "If you're straight with me, you can. If not, you better run."

I offered her my hand.

Mott didn't move. "Hang on. I want to know if I can trust *you*."

I offered her the rings, showed her how to use them. "Ask me anything."

"Can I trust all of you?"

"Yes."

Mott raised her gaze toward the ceiling. "Who's on the roof?"

The question took me by surprise. "My mom, and a vet named Beltane."

"Are you good to your mother?"

I laughed at that one. "I try my best."

Mott held out her hand, and we shook. She turned to Rebe. "I'm guessing you're the person I'm talking to about the sneaky stuff." Mott worked her phone. "If I set up a ghost account, will you know how to tap it?"

"Not a problem," Rebe said.

36

The liquid skin Basquiat and Molly had molded onto Mom's cheeks and chin made her look vaguely elf-like. They'd given Kelsey big jowls and a heavier brow.

After Mom dropped Kelsey in Philadelphia, where he would buy the neodymium magnets, she'd push on to Farmville, Virginia, where Rebe had rented a P.O. box. It would be at least another twenty-four hours before the materials were delivered to the P.O. box, but if Mom was there waiting, they'd be on the way to us the moment they arrived.

"Do what Beltane says until I get back," Mom said through the window.

I rolled my eyes. "Mom, we don't need a babysitter."

"Work with me here, Sam. A year ago I was grounding you. Now I'm laying down cover fire. It's a strange situation."

I nodded. "You're right."

Mom looked off through the windshield for a moment.

"After Theo died, I kind of went off the deep end for a while."

"I noticed. You seem better now."

"I am. But when you offered to get my legs working again, all I could think was, if I had my legs I'd be able to protect you. I didn't think about the danger I was putting you in by fighting back against those bastards. Now I'm wondering if I made a terrible mistake that we're all going to regret."

"It wasn't your mistake to make. If you hadn't agreed, we would have gotten someone else."

Mom pounded the steering wheel. "No, you wouldn't have. You're *seventeen*, and I'm still your mother."

"You're right. I'm sorry. I'm just glad you can see how important this is."

"*Do* I see that? Or did I jump onto a train, and now it's too late to hit the brakes? I'm not sure."

"Either way, it's the right thing. I keep thinking about this loaf of bread that Theo baked for us after we had an argument, because he loved us like we were his brothers and sisters. But if he'd passed a hungry kid on his way to Rebe's house that morning? I think he would have handed the bread to that kid, because he cared about *everyone*. Not just his friends and family—*everyone*."

Mom considered that for a moment. "I'm not sure this is the equivalent of giving bread to hungry kids. I'll have to think about it." She threw the truck into drive.

I stepped back, raised my hand as she pulled away.

We set to work clearing extra chairs and tables out of the cafeteria so we'd be ready to ramp up production as soon as Mom and Kelsey returned with the materials.

"Can someone put on some music?" Basquiat asked. He was carrying a chair in each hand.

"I got it." Rebe paused to work her phone.

Beltane, who was carrying a table over her head, nearly bumped into her. "Watch out, sandbag."

Rebe reacted as if someone had dumped a bucket of ice water over her. "You want me to draw you a map so you can find your way around without running into people, *dim bulb?*"

"'Dim bulb'?" Beltane said. "For someone who's got nothing going for her except her mind, supposedly, that's pathetic."

"Oh, I've got plenty of better words to describe you."

Basquiat put an arm around Rebe and turned her away. That left Beltane for me. I stepped close enough to see the pores on her nose. "Come on. We're supposed to be backing each other up, not tearing each other down."

Rebe pushed past Basquiat, stabbed a finger at Beltane. "What turned you into such a bitch? Was it the war? Because I wasn't even alive then."

"You don't know what you're talking about. The war's got nothing to do with this."

"Lie," Boob said.

Beltane shoved me out of her way. It was like being shot from a cannon—I went over a table, flipped, and landed butt-first on the floor. *"Get that thing out of my face,"* Beltane said.

A gunshot rang out. Beltane froze, halfway to Boob.

"What is your *problem?*" Rebe shouted at Beltane, gun pointed at the ceiling. She'd pulled it from her pack, which was now on the floor, most of its contents spilled out.

Beltane glared at her. "Shoot that thing again, and I'll end you." She turned and jogged from the cafeteria.

We watched her go in stunned silence. My tailbone was throbbing.

A *bang* echoed somewhere in the building. Then another. Then crashing and clattering that must have been Beltane either throwing desks or smashing them.

"You really hit a nerve," I said.

"Boob, you don't have to announce it every time someone is lying," Basquiat said.

"I *don't*," he said.

Rebe barked a laugh. "Oh, *that's* reassuring."

As we headed to our rooms to get a few hours of sleep, I ended up beside Basquiat, who looked straight ahead, saying nothing. I was pretty sure he was angry with me. He was normally so cheerful that it was easy to tell when he was brooding. I also thought I knew what he was angry about. When Basquiat turned into his room, I paused in the doorway.

"Do we need to talk?" I asked.

"I don't know. Do we?" Basquiat pulled off his T-shirt, dropped it beside his sleeping mat.

I threw my hands in the air. "I just put my arm around her. Nothing's happened between us."

Basquiat's clenched brow relaxed a little. "All right."

The clacking of Beltane's blades on the linoleum came from the hall. I waited until she passed without a word and turned into her room.

It seemed ridiculous for Basquiat to be angry about me having my arm around Molly, with everything that was going on, though I had to admit, it would have bothered me if the tables were turned.

"Sometimes I get the sense you think I stole Molly from you, but you can't call dibs on a person," Basquiat said. "Everyone gets to choose who they want to be with."

"You could have had any girl in school. Why would you pick the one girl I've liked since freshman year?"

Basquiat spun toward me. "She's the *one* girl you fell for because she's a wonderful girl."

Truth.

Basquiat ran a hand through his hair. "She needs me. When her father left, I was about the only thing that kept her from falling apart. I'm doing my best not to be in your face with this, so you probably can't see it, but we're good together. Molly needs me."

I wanted to be that person for Molly. Basquiat was right, though; if Basquiat liked Molly, and Molly liked Basquiat, that was that.

"I do get what you're saying. I'm sorry I put my arm around her."

"No, honestly, that's no problem. Just, don't resent me, you know?"

"I don't resent you." I caught myself looking around for Boob, half expecting to hear him shout, "Lie!" I thought I'd put that anger and resentment behind me after Theo died, but I hadn't. Not completely, anyway. "I won't anymore."

We shook hands.

37

I found Beltane squatting behind a dumpster, watching the road. She stiffened when I stepped into view, then pointed her rifle at the sky. "Jeez. I could have shot you."

"I didn't think it was a good idea to call out." I joined her behind the dumpster.

"Your best bet is staying inside, out of sight. What do you need?"

I shrugged, my hands in my pockets. "Nothing. I just wanted to see how you're doing."

"How I'm doing?" There was an edge to her tone.

"You've been keeping to yourself since we had that argument. I just wanted to see—"

Beltane pointed toward the doors. "Get your ass back inside. I'm breathing. You're breathing. It doesn't matter how I'm *feeling*, and I don't give a flip how you're feeling."

I marched back inside. Jeez, she was hard-core.

As soon as I was through the doors, I heard Rebe shouting my name.

I ran for the cafeteria.

When Rebe saw me, she gave me this look I couldn't read. Pity? Dread?

"What?"

"I—" Rebe pinched her temples. "It's bad, Sam. Really bad."

I rushed over, slamming my shin into a table leg on the way.

Mom was on News America. She was in a chair, a bright light shining on her face from above. Her legs were gone—the exposed stumps red and raw where they'd been removed. She looked like she was in shock. Her upper lip was split and bleeding, her left arm covered in dried blood.

"It could be fake," Rebe said. "You know what they're like."

"Look at her face." Liquid skin clung to her cheeks and chin where her disguise had been pulled off. If they knew she'd been wearing a disguise, they had her. "Mom." I had to do something. Now.

I flinched as a hand rested on my shoulder. Basquiat, standing behind me, his eyes filled with tears.

"Oh God, Sam." Molly pressed against me.

"We have to turn ourselves in," I said. "They'll torture her. Kill her." They'd already tortured her. That's why she looked the way she did, the wide-eyed shell-shocked stare. They were torturing my mom.

"If we give up, they'll kill all of us." I hadn't heard Beltane come in. "I'm sorry. She was the best."

"Don't talk about her like she's dead."

Beltane swept tears off her cheek with her forearm.

"We'll get her back." Basquiat squeezed my shoulder. "We will."

"How?" How would we get her back? Storm the Pentagon with two broken-down vets and a few teens who'd never shot a gun?

"The truth app." Molly shrugged. "If people knew Vitnik was lying, if they knew what she'd done, she couldn't get away with killing an innocent war veteran."

I turned to Rebe. "Did they say where she was captured? Do they know about the P.O. box?"

"I don't know."

"Can you check on the materials? Has anything been delivered yet?"

"We have to get out of here," Beltane said. "Sooner or later, she's gonna crack, and then all they have to do is send a drone to drop—"

"We can't leave!" I shouted. "Kelsey and Mr. Chambliss won't know how to find us."

"Fine. I'm just saying," Beltane mumbled.

"Nothing's been delivered yet," Rebe said, eyes on her phone's readout. "The first package arrives in ninety minutes."

"So they didn't pick her up at the post office. It may still be safe to pick up the materials."

"And it may not be," Basquiat pointed out.

"We just have to take a chance. I'm going to pick up the packages," I said.

"I'll go," Beltane said.

"No, it's—"

"I'll go." Beltane gave me her thousand-degree glare. "Stay out of sight until I'm back."

38

Kelsey pulled up in a black pickup while Beltane was on her way to the post office. I could tell from his expression that he knew about Mom.

He flipped a tarp off a half-dozen cardboard boxes in the back of the truck. "Neodymium magnets." His tone was flat.

Now we needed Beltane to come through.

I held the newly manufactured rings in my trembling palm. "How many can we make per hour?"

My friends looked at each other, uncertain.

"Maybe ten?" Rebe said.

Ten. "Two hundred a day, if we work twenty hours and sleep four." No one protested at the schedule.

There were four hundred million people in the United States. If one in a hundred had a truth app, Vitnik wouldn't be able to open her mouth without being exposed. How could we expose her with only a few hundred? News America would go on releasing its videos and altering ours, and most people would believe theirs. We had an undercurrent of buzz going through BuckyHead, but it wasn't nearly enough.

"We have to get them into the right hands," Boob said. "Difference makers. Like Silhouette Lark. If Silhouette Lark had a truth app, tons of people would see it in action. Plus, she'd make it cool."

"It's not as if we can ask Silhouette Lark to drive to one of Vitnik's reelection rallies, point the app at her, and ask the one question she'd need to ask," Basquiat said.

A red light went off in my head. "No. *I'm* going to do that. Once we've got more buzz going."

"They'll drag you away before you can get the question out," Basquiat said. "Or shoot you on the spot."

"Then I'll ask the question, from another part of the room," Molly said.

Basquiat held out his hand, a pair of rings sitting in his open palm. I took them, shoved one on the ring finger of my left hand and the other on my index finger, then synced them to my phone.

As Basquiat solemnly offered a pair to Rebe, like a priest offering the sacrament, I grabbed a water bottle from the table and wandered into the hall to rest. Under other circumstances this would have been a triumphant moment. Vitnik had taken that away from me.

I slid down the wall of lockers until I was sitting, then chugged until the water bottle was empty.

Four hundred. Two days of production and I was already feeling like the work and lack of sleep were making me crazy. Were four hundred truth apps enough to change the world?

"How are you doing?" Molly plopped down beside me. Her eyes were glassy, her face shiny with sweat.

How was I doing? It was hard to think straight enough to form an answer. "Every minute my mom's with them hurts. I've had bad times before, but there's no letup to this, no moment I'm not on fire inside."

Molly squeezed my shoulder. "I know I can't make it better, but I'm here for you. We're all here for you."

I nodded thanks. The pattern on the linoleum floor seemed to be weaving and twisting. "They're torturing her. Right now, at this very moment. I don't want to imagine what they're doing, but I can't help it."

I hated Vitnik. I hated her so much it hurt. I wanted her to die. I'd kill her myself if I had the chance.

I struggled to my feet. "I need to get back to work."

The others were grouped around one table, searching for addresses on the net and addressing envelopes.

"What about Hennie Jeckyl?" Boob asked.

"No politicians," Basquiat said.

"He started out as an indie news dog."

Basquiat waved a dismissive hand. "Fine. Send one to a politician. Good idea."

"Don't talk to me like I'm an idiot," Boob said.

Basquiat squeezed his eyes shut. "Just . . . do what you want."

Rebe stuffed two rings and an information sheet into an envelope, sealed it, and dropped it onto the growing pile in the center of the table.

Another hour to finish packing the rings, if we didn't kill each other first. Two hours for Beltane to mail them, if she didn't get caught. Express drone delivery times varied from two to eight hours, depending on the location.

Then, hopefully, all hell would break loose.

39

Rebe sat cross-legged on a cafeteria table, staring out into the parking lot, her lips moving silently. On another day I might have made some crack about what she was doing, but now it only worried me.

"The missiles are flying."

I sprung from my seat as Beltane strode into the cafeteria, her bladed feet clacking on the linoleum, her hair and the front of her shirt soaked with sweat. "I drove an extra sixty miles, just to be safe. Dropped them at a bunch of automated kiosks."

I let out a hoarse whoop, while Basquiat clapped Beltane on the back. Just a few more hours, and the truth app would be out there.

Beltane sat heavily in one of the cafeteria chairs, rested her head in her hands. "Don't point that thing at me." She looked at Molly.

"We're not even *talking*. Relax."

"I *am* relaxed. Even if we're not talking, I don't want that thing pointing at me."

Basquiat perched on the edge of one of the tables. "Beltane, there's nothing we could learn about you that could make us think any less of you."

We all burst out laughing, except Beltane and Basquiat.

It took Basquiat a moment to realize what he'd just said; then he buried his face in his hands. "Fatigue. Let me try that again." He steepled his fingers. "Whatever secrets you have, it won't change how much we like and appreciate you. And you'll feel better if they're out there."

"I don't want to feel better," Beltane said.

"*Lie,*" Boob said.

Beltane spun to face him. "Do you *want* to die?" She pounded the table. Plastic splintered as her fist went right through it. "Are you provoking me because you want me to snap your neck and put you out of your misery?"

"There are days I want to die, but today, surprisingly, isn't one of them," Boob replied.

And that, according to my truth app, was true.

Basquiat stepped between Beltane and Boob. Not that that would slow Beltane much, as I'd recently learned. "We need to come up with a more polite way to tell someone they're not being totally honest."

"Are you suggesting shouting 'lie' at people isn't polite?" Rebe looked Boob's way. "Especially coming from someone who's still casting a little shadow of his own."

Boob looked up. "What do you mean?"

Rebe folded her arms. "The very first time, I asked why you broke up with me, and you still haven't answered."

"Jeez. Teen angst." Beltane grabbed her rifle and headed for the exit.

Boob looked both annoyed and uncomfortable. Which, when I thought about it, was pretty much his resting expression.

"Go ahead, Boob," Basquiat said. "Tell her. She wants the truth, even if it hurts."

"It won't hurt *her*. It'll make me look like the biggest loser on the face of the Earth."

Basquiat gave Boob a big, warm smile. "And you're strong enough to handle that."

Boob raised his eyebrows. "Oh, really? You know, you'd make a good priest."

"I'll try to take that as a compliment," Basquiat said. "Come on, spill it."

Boob gave us one of his signature sighs, like someone had just pulled a plug out of him. He turned to Rebe. "I was waking up in the middle of the night terrified, because we were getting to the point where we were probably going to kiss pretty soon, and I've never kissed anyone and I was afraid I would do it wrong."

Molly suppressed a laugh.

Boob waved in her direction. "Go ahead. Laugh. I know I'm ridiculous."

"Let's discuss who's the most ridiculous person in this room, but give me a minute to go puke up my lunch first," Rebe said.

The thing was, I could relate to what Boob was saying. Last year, the first—and so far only—time I'd ever kissed a girl, I was so nervous I thought I was going to vomit. It was after a concert I'd performed with my band for a sweet sixteen party. She was a cousin of the birthday girl, visiting from Staten Island.

"You think you can out-ridiculous *me?*" Boob said. "I'm terrified of being late for a class, because if I'm late everyone will watch me walk to my seat. When people watch me walk, it's like torture—my arms feel like big salamis hanging from my shoulders. My feet feel like they're half a mile away. I don't feel like I can do *anything* right."

Molly was looking pointedly at Rebe. "Are you going to do it, or am I?"

Rebe frowned. "Do what?"

"Kiss him."

Boob looked mortified. *"What?"*

I burst out laughing at Boob's reaction. I couldn't help it.

"It's ridiculous for him to agonize over something so stupid," Molly said.

"*I'm* not kissing him." Rebe folded her arms across her chest.

"*I'd* do it, but I don't think Boob would appreciate that as much," Basquiat said.

"In five seconds you can erase all that anguish," Molly said to Rebe.

Boob took a half step back.

"All right, fine." Rebe huffed in annoyance and went to Boob. "Come here." Before Boob could say anything, she planted her lips on his.

Basquiat and I burst into spontaneous applause.

Finally, Rebe stepped back. "Was that so terrible?"

"No," Boob admitted, a little grudgingly.

"It's not something you do right or wrong, moron. You just *do* it."

"Okay." Boob looked uncomfortable, a little stunned, but also pleased.

I cleared my throat. "You know, I've got the *exact same* problem as Boob. I could really use some help with it."

Rebe reached out and shoved my shoulder. "Smart-ass." She turned toward the assembly line. "We should get back to work."

Fear and anguish flooded back in, and I realized that the invisible boot pressing on my chest had lifted for a few minutes. I felt like crap for forgetting about Mom, for laughing and having fun. How could I forget for even a second what she was going through because of me?

"Hang on." Rebe checked her flashing phone. "Oh, baby. *Oh, baby.* We've got our first sighting."

Basquiat squeezed in beside her to see the screen. "Expand it. Expand it."

Rebe expanded her screen. I recognized Silhouette Lark immediately, which isn't hard, what with the gold Afro and diminutive height. It was a live user-POV feed. Silhouette was strutting down a city street, riff dub music playing in the background.

"So the security camera picked him up about ten minutes ago. Let's see if the little rodent is still gnawing on his burger." Silhouette entered a Burger Boy restaurant. Her state-of-the-art phone system quickly analyzed faces. A guy sitting near the back lit up, glowing yellow.

"There we go." Silhouette headed across the black-and-white checkerboard floor toward a fortysomething guy sitting in a booth across from two friends. "Corey Carlton Seager." She sounded like a teacher taking attendance.

Corey Carlton Seager looked up, and stopped chewing. "Yeah?" It was clear he recognized Silhouette, although from the way he was looking at her, he couldn't quite place *how* he recognized her.

Silhouette sighed heavily, like she was deeply disappointed in this stranger. "Let's see if I've got this straight. You propositioned Verily Stuart, your student, who's seventeen."

Corey Carlton Seager tried to interrupt, but Silhouette raised a finger, silencing him.

"When she reported you after you tried for, like, the eighth time, you inserted plagiarized lines into a paper she'd handed in, and then you hacked her personal files to change the same lines in her copy of the paper. Then you claimed she was accusing you of harassment to try to beat the plagiarism charge. Is that about right?"

Corey ran his hand through thinning hair, looking disgusted. "No matter how many times Verily tells that story, it's still not true." The readout on Silhouette's truth app shot into the red. "I'm sorry, who *are* you?"

Silhouette gave Corey Carlton Seager a bright smile. "Silhouette Lark. And friends. One point six million of them at the moment." A swarm of raindrop-sized faces materialized around her. She held out her hand, displaying the rings. "This is my shiny new truth app, and it just caught you lying through your teeth, jackass."

She lifted the ketchup, spelled out LIAR across Corey's french fries. "I hope you have superwicked security on your various electronic devices, because my friends are probably ruining your life as we speak."

Corey Carlton Seager had a nice phone. Not as nice as Silhouette's, but no more than a year old. As Silhouette turned on her heels, all four foot ten of her, and strutted out of Burger Boy, Corey's phone began to smoke.

"This is the coolest, most vascular thing I have ever owned." Silhouette kissed one ring, then the other, then looked directly into the camera. "Thank you, Team No More Bullshit. Listen up, everyone: As usual, News America is full of it. These kids aren't terrorists, they're revolutionaries."

With tears in our eyes, we whooped, we punched the air, we hugged.

On Rebe's phone, Silhouette said, "Stay safe, my friends.

If there's anything Silhouette can do for you"—she turned her palms up—"just ask."

"You know, Silhouette Lark lives only about three hours from here," Boob said as Rebe switched off the feed.

"So?" I asked.

Boob grabbed my arm. "So *you* don't ask the question, you bring her, and she does. They can't drag Silhouette Lark away to those not-so-secret rooms under the White House without starting a riot."

40

I had an itch on my nose, but I couldn't scratch it because of the liquid skin. A man in a suit cruised past us in a late-model NVUS, its polished chrome grillwork sparkling. He slowed and pulled into a driveway.

"Is that her house?" I asked.

"Next one down." Boob's eyes were bright with anticipation. "I know this neighborhood better than I know my own."

I had to admit, I was excited to meet Silhouette as well. The event that launched her career was the stuff of legend. It was twelve years ago, in her high school cafeteria. This rubbery-faced hulk was using a spoon as a catapult, shooting peas at two overweight kids—a guy and a girl sitting together—while his Neanderthal buddies snickered. Suddenly, Silhouette was standing before the hulk, one hand balled into a fist, the other behind her back. Only, because of the camera angle, we could see what she was holding behind her back: a heaping, dripping handful of gooey cafeteria lasagna.

"You think throwing food at people is funny?" The cafeteria had gone deadly quiet. The hulk didn't seem to know what to do. You can't pound a girl who weighs less than your foot. He was smirking, but the smirk was wavering; his eyebrows were clenching and unclenching in confusion. "Then you're gonna think this is hilarious." Silhouette slung the lasagna into the hulk's face. It made the most satisfying, distinct plopping sound, and most of it just *hung* from his cheek and nose, seemingly defying gravity before a big chunk finally peeled off and dropped to the floor.

The hulk finished off Silhouette's masterpiece by turning away, looking stunned and a little scared, as Silhouette stormed off. It would have been cool if everyone cheered, but they didn't. There was a rising buzz of conversation, and that was it—fade to black. That clip was more recognizable to people under thirty than the *Mona Lisa*, and it might well have been a more beautiful work of art.

The guy who'd pulled up in the NVUS studied us, frowning, as we passed his driveway.

"Afternoon," Boob called.

"Afternoon," the guy said, a bit grudgingly.

"I'm sending the message." Boob tapped Beltane's phone, which was strapped to his wrist, and sent the cued-up message that Rebe was hoping would be untraceable.

Turn off your feed. Team No More Bullshit.

Silhouette's reply came in seconds. Boob showed it to me.

Done! What's blowing? All atwitter.

We headed up Silhouette's long, curved driveway, which was framed by a country club lawn. The door swung open two seconds after Boob knocked.

Silhouette Lark clapped a hand over her mouth. She didn't quite come up to my shoulder, even with her Afro. Her legs were about as thick around as a stork's. If not for gold makeup ringing her eyes and lips, she would have looked more like thirteen than late twenties.

"Oh. My. God." She pulled us both inside. "This thing is *amazing.*" She wiggled her fingers, displaying the truth apps. "*Everyone* wants one. I mean, *everyone.*"

We were standing on a bright-gold marble floor, in a vestibule decorated with photos of Silhouette with various celebrities, mostly pop singers, mixed with a few athletes and microchannel personalities.

"As soon as we can stop President Vitnik from trying to kill us, I promise we'll make enough for everyone," I said.

Boob was standing frozen beside me, gawking at Silhouette. "I'm a huge fan of yours."

"And I'm a huge fan of yours," Silhouette said. "So we have something in common."

"You said if we needed your help . . . ," I said.

Silhouette beamed. "What do you need?"

"We want you to help us take down the president."

She went very still. "Anything. Anything you need. I hate that woman." From the venom in her tone, she could give me a run for my money on which of us hated Vitnik more.

"For something in particular, or on general principal?" I asked.

"There's nothing general about it. My father was a lieutenant in a division under her command during the war. The history's all been rewritten, but Vitnik sent my father and ten thousand other soldiers into Krasnoyarsk because she needed combat footage for the documentary they were doing of her. Krasnoyarsk was worthless, nothing but bombed-out buildings. My father died feeding that leech's ambition." Silhouette lifted her hand, examined the truth app rings. "I was hoping you guys weren't just another bad TV show. I was hoping you were the real deal, but this—if you really have some idea how to pull it off—this is truly epic."

"We were hoping the same about you," Boob said. "That you weren't just another TV show."

Silhouette laughed. "I'm definitely another bad TV show, but I'm also the real deal. A lot of people think what I do is a joke, but if you live just about every moment of your life in front of an audience, live, with no computer distortion? You better be authentic."

I'd never thought of it like that before. In a way, living your life in front of an audience was a lot like living it with truth apps. In both cases, you couldn't get away with much.

"Tell me what you want me to do," Silhouette said.

41

When we reached the park across from the Musk Civic Center in downtown DC, Boob and I hung back at a picnic table where no one would notice us and watched Silhouette work. Everyone from teen microchannelers to white-haired journalists in suits came to pick up the truth apps we'd been cranking out for the past twelve hours. All participants had been handpicked by Silhouette.

Boob nudged me. "Paul Park."

I squinted at what looked to be a white man in his seventies, trying to see what Boob was picking up on.

"Is it?"

"I'm telling you," Boob said.

Paul Park was hugely influential on the guerilla news circuit. He came up with incredible disguises to get into places no one else could. We watched as Silhouette gave him a quick lesson on how to operate the truth app, then he headed toward the civic center.

Vitnik typically took a few questions after her events. Silhouette needed to be one of the people Vitnik called on, even though the questions were vetted ahead of time and asked by actors planted in the audience. Boob was the one who'd come up with the solution; now we had to hope it worked.

"This is like a dream come true," Boob said. "We're teamed up with Silhouette Lark. I can't believe it." He stood. We'd been watching people pick up truth apps for about twenty minutes. "Why don't we head inside? I can't wait to see her in action."

Pretty much every seat in the arena was taken. Vitnik had people waiting to fill empty seats so every one of her campaign appearances looked like a sellout.

The floor was a mosh pit. The event in the Walmart parking lot had drawn mostly older people, but there were a lot of teens and twentysomethings this time. They were Silhouette's troops, come to execute Boob's plan. I picked a spot on the far side of the room, close to the older man Boob had insisted was the legendary Paul Park. My job, along with Boob, Molly, and Basquiat, was to raise a ruckus if Vitnik refused to let Silhouette ask her question. None of us had brought our rings.

The music swelled, and Vitnik appeared to thunderous applause, much of it prerecorded and piped in over the sound system. She was dressed in a golden outfit that caught the light and shimmered, reflecting yellow beams as if the outfit was made of gold. Black boots and belt matched her dyed hair.

"There's a golden sun rising over this great nation. Jobs and growth and lower inflation. Seela wants to bring us down, what they'll get instead"—Vitnik made a slashing gesture—"is castration."

I could barely look at her strutting around up there, knowing what she was doing to Mom. She was ten points ahead in the polls. How could she not be, with a five-billion-dollar campaign war chest, most of it self-funded?

When her performance finally ended and she took a bow, my heart started pounding slow and hard.

Vitnik spread her hands toward the audience. "How about a few questions before I get back to work for you?"

The woman standing to my left stepped on my foot. She was being shoved by other people, all shuffling and stumbling in the same direction as Silhouette's troops created space in the center of the floor.

Silhouette stood alone at the center. She raised her hand as thirty thousand people looked on. "I'd like to ask a question, Madam President."

Vitnik kept her smile frozen in place. "And who are you?"

"My name is Casey Simkins." Silhouette's voice sounded wavery, like she was nervous, but that was an act. The fake name was to throw Vitnik's people off-balance for a moment so they couldn't get a read on who Silhouette was, and how risky it was to let her ask a question.

Vitnik surveyed the circle. "I see you brought friends."

"I have a lot of them."

"You certainly do." Vitnik was sizing Silhouette up, the slightest squint in her eyes. Maybe she even recognized Silhouette vaguely.

Vitnik gestured toward Silhouette. "What's your question, Casey?"

Silhouette clasped her hands behind her back. "Did you purposely let the Russians wreck our economy to get reelected?"

Vitnik's smile collapsed. Her eyes got wide, wider. Out of the corner of my eye I saw a figure running.

It was Xavier Leaf.

"Have you taken your medication today, sweetie?" Vitnik said, recovering her composure. "Of course not—that sounds like something out of a bad Hollywood thriller."

Someone behind me and to my right gasped. Whoever it was whispered urgently to whomever she was with.

"How about a serious question?" Vitnik looked around.

Dozens of hands were in the air, waving, and Paul Park called out to Vitnik, desperate to get her attention. Ignoring him, Vitnik called on an old woman who asked Vitnik about her cat. It was difficult to hear the woman's question over the growing rumble.

Vitnik gave a quick, cursory reply, then held up her hands. "Thanks for coming." She all but sprinted from the stage, disappearing down a breezeway flanked by Secret Service.

Paul Park was commenting to his followers in a harsh, almost-panicked whisper, right there on the floor, and he was one of thirty or forty influential microchannel journalists who were spreading video of what the truth app had just revealed. By now their followers had seen the truth app in action, because of the four hundred we'd mailed far and wide. They knew it worked. Was it enough? It had to be. For Mom's sake, it had to be.

Silhouette's friends had closed ranks around her. As they shuffled toward the exit, Silhouette lifted her chin and looked around. I raised my hand. Silhouette spotted me, broke into a grin, and raised her hand in return.

"*There!*" someone shouted.

I looked up, right into Xavier Leaf's eyes. He was pointing at me, speaking frantically into his phone.

I pushed toward the exit. The liquid skin fooled facial recognition programs, but not necessarily people who knew you. Especially when you drew attention to yourself by raising your hand like an idiot.

Two Secret Service agents pushed into the crowd and headed toward me. They had a long way to go; there was a chance I could make it outside and disappear in the crowd.

I spotted Molly and Basquiat hovering uncertainly close to the exit, the crowd flowing past them.

Go, I mouthed silently, urgently, as I tugged on my shirt, which was suddenly uncomfortably warm.

Then hot. Hotter.

A woman near me shrieked in pain; others joined in as I fell to my knees, feeling like I was on fire. My skin was burning, but there was no fire. I dropped to the floor, writhing, trying to make the pain stop.

"There. Him." Leaf's voice cut through the searing agony, much closer now. "Him."

All at once the burning stopped. Leaf lowered the heat gun he was holding.

A big, crew-cut Secret Service agent rolled me onto my stomach, stepped on my back, and yanked my arms behind me, handcuffing them. He pulled me to my feet.

Boob was standing handcuffed a dozen yards away, Secret Service on either side of him.

Leaf reached up and yanked the fake nose from my face. "Who else is here?"

"No one."

He gave me an impatient look. "Let's go. Load 'em up. Sweep the area for their friends."

42

It looked like a regular chair. The seat and back were cush-
ioned, the arms grooved, a reddish wood. I didn't notice the
wrist restraints until Xavier Leaf and a male Secret Service
agent strapped my arms down.

President Vitnik paced the room, her arms crossed.

"Who told Silhouette Lark to ask that question?"

It took me a moment to realize Vitnik was speaking
to me, because she was facing away, toward a blank video
screen. I couldn't see what harm it would do to answer the
question. The problem was going to come when she asked
where my friends were hiding. I wanted to think there was
nothing they could do to make me betray my friends, but I
wasn't a hardened war veteran like Mom. I was a seventeen-
year-old kid in the basement of the White House, and I was
scared to death. I had to go to the bathroom, but I knew
better than to ask if I could.

"I did."

Vitnik turned to face me. "Why?"

"Because you're trying to kill us. Because you killed Theo Harlow." My mouth was so dry it clicked when I swallowed. "If you'd just left us alone, I wouldn't have done it."

"And I would have left you alone if you'd stopped working on the single biggest threat to civilization since the nuclear bomb." Vitnik pointed at me. "You have *no* idea what you're screwing with."

I managed to look her in the eye, but I stayed silent.

"We did *not* purposely ruin the economy," she continued. "It was a strategic action undertaken with the blessing of key figures in the financial industry that had an unexpected cascading effect." She swept her hair out of her face. "This world is *complicated*, little boy. Knowing someone is lying is not the same as knowing the truth, and sometimes lies are more true than the truth. Releasing that app will only serve to confuse people. The average person can't handle the truth without interpretation."

Interpretation. That was an interesting way to put it.

The door opened. A woman wheeled in a large, rectangular electronic device. It looked like an oversized stereo.

"Where's my mother?"

"You want your mammy, little Sammy?" Vitnik gestured to Leaf, who tapped his phone.

The screen on the wall flashed to life. It was Mom. She was strapped to a chair. A funnel jutted from her mouth and she was making terrible gagging sounds. A woman turned. She clutched something between her fingers—something that wriggled. She dropped the wriggling object into the funnel as Mom bucked and twisted, trying to get the funnel out of her mouth.

The screen went blank.

"Where are your friends?" Vitnik asked.

"Mom," was all I could manage.

Vitnik smacked the side of my head. *"Where are your friends?"* Another smack. *"Where are your friends?"* Again. *"Where are your friends?"*

"They keep moving. They've moved by now." At least I hoped they had. I hoped they were far away. The spot where Vitnik had slapped me throbbed.

Leaf pulled the electronic device closer. "I told you to listen to me," he said under his breath. He put a set of earbuds in my ears, then turned to his phone.

Music tore into my eardrums like an ice pick. I doubled over, trying to escape the agony, but it followed me.

It stopped.

Vitnik stuck her face close to mine. "Where are your friends?" My ears felt like they were stuffed with red-hot cotton.

I didn't answer. I wasn't sure I could. I wanted to go home, to my room. It was just an idea I'd had. The truth app—it was just an idea, like airbags, or Twitter.

The deafening music blared again. Longer this time. It felt like pins, dozens of them, shoved deep into my ears, again and again.

When the music finally stopped, Vitnik's voice sounded very far away.

Blood dribbled from my left earlobe and onto my shoulder. Vitnik's lips moved. Her voice was nothing but a deeply muffled hum. I thought what she said was, "Get the force feeder."

The door opened.

"You need to see this." I could hear because the man was nearly shouting, a vein in his neck bulging. I thought I recognized him from TV. The vice president? The press secretary?

The TV screen flashed on, showed the White House lawn, and beyond that the twenty-foot-high security fence surrounding it.

And beyond the fence, a crowd.

"Riots in at least eleven locations," the VP or press secretary said. He lowered his voice. I couldn't make out any of what he said, except "exponentially."

"Shut down all communication satellites," Vitnik said. It was like listening to TV with the volume turned close to zero.

"If we shut"—muffled, muffled—"coordinate our response. We can block—"

"There's no time to finesse this. Shut it down." As Vitnik swept hair out of her face, she glanced my way, almost like she'd forgotten I was there. "You like this? There'll be no way to call for an ambulance, for the police. People are going to die because of you." She turned back to the VP. It must have been the VP. "Shut it down. Now."

He studied Vitnik with half-lidded eyes for an instant longer than seemed polite, then turned.

Vitnik studied me the way you might study the bottom of your shoe after you step in dog crap, then she left as well, with Leaf on her heels.

They left the TV on. I watched crowds grow outside the gates until there was no more room. Helicopters buzzed overhead, dropping tear gas, itch gas, sweeping the crowd with heat cannons, but even if the crowd wanted to leave, there was nowhere to go, because more people kept pouring in.

My throat was so dry I couldn't swallow. My bladder ached. Maybe it was time to let go and wet myself. In another hour I wouldn't have a choice.

Should I shout for help? It seemed like a bad idea to draw attention to myself. Better they forget about me. No one had passed in the hallway for what seemed like hours; I was beginning to suspect the building had been evacuated, maybe by helicopter.

On the screen, the front gates finally burst open. People poured onto the grounds, like sand pouring through the neck of an hourglass.

I listened, my ears throbbing in time with my heart.

There was a distant, muffled crash.

Someone shouted, "Come on!"

"*Hey,*" I cried, not entirely sure how loud I was calling. "*Help!*"

More crashes. Two guys ran past the door.

"*Wait!*"

Five or six more people passed. I called again. This time a face appeared—a guy with a wispy mustache and wearing a ski cap.

"Can you unstrap me?"

He gave me a big, friendly smile. "No problem, cousin."

When he figured out how the restraints worked and pulled the first strap loose, I had to fight back tears of relief.

"What'd you do to end up here?" he asked.

"I invented the truth app."

His face lit up. "Seriously?" He loosened the other strap, then offered me his hand. "In that case, it's an honor to set you free."

I shook his hand.

"Hey, do you have any of those things on you? Can you set me up?"

"Sorry, I don't." The guy looked crestfallen. "If you give me your contact info, I'll send you one."

Brightening considerably, he emailed me his address. His phone was still working. I was about jumping out of my skin I was so desperate to find Mom and Boob. I thanked him again, then ran off down the hall.

People were making noise on the floors above, but only a few were on this level. Most of the doors were locked.

"*Mom? Boob?*"

A faraway voice called, "Sam."

I picked up my pace. *"Boob?"*

I turned a corner, and there he was.

We came together in a hug. "I didn't crack," Boob said. "I didn't tell them anything."

"I knew you wouldn't. I never had a doubt." I gestured down the hall. "She's here somewhere. I saw her on the TV." At least I thought I had. It could have been old footage, or computer generated.

Three people passed, each carrying a box of what looked like food.

"Ms. Gregorious?" Boob called.

We found a stairwell and headed down. The level below was uglier—bare concrete floors and walls.

"Mom?" I called. We waited, silent except for our labored breathing.

Boob tapped me. "I heard . . . something. It could have been a voice."

I hadn't, but that wasn't surprising, given the state of my hearing. As we headed down the hall, I called again.

"There it is again. *Ms. Gregorious?"* Boob called.

Light leaked from a door cracked slightly open halfway down the hall. I raced to it, pushed the door open.

Mom was strapped to a chair, blindfolded, the force feeder still in her mouth.

"We're here, Mom. It's over." I touched her shoulder, then, as gently as I could, I withdrew the force feeder. There was a tube on the other end that must have gone straight into her stomach. Mom gagged as I pulled it free. I undid the blindfold while Basquiat released her hands.

Although I'd been talking in a low, soothing voice the whole time, Mom still seemed shocked to see me.

"Sam?" Her voice was a horrible croak.

"We got her, Mom. We took down the president."

Mom nodded. "Is she dead?"

"I don't think so."

"She's going to be."

I lifted Mom from the chair while Boob retrieved her legs from the floor.

"Is everyone safe?" Mom asked as we rested before heading up the stairwell.

"Everyone's fine. You saved us, Mom."

The ground floor was packed with people, mostly young men hooting and dancing around. The place was trashed, the walls already covered with graffiti.

"Make way, please. Injured person," Boob called every few seconds.

People turned to stare at Mom, to pat my back as I passed, a few calling my name, evidently recognizing me from TV.

People were milling around on the lawn, not sure what to do now. Others were lining up bodies by the gates.

"*Sam.*"

I stopped, looked around. "Molly?" I didn't see her.

Then I spotted Beltane, threading her way toward us, rifle pointed in the air, leading a group through the crowd:

Molly, Kelsey, three more bionically enhanced vets carrying rifles. Mr. Chambliss had been busy.

Beltane took Mom from me, handed her to a vet I didn't know. Molly hugged me fiercely. "Are you okay?"

I nodded. Molly grinned and said, "You did it. You really did it."

"Where is Vitnik?"

"There's a bunker where the president's supposed to be taken in case of a nuclear attack. People think she's there."

Beltane grasped my upper arm to get my attention. It was hard to miss how strong and firm those fingers were, how easily they could snap your bones. "We're going to move out fast, Napoleon. Sooner or later, the army's going to turn up and clear this place out."

Molly said something I couldn't hear.

"You have to speak up. They hurt my ears."

"Mott is setting up a production facility."

"A production facility," I echoed as we jogged after Beltane.

"Out of the way. Move. Move!" Beltane barked at the people blocking our way. They parted like the Red Sea. Who wouldn't get out of the way for a group of armed vets with operational bionic parts? It was not a sight you saw every day.

The crowd thinned as we got farther from the White House. Store windows were smashed. People were carrying looted food, clothes, electronics. Not just young people—

parents trailed by kids also rushed along hauling stuff. We passed a police cruiser that had backed through the window of an electronics store. The officers were loading up the trunk.

Beltane led us to a school bus parked halfway on a sidewalk alongside a row of apartment buildings. Two vehicles lay on their sides, and a third was upside down, evidently shoved out of the way by vets to make room for the bus.

As soon as we were moving, Molly, Basquiat, and I huddled around Mom, who was lying across a seat and wrapped in a blanket. In the seat behind hers, Rebe sat with her arms wrapped around Boob.

I choked up as I looked into Mom's face. She didn't seem to see us.

"Mom?" I said. "Is there anything you need?"

Her eyes focused. She looked from me to Molly to Basquiat. I thought she might smile when she recognized Basquiat, but her scowl never wavered.

"Find Vitnik." The focus went out of her eyes, and she was gone again.

"Relax. The army's not coming," Beltane called up to Kelsey, who was driving. She was looking at her phone.

Kelsey turned in the driver's seat. "Why not?"

Beltane expanded her phone's screen and played a clip of an interview with a slim, gray-haired woman in a military dress uniform who was responding to a question from a journalist.

"As soon as we establish who is commander in chief of

the U.S. military forces, I will carry out his or her directives. I will not take orders from a traitor."

Beltane closed the screen. "That's General Alante Austin, chairwoman of the Joint Chiefs of Staff. Vitnik is cooked."

A ragged cheer broke out. It hurt my ears, but I didn't mind.

43

I woke when the bus's engine downshifted from a rumble to a mutter. We were cruising along an industrial road lined with cyclone fencing.

"Where are we?" I asked.

"Jersey. Outside Trenton." My hearing was a little better. Molly didn't sound as muffled.

We pulled into a huge, empty parking lot with a long, flat factory at the far end.

"Mott rented this for us?"

"Everyone wants a truth app," Basquiat said. "Instead of worrying about someone trying to stop us, we have to worry about people trying to steal apps."

I spotted at least six armed vets patrolling the grounds, and three more on the roof. And those were just the ones in sight. "Anyone coming here to rob us better come in a tank."

Inside, people were rushing around a factory floor lined with rows of heavy machinery. Not enough people by a long shot, but it was a start.

Mott, who was talking to a guy in blue coveralls, spotted us and headed over.

"Where's your slingshot, David?" she called out, grinning.

It took me a minute to get the reference. I held up my hand, wiggled the fingers with the truth app rings on them. "Right here."

"That reminds me—I need one of those, and I need someone to train a couple of my people on how to use them." Mott joined us. "I'm all in on Chambliss's idea of hiring vets to work the factory, but I still want to make sure we don't let any bad element through." She pointed to a glass wall twenty feet above the factory floor. "We'll set up a bunkhouse up there with cubicles for a little privacy. Install showers. Kitchen." She put her hands on her wide hips. "*Good* food. Steak and seafood. These are vets. We treat them right, pay them damned well."

Vets. I loved it. I put a hand on Mott's shoulder. "I'm happy to leave business operations to you while we focus on getting the factory up and running."

"Those should help you." Mott pointed toward the far wall, where crates were stacked four high from one end of the floor to the other. "3-D printers."

There were dozens of them. Big ones—industrial-grade. "Oh my goodness." This was beautiful. We were finally going to get the truth app out there in numbers that mattered. Soon all the people who'd got where they were by lying would come tumbling down. Every crooked politician and CEO, every killer who'd gotten away with murder would be exposed.

There was a big board mounted on the wall above the printers. On it were two rows of names. Mom's name was at the top, beside Emma Marshall's. I recognized that name: she was the vet we'd dug up to get Mom new legs. So the board was a remembrance of the vets who'd made this all possible. My guess was it had been Mr. Chambliss's idea. I was glad to see he'd been keeping track.

I looked around. "Where's my mom?"

"They set up one of the offices as a room for her," Molly said.

I headed off to find her.

She was sitting in a big stuffed chair, facing a window that looked out on the parking lot.

"Do you want to be alone?" I asked.

Mom looked up. I couldn't get over the sense that she was blind, the way she struggled to find me.

"I don't know what to do to help you. I'm so sorry I got us into this. I didn't know," I said.

"It's not your fault." Mom sounded out of breath, like it took everything she had to form the words. "I'm the one who screwed up." She looked at the floor. "When I got to that town in Virginia and checked into a room, I was so filthy, and the shower was right there. I felt guilty, but I did it anyway—I took a shower. And then I went out to get something to eat. . . ." She shook her head. "I forgot to re-apply the damned liquid skin, I was so tired."

I'd been wondering how they found her, but I hadn't wanted to ask. "We've all made mistakes along the way, Mom. When I've got some time, I'll write up a list of mine. I'm going to need a lot of paper."

Mom didn't respond.

"What can I do? I don't know what to do to help you."

"I'm supposed to be the one taking care of *you*. I'm the mom. You're the kid."

"You have been. I'd be dead three times over if it wasn't for you."

She didn't answer. I kissed her on the cheek. "I love you, Mom." I left her staring into the parking lot, although I didn't think she could actually see it.

"You were right," Mom said as I was closing the door.

I paused. "When was that?"

"When I didn't want you to sell your shoes. You said I wasn't taking you seriously. I wasn't. My little boy, thinking he could start his own company."

"And it turned out I couldn't. Not without your help." I eased the door closed, afraid the sound would startle her. I turned to find Mr. Chambliss heading toward me.

"How is she?"

"Not good. It's like she's not all there."

Mr. Chambliss nodded. "The trauma she went through dredges up all the old war trauma. Maybe I can help. Sometimes it's easier to talk to someone who's been there."

Mr. Chambliss rapped lightly on the door as I headed off to see what I could do to be useful.

44

"Oh. My. God." Rebe looked up from her screen, a cheese-steak in her free hand. "Take a guess what they're selling for on BidBuy."

It hadn't even occurred to me that people would be re-selling truth apps this soon. We were making it as hard as possible for people to buy more than one, but I guess there were always ways to game the system.

"Eight thousand?" We were selling them for four, al-though even that amount was offset by the ones we sold at cost in poor communities. That had been one of Theo's ideas, months ago, to level the playing field. At the time I'd thought he was out of his mind.

"Try forty."

"What?" I sprang up. Rebe expanded her screen and scrolled down sales figures. Forty thousand dollars, give or take. No wonder people were selling them.

"The price will come down as more hit the market.

Supply and demand," Rebe said. "Right now, truth apps are *the* status symbol. Oh, and I found yet another factory making knockoffs. That makes six."

"Good." We should have expected people would reverse engineer truth apps and start manufacturing them. I didn't care. I wanted as many out there as possible. "Let's release the plans on an open-source forum. Let's give them away."

Rebe raised her eyebrows. "You're getting hard-core, you know that? You're turning into Theo."

Her words startled me. I was, wasn't I? When all this started, I thought Theo's ideas were strange and eccentric. To me, the way he'd seemed to care about strangers in the Sudan as much as his own mother had been endearing and vaguely admirable, yet also tiresome and unrealistic. Not anymore.

I would have given anything to talk to Theo for five minutes, to tell him that I got it now, that I understood what he'd been saying. The four of us making tons of money was meaningless when compared with the chance to make things better for a billion people.

"I wish Theo was here to see this," I said.

"I know. I miss that dork every day."

"Hey, boss." I looked down. Beltane was looking up at me from the factory floor. "We're buying a helicopter."

"Okay."

Beltane shrugged. "Okay." She wandered off.

We were buying a helicopter. Unbelievable. We had a

security force of thirteen repaired vets, a bunch of weapons, bulletproof clothing, and now a helicopter.

"Wow. Another bank went under," Rebe said.

"Good." Let the rich come tumbling down. Just as Theo had predicted, powerful people—and powerful corporations—had already been brought down by a new breed of guerrilla journalists packing truth apps. And that was with less than a few million truth apps out there. Wait until there were half a billion.

Of course, it cut both ways—a lot of corporations were requiring employees to take a truth app screening to keep their jobs, and they were laying off a decent percentage of their workforce. And it wasn't like the people who got laid off could find another job, because they were damaged goods—thieves, embezzlers, liars—and all you needed was a truth app to know that.

Rebe's phone rang. She spoke for a few moments, then turned to me. "Roshanna Lupe at News America wants to interview us."

I barked a laugh, then saw that Rebe wasn't smiling.

She held out her phone. "You want to talk to her?"

"Here." Basquiat pulled a tissue from my pocket and dabbed sweat off Molly's forehead.

"I think that's a good background," Rebe was saying to Mr. Chambliss, who nodded.

I looked past Molly at the factory floor below, bustling

with activity, machinery humming, then put a hand on her shoulder. "Boob and Rebe will be monitoring the live feed, watching for shenanigans. If they alter *anything*—the background, one syllable you utter, the color of your *shirt*—I'll signal to you. Inform Roshanna Lupe that the interview is over because they violated the agreement, and cut the feed. Got it?"

Molly nodded as Basquiat got behind her and massaged her neck and shoulders.

"This is our chance to set the record straight with all the people who get their news from News America," I said.

Rebe's phone rang, sending a thrill of terror and excitement through me.

"Yes. Molly's ready." Rebe expanded the screen to the max. Roshanna Lupe was sitting in a director's chair in front of an American flag.

"I'm speaking live with Molly Burroughs, spokesperson for the so-called TruthCorp, manufacturer of the truth app. How are you today, Molly?"

"Doing well, Roshanna."

Roshanna crossed her legs. "Ms. Burroughs, are you aware that the distribution of your product is directly responsible for the failure of sixteen American corporations, including most recently Patriot Bank?"

"I'd say fraud and corruption are responsible for those failures," Molly shot back without missing a beat. "If no one had lied, there would have been nothing for the truth app to expose."

"How about the two hundred eighty-seven suicides your truth app has been linked to? I guess that's not your problem, either?"

"The truth app lets you know when people are lying to you. That's all. Are you saying that's a bad thing?" Molly licked her lips. The contempt on Roshanna's face was withering.

"Why don't we ask Ellory Mika, whose daughter Claire was one of those suicide victims?"

A subscreen opened in the air beside Roshanna, showing a stone-faced woman with unkempt hair.

"Mrs. Mika, I am so sorry for your loss," Roshanna said.

"Thank you," Mrs. Mika croaked.

"Your daughter Claire was twelve? Is that right?"

"Twelve. Yes."

"And she'd had surgery that required her to wear a colostomy bag."

"That's right." A tear rolled down Mrs. Mika's cheek. "She wore loose clothes so no one at school would know. She was terrified the other kids would find out. Then, two weeks ago, one of them brought one of those tattle machines to school and started questioning everyone, trying to dig up dirt, to humiliate his classmates." Mrs. Mika wiped tears from under her eyes. "She was such a beautiful girl."

A photo of Claire appeared on the screen.

"Is there anything you want to say to Molly Burroughs, Mrs. Mika?" Roshanna asked.

Mrs. Mika raised her gaze. "Are you making a lot of money? Enough to make it worth my daughter's life?"

It felt like there was a fist in my stomach.

Molly's eyes filled with tears. "My God, we never meant for anything like that to happen. We're trying to make things better for people—"

"How many more suicides and bankruptcies will it take before you figure out that you're not making things better?" Roshanna asked. "Is your mother proud, Molly?"

I signaled to Molly to end the interview. She ignored me, leaned forward in her seat. "President Vitnik tortured my friend's mother. Vitnik lied, and *you're* the ones spreading those lies. You told everyone we were *wiping people's memories.*"

"And it turns out all you're really doing is crippling the U.S. economy and causing thousands of deaths."

Molly pointed a trembling finger at Roshanna's perfect little nose. "We exposed the worst traitor in American history."

Roshanna Lupe raised her eyebrows. "Are you sure about that? I think I know a worse one."

"Cut the feed," I said to Rebe. The screen went blank. "We should have known it would be an ambush. Unbelievable. They can twist anything." I tried to sound outraged, but the dead girl's face was dancing in my vision. People had died because of us. Good people. An innocent kid.

Basquiat gave Molly a hug. "You did wonderfully."

"You did. Awesome job," I said. Below us a forklift rolled

by, carrying sealed crates filled with truth apps hot off the assembly line.

Molly wiped tears from her cheeks. "That poor girl."

Beltane was jogging toward us from the far end of the floor, the *clack-clack-clack* of her bladed feet echoing off the concrete.

"There's a crowd forming outside the gates. Someone figured out our location from the background," she said to Mr. Chambliss. "They want truth apps."

We followed Mr. Chambliss and Beltane outside.

There were about a hundred people gathered, with more arriving. The road was lined with parked vehicles.

"Sam!" I heard someone call through the noise when we were about fifty feet from the gate. *"Come on, Sam, buddy, set me up?"*

"Come on. How much?" someone else shouted.

People were waving credit cards, even cash.

Off to our right, a handful of twentysomethings were rattling the fence, which was topped with barbed wire.

Beltane strode toward them. "Cut that out *right now*, or I'll pull your damned arms off."

"We're not selling them here!" I shouted.

People booed.

They booed even louder as we headed toward the factory doors. This was insane. We shouldn't have agreed to the interview. My stomach was in knots after seeing that poor girl's mother.

They were packed twenty deep. It reminded me of the mob that had circled the White House. In a few places the fence rattled and swayed as the mob pushed against it.

"This is not good," Beltane said.

Kelsey spit sunflower seed shells into the grass. "We have a dozen heat guns. We could turn them on the crowd."

"Except the people you'll hit are the ones closest to the fence, and they have nowhere to go." I studied the crowd. "We have to get the people in the back to move first."

"What are we going to do?" Beltane said. "Ask them nicely?"

"No. Just give them what they want. Once the crowd moves away from the fence, keep them away with the heat guns." I turned to my friends. "Who wants to play Santa with me?"

The helicopter was black and silver, narrow at the front and fat at the back, like a flying lightbulb. With one of the newer vets, a guy named Cliff, piloting, we rose from the roof and headed out, beyond the fence.

"Right here," I said. We hovered thirty feet off the ground, fifty yards out from the crowd. I turned to Molly and Basquiat. "Bombs away."

Laughing, they began dropping handfuls of boxes. Truth apps. The boxes rained down into the weeds.

The crowd raced for the apps.

"Now move slowly away from the fence," I said.

Cliff inched us away, with Molly and Basquiat feeding a steady stream of truth apps out the side of the helicopter. The crowd followed, which took them farther and farther from the fence.

"I'm out," Basquiat announced after a few minutes.

Molly dropped a double handful. "Me too."

We rose and headed back to the roof. At this point, Rebe would be telling the crowd that was all we had for now and they should go home and, whatever they did, to stay away from the fences.

Some people headed back toward the fences anyway. They didn't get within fifty feet before they were brought to their knees by the heat guns. They'd been warned.

I twitched, recalling the agony of my close encounter with one of those guns. We couldn't let a mob overrun the factory, though, and we'd asked them nicely to leave. Still, the irony wasn't lost on me.

Within twenty minutes, there were only a few hundred stragglers, and they kept their distance.

45

My attention was immediately drawn to the gigantic, tube-like gun in the corner. "Is that a rocket launcher?"

Beltane, who was rummaging through a rack of cream-colored head-to-toe catsuits, glanced my way. "Yep."

We owned a rocket launcher. Jeez.

Beltane pulled a catsuit from the rack. "Try this one."

I took the suit from her. "Hard to believe these can stop a bullet."

"It won't keep a head shot from fracturing your skull, but bullets can't penetrate the material."

I wanted to see for myself what was going on out in the world. These high-tech long johns were the price of admission. I looked around for somewhere to change.

Beltane noticed me looking around and burst out laughing. "You can leave your underwear on."

"I know." I turned around and pulled my shirt over my head. I was a little sensitive about undressing in front of people, due to my scrawniness. I kept hoping I was going to fill out one of these years. It wasn't like I didn't eat.

Out of the corner of my eye I caught a glimpse of Beltane. She was changing into a suit as well, three feet away from me. A series of wide, ragged scars ran from her left shoulder blade down to her rib cage and then wrapped around her side.

I caught her eye reflected in a shiny silver canister of ammo for the rocket launcher. "Shrapnel from a four-legged drone," Beltane said without turning around. "It took a direct hit from an RPG. Half of the thing flew right at me. Took my left arm at the shoulder, my left leg at the knee."

Busted as a Peeping Tom for the second time. It hadn't been intentional this time—if I'd realized Beltane was undressing, I wouldn't have turned. But the similarity reminded me of Molly, and suddenly I felt so ashamed, remembering what I'd done. When I got back I needed to apologize to Molly again, and do it right this time.

Beltane finished dressing and turned around. "How does that fit?" She pulled the hood onto my head, tugged the suit at my shoulders and stomach. "Good. It's needs to be snug."

I felt like I was wearing too-tight underpants over my whole body.

"Let's get moving. We're burning daylight."

There were more bicycles on the road than cars. We passed a gas station; the price on the sign out front was $9.99 a gallon, twice what it had been a few months ago. Below that outrageous price was a handwritten sign: *No Gas.*

"Once this tank is empty, I'm not sure how we're going to fill it again," Kelsey said.

The roads of downtown Trenton were clogged with pedestrians. It was ten a.m. on a Tuesday, but no one seemed to be at work.

A man was hanging from a telephone pole outside City Hall. A black dress shoe was on one foot, nothing but a sock on the other. The sign around his neck read *Liar and thief.*

"Oh my God." It struck me with a sickening, crystal clear clarity: That man was up there because of us. Because of me.

Beltane watched out the window, an assault rifle across her legs. "I said this was going to get ugly. But I had no idea *how* ugly."

Neither had I. For every outright criminal who was being exposed the way Vitnik had been, two politicians were getting tripped up by one simple, straightforward question that people with apps kept asking them: *Can we trust you?* It was amazing how few could say "You can trust me" without goosing that needle. (That was becoming a thing—instead of calling it lying, people were calling it *goosing the needle.*) Some politicians were passing the test, and they were on the rise, replacing the liars. The question was, were there enough of them to avoid a leadership vacuum?

The left side of the access road leading to the Target parking lot was lined with people begging exiting shoppers for food. There were hundreds of them—old people, young people, families with kids. Some were holding handwritten signs. A mother with a crying baby in a carrier on her back knelt in the grass, hands clasped, as cars passed. I'd watched scenes like this on the news, but actually *seeing* it hit me hard. When banks collapsed, real people lost their jobs, their savings. It cascaded down. I was responsible for this.

Not all of it, I reminded myself. The economy had sucked before we released the truth app. There had always been people hanging around store parking lots asking for food and money. But not hundreds of them.

The parking lot was a madhouse. There were lines out the door, and people selling food, water, batteries, and guns out of open trunks in the lot. Two heavily armed guards in tan camo patrolled the entrance.

When three armed vets piled out of our van, I could see the security people tense. One came to intercept us in the lot.

"You can't come inside like that."

"Like what?" Beltane asked.

The guy gestured at Beltane's rifle. "Weaponized like that."

"Do you know who this is?" Beltane pointed at me.

The guard cursed under his breath.

Beltane folded her arms. "We're here for his protection, not to cause trouble. We need supplies. You want to shop for us, or can we go inside?"

The security guy pulled a walkie-talkie off his belt and consulted with someone. "Go on in."

We passed an armed, broad-shouldered female security guard who was asking each person the same question as they exited the store: "Did you steal anything?" She was wearing a truth app.

Inside, the shelves were half empty. They had one brand of ketchup—seven dollars a bottle. Squat tuna fish tins, only with chicken instead of tuna, for eleven dollars a can. Two-liter Pepsi for twelve dollars. As my companions began filling three carts, I grabbed a fourth.

Kelsey waved me off. "We got this. You're here to gather intelligence, so go gather it."

I shook my head. "This cart's for those people out on the road."

Beltane rolled her eyes toward the ceiling. "You want to *stop* the van and *hand out food*? Before you know what's happening, a mob will be tipping over the van and taking *all* the food."

"We'll figure something out." I dropped a dozen cans of the chicken stuff into my cart.

As Kelsey and Beltane loaded the van, I set about creating care packages using the extra plastic bags I'd bought in Target. I didn't have enough bags to give one to each person along the road, so I'd target the kids.

"What the hell is *this*?" Beltane was looking toward the access road, where a dozen or more vehicles were fanning out, circling the perimeter of the parking lot.

A bus in the convoy had *Pilgrims of Truth* painted across its side. There was also a police car with *Truth* stenciled in front of *Police* across its doors, and half a dozen motorcycles, their riders wearing gold helmets emblazoned with *PoT* in red. As the bus squealed to a stop, people poured out, all of them armed.

"Crap." Kelsey slammed the van's rear doors shut and unslung her rifle. "What's the plan? Try to drive our way out?"

"Too many guns," Beltane said. "Let's hang tight and see what happens."

Pilgrims of Truth. There was a truth app involved in this somehow.

Four heavily armed "pilgrims" jogged through the parking lot. One, a young woman, pointed at us and shouted, *"Weapons!"*

A dozen pilgrims converged, surrounding us. Beltane and Kelsey pointed their rifles at the pavement halfway between us and the pilgrims.

"Put them *down*," said a thin guy in jeans and an oxford shirt who could have been an English teacher in a former life.

"Tell us what this is about, and we'll consider it!" Beltane shouted back.

"You're free to go after you pass the test," the thin guy said. "If you're not murderers, rapists, or child molesters, there's nothing to be afraid of."

Vehicles were being waved through the access road a few at a time by gun-toting pilgrims. Other people were standing beside their vehicles as pilgrims with truth apps on their fingers interviewed them. It wasn't hard to piece together what was going on: they were using truth app to search for bad guys.

We'd hoped the truth app would expose criminals, but we never imagined this. I explained what I thought was going on to Kelsey and Beltane, and after a quick consult, they set their weapons down.

The thin guy approached as others snatched up our weapons. I hadn't noticed the truth app he was wearing. He came to me first, opened his mouth to say something, and stopped.

"Holy . . . You're Sam Gregorious."

I nodded, hoping being Sam Gregorious was a good thing to people who seemed to be heavily into the technology I had helped develop.

He stuck out his hand. "It's a pleasure to meet you. More than a pleasure—an honor. Marcus. Marcus Hamlyn." He put a hand on my shoulder and turned. "Hey, can you believe this? This is Sam Gregorious."

Surrounded by grinning faces, I shook a dozen or more outstretched hands as people talked excitedly about how no one was going to believe it back at the center. One woman asked to have her picture taken with me.

Beyond the ring of admirers, three men were being led at gunpoint toward the building.

"What are you going to do?" One of the three men—short,

maybe twenty—asked. The pilgrims with the guns didn't answer.

Seeing the woman take a picture with me, a half-dozen other pilgrims had lined up to do the same.

A guy put his hand on my shoulder. "Thank you. It's an honor." He smiled as the next person in line snapped our picture.

The three men were being lined up against the wall.

"I was *sixteen*. It was forty years ago. I'm not that person anymore," one of the men against the wall said. "There's a statute of limitations—"

One of the pilgrims raised a handgun to his ear and fired.

"We already know you haven't killed anyone, don't we, Sam?" Marcus Hamlyn said, grinning.

"Yes, we do." I tried to match his friendly tone.

Marcus turned to Beltane. "Let's get you people cleared so you can be on your way."

A second shot rang out. The short guy, who had squeezed his eyes shut, dropped.

"Have you ever murdered anyone?" Marcus asked Beltane, ignoring the gunshot.

"Yes," Beltane said.

Marcus froze. "That's the truth."

Beltane gave Marcus her best Beltane glare. "Everyone I killed was Russian."

"Oh, right." Marcus looked down at her legs. "Duh. And you haven't raped or molested anyone, or tried to?"

"No. I haven't molested anyone." Her eyes were blazing with anger. I'd never met anyone who could convey so much anger with her eyes.

The crack of a third gunshot echoed through the parking lot. I flinched, even though I knew it was coming. Marcus turned to ask Kelsey questions.

I wanted to tell these people what I thought of their vigilantism, but this wasn't the time or the place.

"They're all good." Marcus stuck his fingers in his mouth and whistled. When a woman near the access road looked his way, Marcus pointed at us and our van and gave a thumbs-up.

The woman gave him a thumbs-up in return.

I had to tolerate one more handshake from Marcus. "Have a great day," he said.

We climbed into our van and headed for the exit.

"Who the hell do these people think they are?" I said.

"As long as they're taking out the worst of the worst? I'm okay with it," Kelsey said.

"But you don't just shoot people in parking lots like they're animals. Even people who've done terrible things."

"You do in wars," Beltane said.

"But we're not at war."

"No?" Beltane gave me a deadpan look.

We were passing the people begging for food along the access road.

I put a hand on Kelsey's shoulder. "*Wait.* I want to give out the food."

"I told you, if you go out there, they'll mob us," Beltane said.

"That's why you're going to help me," I said.

"Me?" Beltane looked horrified.

"That's right. Be pleasant and help me pass out the bags. If things get out of hand, get us back to the van."

I pulled bags from the back and held a bunch out to Beltane. "There's not enough for everyone, so we only give them to kids. Not their parents—give them right to the kids so the adults not getting them can see why we're doing it the way we're doing it."

Beltane snatched the bags from me, cursing under her breath.

"Kelsey, can you pass the rest out the window once we've given these out?" I asked.

"Yeah, yeah." Beltane slammed the door, went right up to a little girl. "Here you go. Merry Christmas."

People surged toward us, shouting pleas. Beltane held up her bionic right arm like a linebacker about to deliver a stiff arm. "Back off immediately. Kids only."

I placed a bag beside a toddler as the child's mom cried out her thanks and grabbed the bag, pressing it to her chest. A little girl with a dirty face, maybe seven years old, came running up to me calling, "Please, please, please!" She squealed when I gave her a bag.

The lump in my throat felt like an egg. There were kids like this all over the country, the world, because of me. Handing out these bags was like feeding one grain of rice to a hungry whale. But it was all I could think to do.

Kelsey crept along in the van, keeping up with us.

"Here you go, kid," Beltane said in a tight voice. The boy tucked the bag to his solar plexus like it was a football and ran. When Beltane turned to get more bags from the van, I saw her face was wet with tears. I didn't know whether she was crying because of the part she'd played in getting the truth apps out there, or for some other reason. I only knew why I was crying. How had this all gone so wrong?

46

I stopped in Mom's doorway. Mr. Chambliss was in a chair facing her, his hands covering hers. He was speaking in a low, soothing tone. I heard him say, "When I was in Siberia . . . ," but the rest was too quiet for me to hear.

Mom noticed me and tried to draw her hands away from Mr. Chambliss, but his hands just followed, until Mom was clutching them to her chest along with her own.

"I'll come back," I managed, and headed down the hall, feeling stunned, slightly embarrassed, and happy for Mom. Their body language said there was something between them. I hoped things worked out for once. Mr. Chambliss was one of my favorite people on the planet.

I passed Rebe's room and nearly burst out laughing when I saw her and Boob sitting shoulder to shoulder on her cot. Another blossoming couple? I picked up my pace, not wanting to pry.

Then their facial expressions registered, and I back-tracked. They were watching TV, both looking like they'd eaten something rotten.

On the screen a line of tanks rolled down a city street strewn with bodies. The tanks rolled right over the bodies and through thick black smoke. The sound of explosions and gunfire punctuated the scene.

"Are we being invaded?"

"No. The army is fighting *itself*," Rebe said without looking at me.

I cursed under my breath. The day before, there'd been a standoff at the Pentagon. The secretary of state had claimed he was in charge, while the four-star general in charge of Vitnik's Elite Guard (Vitnik was still in hiding) insisted *she* was still in charge. There was no mention of General Austin, the chairwoman of the Joint Chiefs. The secretary of state had pulled out a truth app and began interrogating the general, who tried to look like he was storming off indignantly, when he was clearly fleeing. No one in power wanted to answer questions with a truth app pointed at them.

I wondered about General Austin. She'd been the first to defy Vitnik, and she'd done it in public, with truth apps pointed at her. I wondered if we should reach out to her and see how she responded.

Molly appeared in the doorway holding Basquiat's hand. They joined us.

It seemed as if all anyone cared about was seeing people nailed by truth apps, whether it was world leaders, religious figures, teachers, or their next-door neighbors. The Internet was packed with videos of "gotcha" truth app confrontations.

"I honestly thought we were going to make things better," Molly whispered.

I wanted to tell her we were—we *were* making things better, but it was impossible not to draw a straight line from the truth apps to the street battle on TV.

We hadn't understood just how many secrets were out there. At seventeen we didn't have spouses to cheat on or employers to embezzle from. That wasn't to say there weren't many people out there who had nothing of consequence to hide, who were going about their honest lives, heads high. You just didn't hear much about them as liar after liar was exposed. And it seemed as if the higher you got in the echelons of power, the more people had to hide. Was it true that the rich and powerful weren't smarter and more talented than the rest of us, just more willing to lie and cheat to get what they wanted? Maybe that was my cynicism talking. Maybe the lies the rich and powerful told just resulted in larger consequences.

Rebe switched to US Green, one of the midlevel news channels. It was showing a feed from someone in Saint Louis, where members of the local chapter of the pilgrims of Truth were going door to door through a suburban neighborhood. It was incredible how quickly the Pilgrim movement was spreading.

On the stock market, half the listings had been suspended; the only stocks still being traded were companies that made basic necessities. And weapons.

Basquiat sprang to his feet. "We need to stop. The more apps we sell, the worse things get."

His words startled me. Every tragedy that could be traced back to the truth app was like a punch in the face, but it felt like we were all in, like there was no going back. We had to have faith that in the long run, the truth was better than lies.

"What would it accomplish to stop now?" I asked. "We've open-sourced the plans. There are dozens of other factories making them. We can't put the toothpaste back in the tube."

"So we might as well get rich off our doomsday machine?" Basquiat said. "Is that what you're saying?"

"It's not a doomsday machine. It's the *truth*. The *lies* were the doomsday machine."

"That's a rationalization." Boob threw his hands in the air in frustration. "When exactly did this become a crusade? We were developing a *product* so we could make money. All of a sudden it became about saving the world."

"It was always about saving the world for Theo. And the product was his idea to begin with."

Molly was staring at her hands as she picked at her fingernails. She'd believed so strongly in the truth app; she'd been the one who showed me Theo's blog, which changed my mind. Had she changed *her* mind? I felt backed against a wall. No one was taking my side.

I pulled up Theo's blog on my phone and scrolled through it, reading passages at random, looking for one I'd read weeks ago.

"What are you doing?" Boob asked.

"Theo should get a say in this."

It wasn't the passage I'd been searching for, but when I saw the words, I was so startled I lost the spot and had to find it again. It was as if Theo was speaking into my ear from his grave.

"Here." I expanded the screen so everyone could see it, then read aloud, "'Our leaders don't know how to tell the truth, and they're too old to learn. Our institutions may not be able to handle what we're going to unleash, but it's a cancer. We have to cut it out, even if, like surgery, it hurts.'"

"Theo wrote that months ago," Basquiat said. "We don't know if he'd have the same opinion once he saw what was going on."

Mom and Mr. Chambliss appeared in the hallway. They'd probably heard our rising voices and come to investigate.

"Mr. Chambliss, what's happening out there?" I asked, seeking an ally who was still alive.

He shrugged. "I don't really know, Sam. Things are getting worse. Not that they were good to begin with."

"Could this be growing pains? Could we end up better

off in the end, or is everything going to keep getting worse until it all collapses?"

"I think either outcome is possible at this point, depending on how things unfold from here."

Rebe had switched back to News America.

Roshanna Lupe was smiling brightly, like it was all sunny days on the horizon as far as the eye could see. "Authorities are asking people in the following cities to stay in their homes while the police, with support from military forces, get the situation under control. Food and fuel rationing remain in effect. . . ." She trailed off, studying her coanchor, who was smirking and shaking his head. "What's that you've got there, Rob? Is that a tattletale machine?"

Rob was indeed wearing a truth app. I hadn't noticed. "It's a good thing our viewers can't watch you through this thing because, whew"—he shook his hand like he was extinguishing a match—"is that needle dancing."

If looks could kill, Rob would have burst into flames. "You want the truth, Rob? Is that what you want?" Roshanna looked at the camera. "All righty. I'm not sure who's in charge, folks. We've got a civil war raging across this beautiful country of ours, while right across the river in Trenton, on Industrial Drive, the bastards responsible for it go on cranking out their tattletale machines, and no one is doing a damned thing about it." She looked at her coanchor. "How'd I do that time, Rob? Did I tell the truth?"

Rob gave her a thumbs-up.

"Did she just give out our location?" Rebe asked.

"You want a little more honesty?" Roshanna went on. "When it comes to President Vitnik, I don't think things are as simple as the tattletale machines claim. What I *do* know is our dear president was keeping this country functioning." She looked right into the camera. "Save us from this anarchy, Madam President."

Roshanna Lupe and her sidekick had me fooled for a minute. I thought they were finally off script, but it had been nothing but carefully rehearsed theater designed to help Vitnik.

"We're bugging out in *ten minutes*. Pack up." Mr. Chambliss went onto the catwalk overlooking the factory floor, stuck his fingers in his mouth, and whistled. "Mott. There's a mob heading our way. Ten minutes."

"I'll find Beltane and get weapons." Mom headed for the stairs.

47

We looked like a band of aliens in disguise, everyone's faces framed in ovals by the catsuit hoods. Our eighty-odd veterans-turned-factory-workers were crowded near the doors, with Cliff in the middle handing out cash to make sure everyone could get home once they were out of here.

"Get in the van," Beltane said to us. Then she turned to our workers. "Haul ass. Keep up with the van."

Except that made no sense, because we were wearing bulletproof catsuits and they weren't. While Beltane readied the security forces, I picked the slower-looking workers out and put them in the van. Kelsey, who was driving, didn't protest.

I spotted Mom near the door, rifle in hand. I wasn't sure if she'd told Beltane to take charge, or if Beltane had just seen Mom wasn't up to it. Either way, Beltane was clearly in charge.

"Let's move out." Beltane pressed the button to open the

big garage door. It rose with a mechanical hum. As soon as it was high enough, Kelsey gunned the van. I jogged behind it, Molly to my left, Basquiat to my right, Boob, Rebe, and Mott on our heels. There were maybe thirty people standing near the fence, nowhere near enough to pose a threat. They backed off as one of the bionic vets pushed the gate open.

It was like being in a strange parade. We jogged behind the van down the mostly deserted road, passing industrial sites surrounded by chain-link fences.

Behind us, our helicopter rose; a moment later, it was hovering overhead. Vets ran along either side of our contingent, their heaters now holstered, assault rifles in hand.

A mile from the factory, Mott pointed out a black van parked in an empty lot. "That's my ride. I can take about ten people and make sure they get where they're going."

She pulled ten workers from the crowd and headed for the van with a wave. "We're not done. I'll be in touch."

We jogged into town puffing and sweating in the chilly air. Our employees gradually peeled away, heading home by bus or rental car. We dropped the last of them at the bus station, climbed into the van, and headed for the highway, the helicopter still shadowing us. Traffic was dominated by pedestrians and bicycles, which slowed us considerably. I had no idea where we were going.

News America was running a live feed of a mob tearing up our abandoned factory. Some of the microchannels were showing it, too, only their feeds also showed the mob looting truth apps. Sure, they wanted us to stop making them . . . right after they got theirs. Another feed opened on News America—a close-up of a face I was hoping I'd never have to see again.

Vitnik was standing on the White House lawn, surrounded by soldiers. In the background crews were working to repair the damage to the White House. Vitnik claimed she was the country's democratically elected leader, that insurgencies would be put down and traitors brought to swift justice. Including us.

"Except the microchannels are saying forty to fifty percent of the military is not backing her," Rebe said.

"What the hell is *that*?" Boob was looking out the window. Off to our left, parachutes dotted the steel-gray sky, drifting toward rooftops two or three blocks away.

Kelsey craned his neck. "Vitnik's Elite Guard. About thirty."

A thump on my window made me jump. "Cut your feeds!" Beltane shouted through the glass.

Rebe cut her feed.

Kelsey turned right, following the vets leading the way.

"If they have access to satellite output, they can still track us with our feeds cut," Rebe said.

We couldn't move very fast because of the bicyclists and pedestrians. I unzipped my backpack and pulled out my handgun as Beltane shouted something outside. The vets spread out, some to the sidewalks, others running ahead of the van or dropping behind.

"Get low. Watch in the directions I can't," Kelsey said.

I ducked between the seats. We were on a side street, four-story brick tenements on either side.

"If there's shooting, cover your face with your forearms," Kelsey said.

Beltane leaped onto a moving bus and dropped to her stomach, rifle raised.

The windows shattered inward. Shards of glass rained down as I dropped to the floor and wrapped my arms around my face.

Pain tore through my thigh, like someone had hit me with a nail sticking out of a plank. I cried out just as I was hit again, below the shoulder blade. Then again in the ass. I curled up into a ball as two more bullets struck me. The suit wasn't working—I could feel the bullets tearing into me as my friends cried out in pain.

"*Drone bomber!*" Kelsey shouted.

An explosion swallowed all other sound. My skin was suddenly hot, my mouth and nose filled with smoke as the van plunged nose-first, as if dropping off a cliff. An instant later, it slammed to a halt.

Someone was pulling my arm. I was confused about where I was. Then it came back to me. I'd blacked out for a moment.

"We have to get out!" It was Molly, shouting over gunfire.

I coughed; pain ripped through my rib cage, and I remembered that I'd been shot five or six times. Only there was no blood. The suit *had* worked. It had just *felt* like I was being riddled with bullets.

I struggled to my knees. The van had crashed into a deep gash in the road caused by the explosion. A drone must have tried to drop a bomb on the van and missed. We'd be an easier target now that we weren't moving.

"Kelsey?" Basquiat was in the front seat. Kelsey lay motionless on the giant marshmallow airbag.

I took a step, my legs trembling wildly, as Basquiat reached Kelsey and unbuckled his seat belt. He grabbed Kelsey's shoulders, slid an arm between his chest and the airbag, and tried to lift him.

"Oh God." Basquiat set Kelsey back down and turned away. "He's gone. Go."

I stared at the back of Kelsey's unmoving head. "Are you sure?"

"Yes." Basquiat's voice broke. *"Go."*

I climbed out of the van. Across the street, a building was in flames. Two silver drone bombers the size of kites cruised overhead.

"Which way?" Basquiat asked. I looked around. Boob and Rebe were nowhere in sight.

I spotted Beltane racing along the sidewalk, disappearing behind vehicles, then reappearing. She reached a soldier I hadn't noticed who was holding a rocket launcher, the black hole at the end pointed directly at us. Beltane punched the soldier in the back.

Her fist came out through his chest.

She was moving again before he hit the ground. She

headed for the nearest tenement, threw a punch at the wall, then pulled, sending bricks sprawling to the sidewalk. She grabbed a handful and looked up.

One of the bomber drones appeared over the roofline. Beltane reared back and threw a brick at it. The brick sailed past in a blur, a near miss.

She threw the other, missed again.

Her third shattered the drone. Pieces of it rained down into the street.

"This way." I turned toward Mom's voice. I couldn't see her through the smoke.

There was a *boom*, a bright flash overhead. Our helicopter was coming down, spinning in a tight circle, black smoke pouring out of a ragged hole in its side. It slammed into the pavement a block away, and the still-spinning rotor burst into pieces that flew in three different directions. The biggest chunk hit the face of a tenement, sending debris flying.

I spotted Mom and Mr. Chambliss in an open doorway.

I looked around for my friends. "Molly?"

Mom was at my side. "She's inside. Where's Kelsey?"

I could barely get the words out. "He's gone, Mom."

"No." She took off toward the van. *"Kelsey."*

Mr. Chambliss grabbed my arm. "Let's go. She'll catch up."

I took one last look at Mom kicking out the van's windshield, then turned toward the door. We passed two more bodies on the way—one of ours and one of theirs. We ran to the end of the hall, where two vets had punched and kicked a hole through the wall, into the building backing the one we were in. We climbed through the hole, ran down another hallway, and came out on the next street over. Mom caught up to us there.

48

Raritan, New Jersey, was blacked out. We avoided main streets as we passed through, eventually reaching an area where we could again see lights in passing windows.

Fires were raging in Allentown, Pennsylvania. We could see on our phones that fires were raging in a lot of places, but seeing the orange glow and smelling the acrid smoke in Allentown made it real.

I felt as if I'd been beaten with a lead pipe. It was hard to sit because of the welt on my ass. I was sure I had a broken rib as well. It hurt to breathe.

Darly, one of our vets, was lying between the seats, staring up at the new van's roof, her eyes glassy from Oxy-Contin. She had a broken femur and lacerations from the same explosion that had killed Kelsey.

We'd had luck hiding in a school once, so we found another to stay in for the night. This time it was an elementary school, tucked away from a relatively busy street in a small Pennsylvania town.

We bedded down in the cafeteria. The tables were smaller and closer to the ground than at the high school.

Boob and Rebe were following the news on Rebe's phone, their heads close together. I had the impression they were back together after "the kiss," although no formal announcement had been made.

Basquiat was lying on a table, hands folded across his stomach, staring at the ceiling tiles. "This tiny furniture makes me think of Trina," he said to Molly. "But there are enough recent dead to mourn if I want to mourn."

I joined Mom on a bench in the corner, where she was looking after Darly.

"I should have listened, when you told me to sell. This is a mess."

She shook her head. "No. You did the right thing."

She still wasn't used to having the truth app around. I didn't call her on the lie. Let her think she could still tell me what I wanted to hear, that she could still protect me from painful truths.

Rebe found a report of a gas station in Point Pleasant that still had gas. We decided to make one last attempt to fill up before abandoning the vehicles.

Point Pleasant was a vacation town that hadn't seen many vacationers in recent years. Most of the souvenir shops, mini golf courses, and snack stands were boarded up. We rolled past the gas station in question. If it had been selling gas, there was no sign of any now.

"Let's just stay here?" Molly pleaded. "I want to swim in the ocean."

Mom and Beltane exchanged a look.

"We could rest for a day or two while we figure out what to do next. Maybe steal a boat and head down the coast," Mom said.

We parked on a deserted street that dead-ended at the beach, and broke into an abandoned beachside seafood dive called Stingray's Grill. There was no food inside. We knew from the news that food deliveries were being delayed by protests and fuel supply disruptions, but this place looked like it hadn't had food for months or even years.

We dropped our gear and headed over the boardwalk and out to the beach. Mom, Mr. Chambliss, and Beltane stayed at the restaurant, but a couple of armed vets followed us.

Basquiat and Boob pulled off their shirts. I kept mine on because of the scrawniness thing. The water had an icy bite, but we pushed on past the breakers, into chest-deep water. Once we got out there, no one splashed or laughed or bodysurfed. We just stood there shivering. There was a big, round purple welt on Molly's triceps, three on Basquiat's back.

"I'm going to head in," Boob said after a couple of minutes, his teeth chattering. We all followed him back to shore and sat in the wet sand. Rebe returned to her news feed. I was determined to watch the ocean's horizon. I didn't want to see any more destruction.

"Look at these guys," Boob said.

Two dogs were trotting along the surf, heading in our direction. They were little guys—a white miniature poodle and a brown-and-black Yorkie.

"Hey, there." Molly held out her hand. The Yorkie came right up and stuck his nose in Molly's palms, then looked up at her and barked. The force of the bark jolted the little guy backward. He barked again.

"He thought you had food in your hand," Boob said. "Their owners couldn't feed them, so they abandoned them."

"That's a depressing conclusion to jump to," Basquiat said.

"What, they both happened to get lost with their collars off? They're obviously not strays."

The poodle, which had one of those poodle-ish hair-cuts with puffs of fur around its ankles, came up to me and ducked its head. I reached out and rubbed behind its ears.

Molly offered it some raisins from a box she must have had in her pocket. The poodle gobbled them up like she had a palmful of prime rib. Molly fed the rest to the Yorkie.

The dogs hung around awhile, but when it was clear there was no more food coming, they continued down the beach together, probably going to look for their owners.

"Do you think this is my fault?" As soon as I asked it, I wanted to take the question back. No one could tell me what I wanted to hear. All I'd get was the truth.

Boob, Rebe, and Basquiat looked at each other, as if hoping someone else would answer. Molly stared at the sand.

Finally, Boob spoke up. "You meant well. But yeah, I think it's mostly your fault." He put his hands on his head. "Half a dozen times I tried to get you to pull out, but you wouldn't let it go. When things went south, you picked up the project and carried it on your back."

I nodded, then looked at Basquiat. "You agree?"

Basquiat took a sighing breath. "We're all responsible."

The needle bounced, settling halfway between *Righteous Truth* and *Pants on Fire*.

"But," I prodded.

Basquiat looked me in the eye. "If you really want me to apportion blame, I'd say more of it falls on you. After Theo died, Boob voted to stop, so I'd say he's not to blame at all. Rebe, Molly, and I, I'd assign twenty percent each. That leaves you with forty."

They had no choice—they had to tell the truth. Still, I couldn't help feeling betrayed.

I looked at Molly until she finally noticed me looking.

"Just . . . go to hell, all right? This isn't helping anything."

In other words, *Yes, you're to blame for this.* I'd never felt as alone as I did at that moment. No matter how bad things had gotten, until now I'd always had my friends.

I went on looking at Molly, waiting. More than anyone, I wanted to know what she thought.

Molly folded her arms. "Basquiat actually voted no along with Boob. He's too kind to point that out, but he did. I, on the other hand, not only voted yes but also dug up Theo's blog and showed you what he wrote. So I'm as much to blame as you." The needle didn't twitch. "*I* killed that girl with the colostomy bag. *I* killed Kelsey. I killed thousands of people, and I'm not sure I can live with that."

When Basquiat reached out to put his arms around her, Molly lunged at him like she was drowning, and clung to his neck so hard it had to hurt, but Basquiat didn't complain. With each breath she pushed every bit of air from her lungs, as if it was going to be her last.

This was killing her. And whatever Molly thought, it was my fault. I pictured the hungry faces of those kids Beltane and I had given food to, and Kelsey slumped over the steering wheel, and I could barely stand being in my skin.

And suddenly I understood what Molly had meant when she called me a boy. It had nothing to do with collecting comics or having a baby face. To Molly, being a boy was being selfish. I'd been a boy because I'd felt my own pain, and no one else's. That's what a boy did. Theo, on the other hand, had not been a boy. I wasn't a boy anymore, either, and now that I wasn't, I almost wished I could go back, because being a man hurt.

Boob stood and brushed off his pants. "This is probably as good a time as any to tell you all. I'm going home. I'll disguise my face and try to swap a couple of truth apps for a junker and a tank of gas."

"I'm not sure that's a good idea," I said. "What if Vitnik finds you? You won't have any vets to protect you."

"I'll stay hidden inside. I need to get out of here. I want to go home and sleep in my own bed."

"I talked him into it," Rebe added. "After the thing at the White House, he's earned a pass."

Boob looked at me. "When we were on that boat and I told you I was scared, you told me, 'We're all scared.' You have no idea what this is like for me. Every minute of this has felt like walking through broken glass in my bare feet."

I could see this was something that had been building inside Boob, something he'd been wanting to say for some time.

"I'm sorry I brushed you off," I said. "I hear you now. I get it. It's harder for you. That doesn't mean you're a coward. It means it takes even more courage for you to do what you've done."

As Boob fought back tears, Rebe put her arm around him and rubbed his shoulder. It was a bizarre sight, seeing Rebe comfort someone. It also choked me up, because it was exactly what Boob needed—someone to show him he was loved. I could stand to do a better job of that myself.

"I'm sorry it's so hard for you, buddy. I truly am."

Boob nodded.

"We'll see you back in New City."

When Boob and Rebe had gone, Molly, Basquiat, and I

sat listening to the hiss of the surf. It was soothing, watching the water come crashing in. The water had no opinion on all this. It had no use for lie detectors. It didn't judge.

"I wonder if it's safe to use our phones," Molly said.

So much had changed. I had no idea if Vitnik was still capable of tracking us through our phones. "We can see what Rebe and the vets think when we go inside. You want to call your mom?"

Molly flung a little shell across the sand. "And my dad. I need to tell them I was to blame for their breakup."

Basquiat put his arm around her. "I'll be standing right beside you. They'll understand. They both love you, and so do I."

Lie, my truth app said.

Molly froze.

"What?" Basquiat said, taking in her reaction.

"You're lying."

"*What?* I'm not lying. I'm here for you, always."

"That's different from loving me."

"I *do* love you."

Lie.

As quietly as possible, I started to stand so they could have some privacy, but Molly put a hand on my arm, urging me to stay. I sank back to the ground.

"I—I would never leave you," Basquiat stammered.

"You won't run away, is what you're saying," Molly said.

"That's right, I would never run—"

I think Basquiat made the connection the instant I did.

"You feel responsible for breaking up my family, so you feel like you have to take care of me, because I lost my dad and I have no one." Molly patted Basquiat's knee. She was crying, her voice husky. "I'm not mad. That's sweet. But I'm not a little girl. I can take care of myself."

Basquiat was staring at the sand. "I didn't mean to lie. I thought I did love you, in my own way."

"You didn't lie. That was the first time you said it. Ever since my parents split you've been telling me you're here for me, and that's true. It's different than loving someone, though."

All five spots where the bullets had struck me throbbed like multiple hearts.

Basquiat nodded slowly, cupped some sand, watched it slip between his fingers. "I'm sorry."

Molly forced a smile. "No. Don't be."

"I thought I was doing the right thing."

"You may have been."

Basquiat gave Molly a hug, then left Molly and me sitting in the sand, staring at our feet, Molly crying silently.

"I'm sorry." I hated seeing Molly in pain, especially now, with everything else we were dealing with.

Molly struggled to her feet, grunting in pain from the bruises, then offered me a hand and helped me up. "It's almost as if he beat the truth app." A seagull landed and looked up at us, probably hoping we'd toss it a Cheeto or something. "But he was telling the truth. I was just hearing what I wanted to hear."

We headed toward the restaurant.

We slipped through the back door to find everyone huddled around a screen, watching a news broadcast. I recognized Vitnik's voice immediately. It made me feel nauseated.

". . . because of the destructive influence this apparatus continues to have on our nation and its security, as of today it is illegal to possess this device in an operational state." Vitnik set a pair of truth app rings on the table in front of her, and lifted a brick sitting beside them. "You do not have to be using the device to suffer consequences. If you are in possession of them, disable them immediately." She slammed the brick down, then lifted it to show the crushed rings. "It's that simple." She leaned closer to the camera. "These devices constitute a national emergency, and we cannot afford half measures. Anyone found with an operational lie detection device will be shot on sight."

Mom noticed us. "She's calling on the military to unite behind her."

"Could we take her out?" Beltane asked. "If she only has her Secret Service force for now, the White House might be vulnerable. A small team could get in and out."

Beltane called up a map of the White House. The vets huddled around, pointing out potential weak points.

After discussing it for a while, Mom sat back. "We don't have any intel. Unless we know Vitnik's location at any given time, how could we execute a quick strike?"

Beltane heaved a sigh and collapsed the map. "Yeah."

The five of us retreated to watch the news at a table overlooking the boardwalk and beach. I'm not sure why we were watching. Maybe we were searching for some sign that we'd hit bottom and things were turning around. All we heard was the steady drumbeat of destruction. There was a severe food shortage in Japan, and soon people would begin to starve to death. Some corporate CEO had set himself up as a warlord and was trying to seize control of much of New Mexico.

"When I was in that room under the White House, Vitnik told me people can't handle the truth, that sometimes lies are more true than the truth," I said. "I think she was right."

"Lie," Boob muttered.

"What?"

Boob shrugged. "Lie. You don't think she was right."

"It was pretty close to Pants on Fire," Rebe agreed.

I still thought Vitnik was wrong, after everything that had happened. We lied so routinely, for so many reasons, that even now I often didn't even realize I was doing it. "Okay, I guess I don't believe it. Maybe that's the problem. I didn't see the cliff, and I wouldn't let anyone else convince me it was there, so I drove right off it."

"For what it's worth, you don't believe that, either," Boob said.

I looked up at the ceiling, laughing bitterly. "How could I? If I did, I'd believe we're better off not knowing the truth." I threw my hands in the air. "You know what? It's true. I can't do it. I cannot believe honesty is bad. I still believe Theo was right."

My rib was killing me. Every breath hurt.

"It's not bad. It's just unworkable on a large scale," Basquiat said. "That's the lesson. On a small scale—with the five of us, for example—it was a good thing."

"So it's a good thing for a small group of friends, but it becomes a doomsday machine if it spreads to a million groups of friends." I let that sink in. "I wish Theo was here. Vitnik knew what she was doing when she took him away from us."

"What could Theo say that would change anything?" Boob asked.

"He'd remind us that the world was in such bad shape because people lied, not because they were too honest. He'd say the liars are to blame for this, not the truth app." I could hear Theo saying it; it felt like I was repeating his words instead of speaking my own. I closed my eyes and listened to his voice. "This is bigger than the printing press, the car, the computer. We're changing everything— government, law, friendship, love—and change hurts. This much change is agony. In the end, though, it'll fix what left us hanging by a thread in the first place." I opened my eyes and looked at my friends. "He'd say we need to share what we learned about how to handle the truth app, because we got it right. Stand up and come clean. Cast no shadow."

Boob cleared his throat. "I have to say, that does sound like Theo. That damned commie idealist."

"Vitnik is telling the world the truth app is to blame, and no one's answering her. We're running and hiding, acting ashamed like we really are to blame."

Molly nodded. The others didn't disagree, at least.

"There has to be a way to fight back," I continued. "We have to get people to see the truth app the way we do. Not as a cudgel to beat people with, but as something to make the world better."

Boob curled his hands into fists and grimaced. "Damn it."

"What's the matter?"

He sighed heavily. "I think I know how. I don't want to tell you, because it would be the most humiliating thing imaginable, and because I don't really want to live in Theo's freaking utopia."

"What? Tell me." For the life of me, I couldn't imagine what Boob was thinking.

Eyes closed, Boob pressed his hands to his head.

"Come on, Boob," Molly said.

Boob heaved a big, fat sigh. "People want drama, not lectures. Don't lecture them about how it's done, show them a dramatic example. Release the video of our confession at the campfire. Molly has it. She records everything."

"Are you out of your mind?" Rebe looked like she was about to beat Boob senseless. "*No.* Do not show that video to anyone."

It was perfect. We were rock stars to some, the Antichrist to many, but everyone knew us. Everyone would watch. It would be humiliating beyond words, but it was a brutally honest way to show them the positive potential of the truth app.

"That's brilliant," I said.

Molly was searching for the clip.

"Hang on," Rebe said. "I didn't say I was okay with this."

Molly paused. "So what do we do? Do we vote?"

"I think this one has to be unanimous," I said.

Molly nodded. "You're right."

I turned to Rebe. "Please."

Rebe's glare softened, but she was still shaking. "I won't stop you. I'm just never going to show my face in public again." She got up and walked away.

I looked around. "Are we unanimous?"

Basquiat and Boob nodded. Molly resumed working.

"Title it 'Cast No Shadow,' " Basquiat said. "Then, below that, a tag reading 'When you have nothing left to hide, you're free.' "

Molly typed faster. "Perfect."

Boob got up and followed Rebe.

Everyone would know what I did to Molly. They'd know Molly broke up her parents' marriage, that Rebe was bulimic and ran Internet scams, that Basquiat ran away, that Boob had no self-esteem. We would all be stripped bare.

Hopefully that would get their attention.

Molly looked up. "That's it. Should I send it?"

I looked at Basquiat.

"Do it," he said.

Molly did it. I pictured a million fingers simultaneously opening our clip. Parties where dozens gathered to watch our video and laugh.

I went to find Boob.

He and Rebe were outside, on a patio set up for dining. They stopped talking when they saw me, so it was pretty obvious they were talking about all this. What else would they be talking about?

"Is it done?" Boob asked.

"It's done. I don't know if it will help, but thanks for coming up with the idea."

"I'm sorry to interrupt." It was Molly, standing in the doorway. "We released that clip six minutes ago. It has been viewed two hundred million times."

"Two hundred *million*?" Boob's eyes bulged.

Molly glanced at her phone. "In the time it took you to ask that question, half a million more people clicked the link."

"I'd call it more of an exclamation than a question," I said.

Molly raised her hand, like she was going to slap me from ten feet away.

"'Going viral' doesn't begin to describe it." Rebe covered her face. "God. Two hundred million people know I'm a bulimic thief."

"We were up in Yakutsk toward the end of the war."

Beltane's voice startled me awake. I'd been drifting off. The room was pitch-dark, everyone bedded down.

"Eva was with us. We called her Clown because of her hair. She was our eyes. Had a little girl at home."

I was completely lost. Why was Beltane telling us this out of the blue while we were trying to sleep?

"We were sweeping an apartment complex after a firefight, and Eva spotted one of those doll-within-a-doll-within-a-doll things lying in a hallway. She stashed it in her pack for her little girl. Only it turned out the smallest doll was filled with C-4. Booby trap. Went off a few minutes later.

"So we thought, the bastards who left this will be back to see if anyone took the bait, because where's the fun in leaving a boom-boom surprise if you don't get to see the results?"

And then it hit me: this was a confession. Weeks ago we'd encouraged Beltane to cast no shadow, and she'd finally decided to take us up on it. That was my best guess, anyway.

"So we went back and dropped a pack in that same hallway, making it look like we'd left it behind when we carried away an injured or dead buddy. We put a couple of boxed meals laced with rat poison in the pack, and *we* came back a day later to see if *our* trap had caught the rats who'd killed Eva."

Beltane got quiet. We waited.

"We came back to find two kids had eaten the meals."

"Oh no. Oh, Beltane," Molly said.

"Seven, eight years old," Beltane went on in a flat

monotone, as if she hadn't heard Molly. "One had chocolate smeared all over his face. I still see his face. Every day I see it."

I heard someone get up and cross the creaky wood floor to Beltane.

"Thank you." It was Basquiat, squatting beside Beltane in the dark.

"Thank you," Molly echoed.

Then, in a chorus, Boob, Rebe, me, even some of the vets.

"I hope it brings you peace, to share it," Basquiat said.

"It doesn't," Beltane said. "Some shadows stick with you whether you confess them or not."

I couldn't even imagine. How did you wake up each morning after something like that?

"I think maybe I figured out a way, though," Beltane said. "When I was handing out food to those kids outside Target, it made me think of Yakutsk, except it was the opposite— I was saving kids instead of hurting them. And it got me thinking, if I can save a hundred kids, maybe that would balance things out, you know?"

"That makes a lot of sense," Basquiat said. "If we get out of this, I'd like to help."

That's why handing out that food had been the one thing to break through Beltane's toughness and make her cry.

And, jeez, when she'd gone through that truth app test with the Pilgrims of Truth, that had been a much closer call than I'd realized. Beltane had told the pilgrims that the people she'd killed had all been Russians. That was true, but if they'd probed a little deeper, they would have learned some of them were children.

"Can I ask all you geniuses a question?" Beltane said.

"Sure," I said.

"We're laying down our lives because we believed these truth apps would make the world a better place. So far that's not happening. But the thing is, I can't even picture what this new, improved world would look like. Everyone comes clean about the shit they've done"—she threw her hands in the air—"and then what? At least Vitnik's got a plan. All you seem to have is self-help advice."

None of us had a good answer. I told Beltane I'd have to think about it.

49

A cry of surprise woke me. Molly was sitting up, working her phone. "There are thousands of them."

"Thousands of what?" Basquiat's voice was thick and sleepy.

Molly expanded her screen, which was filled with thumbnails. "I'm not sure. Videos. They're all tagged *Cast No Shadow*." She scrolled down until the thumbnails were one continuous blur. They just kept going.

"Silhouette posted one of the first." Rebe expanded her screen.

Silhouette was sitting alone in her house, uncharacteristically stone-faced. "I've got to be honest, I'm a lot more comfortable getting others to fess up than I am doing it myself, but I'm going to do this." She rolled her eyes toward the ceiling. "Let's see. I'll start with the big ones, since that's how it's supposed to be done. My first video, the one that made me, was staged."

"She's doing her own confession," Molly whispered.

"Look at this one. It's from a *nursing home.*" Boob expanded his screen. A dozen elderly people were sitting in a circle, a TV playing in the background, ignored. An old woman, her face a rugged landscape of wrinkles and age spots, was crying.

"I must have told my kids that story a hundred times. I got it from a romance book I'd read. The truth wasn't nearly as romantic. I was *married* when we met. Our marriage began as an affair, sneaking around behind Peter's wife's back." She paused to wipe her eyes. "To this day my kids don't know."

An old man who was wearing truth app rings said, "Thank you, Angela."

"They're all risking execution," Molly said. "I mean, Vitnik can't track down all of them, but she could make examples of some of them."

Meanwhile, we were hiding. But, what else could we do? If we came out of hiding, Vitnik wouldn't *maybe* make examples of us, she'd throw everything she had at us. Especially now that we'd released the video. If it was turning people to our side, we were a bigger threat to her than ever.

"What do we do now?" I asked.

"What do you mean?" Boob asked. "We lie low and wait for things to stabilize."

That didn't make sense. This was our chance—people were paying attention to us. We needed to keep the momentum going. I just didn't know how.

Beltane was sitting on the edge of a table with a rifle across her knees, watching from a distance. I still hadn't come up with an answer to her question from the night before.

It was the same question, though, wasn't it? Beltane wanted to know what came next, what our vision was. That's what we needed to tell everyone, except, as Boob had pointed out, people didn't want you to *tell* them, they wanted you to *show* them.

"Rebe? Can I communicate with Silhouette without giving away our location to Vitnik?"

"Vitnik's fighting for her life," Mom said. "I seriously doubt she has the time for surveillance." She looked to Rebe. "Is Vitnik even in control of the Pentagon?"

Rebe consulted her phone. "General Austin is."

"Then she doesn't have the electronics to track us. And I don't get the sense that Austin is focused on us."

"I'll still baffle the message." Rebe worked her phone.

Silhouette's face filled the screen. "Oh, thank goodness! You're still alive."

"Most of us. We lost some good people getting out of Trenton."

"I'm sorry to hear it."

"Keep it short," Rebe said.

"The video thing was brilliant, just brilliant," Silhouette said.

"Thanks. It was Boob's idea. But we need to follow up now."

"Yes, you do. Keep the momentum going. You have any ideas for an encore?"

"I do. It won't be easy, though."

"Assuming everyone doesn't hate me after the bombshell I dropped last night, I'm ready to help," Silhouette said.

"Thanks. What I'm thinking is, we have a summit and broadcast it live. Gather a bunch of smart, honest people and come up with a vision, a plan for moving forward."

"Yes." Silhouette moved closer to the screen. "I like it. Yes. Yes."

When we finished talking to Silhouette, Molly asked Rebe to set it up so she could call her mother and father. She promised to keep the calls short, then went outside where she could have some privacy.

50

It was a large, unremarkable movie theater with a redbrick-and-concrete facade on a block of office buildings and stores. We stood out more than the building: five teens flanked by a dozen heavily armed cybervets.

Silhouette was waiting out front. She led us inside.

"We have sort of a good problem. I invited forty people and told them to tell no one else the location, but it seems like half of them brought a few others with them. We're going to be packing well over a hundred into the theater. Maybe more."

Mom was shaking her head. "This is not good. What if someone figures out our location before we finish?"

"It's a chance we have to take," I said. "If we're going to meet a bunch of people, we have to meet *somewhere*. Movie theaters all look about the same from the inside. It's the best we could come up with."

Mom squeezed her eyes shut.

"What about General Austin?" I asked Silhouette.

She shook her head. "I reached out. Austin's not necessarily against the meeting, but it's too risky to ally herself with us."

That was a blow. I'd been hoping Austin would back us. That would have made things so much easier.

The vets had fanned out, one each at the entrances, two interrogating the handful of early birds using the truth app.

The theater was small, but it had a high ceiling and a balcony.

People were arriving in a steady stream now. A woman with long white hair touched another woman's shoulder and gestured toward me. When she saw I was looking her way, she gave me a warm smile.

"I'll wait a few more minutes, then I'm going to kick things off," Silhouette said. "I'll introduce you, then you can get the ball rolling."

"*Me?*" I poked my chest.

"This is your rodeo, Sam."

"No, Molly's our spokesperson."

"I'm our spokesperson, but this is a business meeting. They'll want to hear from the person in charge." Molly patted my back. "And that, my dear, is you."

As Silhouette hurried off to take care of something, I could almost hear my palms sweating. I didn't know who most of these people were, but they were all older than us, and most moved in the self-assured manner of people who knew they were important.

Molly put a hand on my arm. "Your eyes are bulging like a fish's. How about you put them back in their sockets."

"I can't. What the hell am I doing up here? We're talking about how to save civilization, and *I'm* leading the discussion? I'm seventeen."

"I'll jump in and help. And you know Basquiat and Rebe will, too."

Silhouette breezed down the aisle, toward the stage. "I'm going to get started."

By the time Silhouette finished speaking, the theater was almost full. The audience clapped as I stepped onto the hardwood stage. There was no podium. I just stood there in the center, my skinny arms hanging at my sides.

"Thank you for coming." I needed to channel Theo again, to let him speak. "The world was hanging by a thread. Not because there was too much honesty, but because of too many lies. President Vitnik—who murdered my friend Theo Harlow—wants to blame this mess on the truth app, but the app isn't the problem. It's the solution." I could feel my heart slowing as the words flowed. "We set out with Theo to create a better world—a bullshit-free world—"

The crowd was suddenly rumbling, people looking at each other. I looked at Molly, who was mouthing a word, but I couldn't make it out.

"Lie," she said out loud. "That was a lie."

A lie? What had I just said? My mind was suddenly blank. I could feel my face turning fire-engine red.

Then it came to me: I'd said, *We set out to create a*

bullshit-free world. No. We weren't nearly that noble at the start. I wasn't, at least.

"I can tell you brought your truth apps." That broke some of the tension, but definitely not all of it. "The truth is, I was in it for the money. I had no idea the truth app would have this sort of impact. But as time went by, I did realize, and it stopped being about the money."

I waited. When no one called me out, I went on.

"So now everything has to change. We don't need juries to guess whether someone's guilty. We can't have secrets. We can't negotiate deals the same way, because everyone knows everyone else's bottom line. And as my friend Boob pointed out, no more surprise parties."

That got a laugh.

"Someone has to figure out the new rules, and Silhouette thought *we* should give it a try." I held my hands out, palms up. "So where do we start?"

Fifty people began speaking at once.

I raised my hands over my head, shouted, "I think we're going to have to resort to raising hands!"

I called on a middle-aged woman at random.

"I'm Jezebel Knox. I run the political microchannel Green State. We need to elect new leaders. Like, right now. Power is going out all over. I heard the Internet could go down soon, and if that happens, things are going to go downhill fast. We need unified national leadership."

"I have an idea for that." A guy not much older than me stood, his hand in the air. "It's got to be quick, so we identify, say, ten qualified candidates. We hold a televised debate with a truth app running in the corner of the screen, and right after the debate, people vote electronically. The tallies show up in real time. An hour later"—he snapped his fingers—"we have an interim president."

"How would that carry any legitimacy?" a gray-haired guy in a sweatshirt called. "Who are we to run a presidential election?"

A woman in a charcoal suit stood. "Well, I'm a U.S. senator. Larissa Wasserman. There are at least two House members present as well—"

A guy in the back of the theater leaped out of his seat. *"Soldiers. Coming this way."*

People headed for the exits, rushing, but not panicking.

I bolted from the stage and huddled beside Rebe, who was on her phone. She brought up a live feed of soldiers packed into speeding transport vehicles.

"Where is that?" Mom asked.

"Six blocks from here."

Shrieks from the lobby pierced the air. It sounded like people in pain. We raced to the lobby as gunfire erupted outside. A dozen people were sitting on the floor, others kneeling beside them or standing over them.

"Heat guns," someone said.

The gunfire went on. It sounded like it was coming from the roof, where some of the vets had taken up positions.

"An advance force, to pin us down until the main force arrives," Mom said. "We have to get out now." The last few words were drowned by escalating automatic weapon fire outside.

"We're too late." Mr. Chambliss was kneeling, peering through the bottom of a window. "Looks like a full battalion."

"What's a full battalion?" I asked Mom.

"Three to six hundred troops." She raised her voice. "Do we know whose they are?"

"Vitnik's," Rebe called over the gunfire.

Mom pounded her forehead with the heel of her hand. "This was so *stupid*. Too many people knew about it. I should have turned us back as soon as I saw all these people."

Most of the gunfire stopped. A megaphone blared to life. *"You are in violation of the ban on possession of lie detection devices. Exit the facility five at a time with your hands up."*

"Don't do it," Mr. Chambliss said. "They'll drag you away and shoot you."

Silhouette was beside me, her feed open, thousands of penny-sized screens swarming above her. Now that we'd been found, there was no need to maintain Internet silence.

"If any of your followers happen to know General Austin, tell her it's time to get her ass off the fence," I said. "Either she's okay with Vitnik slaughtering civilians, or she should get down here and stop it. We could use a little help."

"That's for damned sure," Silhouette said.

"We could try to punch a hole in their perimeter, get the kids out," I heard Beltane saying to Mom.

"They'll close ranks around us as soon as we're outside," Mom said.

"Maybe use that against them? One group tries to punch through as a diversion, then another punches the kids through a thinned-out spot?" Beltane suggested.

"Vitnik's here," Rebe said, eyes on her screen.

Mom turned. *"Where?"*

"A kid snapped a picture of her coming out of FBI headquarters two blocks away, and posted it to Patterlink."

"She wants to be here to gloat when they drag us out," I said. They were going to broadcast our execution live on News America.

Mom was staring into space with that unfocused look, her mouth a tight, angry line.

"Mom?" I said.

She snapped out of it, turned to Rebe. "I need a map of this area."

The map flashed to life. Rebe expanded it, rotated it to face Mom.

"Beltane?" Mom pointed at the map as Beltane joined her. "We go roof to roof to the far end of the block. Then a fifty-four-foot jump over Ninth Street to the roof on the far side."

"Piece of cake," Beltane said.

"Drop to ground level on Eighth, circle around to the FBI building. Let's assume they're all in bulletproof gear, so we close and dispatch hand to hand."

I had to stifle the cry of hope rising in my throat. They were going to try to take Vitnik. Brilliant. My mother was brilliant.

"Rebe, any updates to Vitnik's location, send them immediately," Mom said.

"You got it."

"Hold them back, whatever it takes!" Mom shouted to Mr. Chambliss as she and Beltane headed for the stairwell.

Outside, the guy with the megaphone had gone from barking orders to making threats. We had eight minutes to comply.

"They've got a howitzer!" Mr. Chambliss shouted from the window. "If there's a basement, everybody get in it."

People headed for the stairwell. We waited until most of them were down before following.

The basement was a dingy, low-ceilinged space with a concrete floor and exposed two-by-fours. It was packed with people.

"I've got live feed of Vitnik." Rebe worked her phone. "I'm sending it to Melissa and Beltane."

The feed was being sent from a window maybe two blocks from Vitnik, who was standing in the street with the vice president, intently watching a feed of the assault on the theater. I counted six soldiers surrounding Vitnik and the VP, plus one Secret Service agent. The agent was Xavier Leaf. One of the soldiers had a grenade launcher mounted on his rifle. Their faces were framed in the tight hoods of bulletproof jumpsuits.

All over the room, people watched the feed, silent.

"Holy crap!" a girl's voice cried over the feed.

Mom and Beltane had gotten a long running start and

were coming around the corner at a good forty miles per hour. Beltane was in the lead, holding a manhole cover in front of her face, with Mom drafting on her heels. They were an awesome sight. Holy crap was right.

They got within fifty feet of the soldiers before anyone noticed. Two of the soldiers were quick enough to open fire before Beltane reached them, but the soldier with the grenade launcher wasn't one of them. Beltane plowed into them with the manhole cover.

It was a horrific sight. Beltane went straight at the soldier with the grenade launcher; the steel plate hit him face-first, and he went down like he'd been yanked. Beltane ran right over him and slammed into another soldier, who was thrown into yet another.

Mom had broken off when they reached the soldiers. She'd taken one down while I was watching Beltane; he was writhing on the pavement. Mom kicked a second in the spine, then spun and threw a side kick to Xavier Leaf's pelvis. Even with the microphone a good two hundred yards away, I thought I heard it snap.

Mom got her hands up to cover her face just as one of the two soldiers still standing hit her point-blank with a burst from his assault rifle. I shouted as Mom fell backward and writhed on the ground as the bullets went on pelting her.

Beltane's fist came out of nowhere, landing right on the soldier's face. He crumpled like a deflated doll.

Beltane looked around, spotted Vitnik halfway down the block, heading toward the soldiers outside the theater.

The president made it three more steps before Beltane tackled her from behind, taking her down hard.

As a roar went through the room, all eyes on Beltane, I watched Mom in the foreground. Almost doubled over with pain, she was standing over Leaf. She said something, then stomped on his leg. Then she stomped the other one.

I knew exactly what she'd just said: *This is for Theo Harlow. And this is for Kelsey Cook.*

"Look out!" someone shouted.

Soldiers had spotted Beltane and Vitnik. Dozens raced toward them, rifles raised. Except they couldn't fire, because they'd hit Vitnik.

Beltane grabbed Vitnik around the neck and took off, dragging her down the street at thirty miles per hour. One of Vitnik's shoes popped off and bounced after her before rolling to a stop. Mom led the way as they disappeared around the corner.

Basquiat wrapped his right arm around my neck and drew me close to him. He had his left arm around Molly. I wrapped one arm around his waist and the other around Rebe's as we formed a tight circle. What a beautiful day it had become. We might not be killed after all.

A clacking sound rose in the stairwell—bladed feet coming down the steps. The door burst open. Mom stepped through and held it open for Beltane, who dragged Vitnik through, then dropped her like a sack in the center of the room. Vitnik thumped to the floor and immediately clutched her neck, gasping. Both of her shoes were missing;

her heels were a raw, bloody mess from being dragged along rough pavement at high speed.

Beltane bent and frisked the president. She pulled something from her jacket pocket and held it out.

A pair of truth app rings.

"We're supposed to shoot you on sight for having these, isn't that right?" Mom asked.

Slowly, carefully, Vitnik sat up. "You can't allow your enemy to have a tactical advantage. No matter how dangerous a weapon, if your enemy has it, you damned well better have it, too." She looked right at me. "I warned you. I told you the world couldn't handle these things."

"I don't recall that. I was having some trouble with my hearing at the time."

"I'll do whatever it takes to protect the American people." Vitnik drew her knees up toward her chest, wincing as her heels left bloody skid marks across the tile. "You still don't get that you are the bad guys here. You're going to be remembered long after I'm forgotten. Whether as evil or just incredibly stupid, I don't know."

The needle on the truth app didn't budge. She really believed that.

"Keep her here." Doubled over, one arm pressed to her stomach, Mom headed for the stairwell. I caught up to her and helped her up the stairs.

"Are you all right?"

"My arm is broken. Some ribs." Her breathing was sharp and shallow.

At the ground floor I opened the door for her.

Mr. Chambliss rushed over. "Are you all right?"

"Nothing serious."

Mom headed for the front doors, pushed one open a foot, and shouted, "Move one step closer, and Vitnik dies!"

No reply.

"You've got five minutes to stand down. If you're not out of my sight by then, we start pulling off her fingers and tossing them out to you."

The graphicness of the threat surprised me, but I was sure it was a bluff.

"We're sending a negotiator to you," Megaphone Man said. "She is unarmed."

"Yeah, yeah." Mom let the door swing shut and sank to the floor.

Mr. Chambliss sat beside her. "What are you thinking?"

"They allow everyone to walk out. I stay behind with Vitnik. Once I get verbal confirmation from Sam that you're free and clear, I execute Vitnik."

"Mom, no way."

Mom squeezed her eyes shut. She was completely spent. "She's not leaving here alive."

"If you kill her, they kill *you*. It's not worth it, just to get revenge."

"It's not about revenge." Mom's voice was hoarse. "If she goes free, she'll keep coming after you until she kills you. She *has* to stop you; it's the only way she can change the narrative and retake power."

"Tanks!" Beltane called.

Mr. Chambliss and I helped Mom up. A line of tanks were rolling down the street. They were shiny and black, bubble-topped.

Mom looked like she might throw up. "They have to know we'll kill Vitnik the second they start firing those."

"The VP got away. Maybe he's giving the orders now," Beltane suggested.

Mom turned to Beltane. "Go downstairs. If they shell the building, put a bullet in Vitnik's head immediately."

Beltane headed for the stairwell.

Outside, the lead tank pulled to a stop. Its long turret rotated.

Away from us.

Toward Vitnik's troops.

The speaker in the lead tank was way louder than the guy with the megaphone. *"Back off, sandbags, or we will turn you into airborne ground beef."*

"Austin," I said.

"How do you know?" Mom asked.

"I called her out on Silhouette's feed. I wasn't sure if she'd come, or whose side she'd be on if she did, but I figured it was worth a shot."

Mr. Chambliss grabbed my head in both hands, bent, and kissed my cheek. "Beautiful. You're beautiful."

Mom pulled a handgun from her belt. "Beautiful is right." She limped toward the stairwell.

"Mom." I knew exactly what she was planning to do. I had

as much reason to hate Vitnik as she did, but the thought of executing Vitnik made my stomach churn. Here, of all places.

I caught her halfway down the stairs. "Don't do this. This isn't who we are."

"Melissa, don't," Mr. Chambliss called after us.

Mom pushed through the door, stumbled from the effort, and fell to one knee. She struggled to her feet and headed toward Vitnik, who was right where we'd left her on the floor.

"We are not the Pilgrims of Truth. We're not Vitnik." I wrapped my arms around Mom's waist and tried to stop her. She pulled me along effortlessly with her bionic legs until she was standing in front of Vitnik.

Vitnik looked up at her.

Mom spit on her, then turned away, into Mr. Chambliss's arms. She pressed her face into his shoulder.

"I think we're safe," I said loud enough for everyone to hear. "General Austin's forces are outside—"

The door swung open. Senator Wasserman came through, followed by General Austin in military dress uniform and flanked by two heavily armed soldiers.

General Austin spotted Vitnik and strode over to her.

"I never liked you. Even before the big revelation, I thought you were a histrionic clown," Austin said.

Vitnik didn't look up. "I guess we'll see if you can do any better."

"Me?" Austin chuckled. "You're so obsessed with being

important you can't imagine someone being motivated by anything but power." She turned to face me, gave me a knuckle-grinding handshake while looking me up and down.

"My ass is not completely off the fence about this. You're going to have to convince me." General Austin looked around, then turned back to me. "Silhouette Lark said there's some kind of a think tank going on here. Fill me in on what the tank is thinking."

51

I wasn't nervous. I should have been, but I wasn't. My friends didn't look nervous, either, except for Boob, back from New City for the moment and sitting in the front row of Ford's Theatre watching the rest of us prepare to moderate a debate that was hopefully going to stave off an apocalypse.

Mr. Chambliss looked nervous. As I scanned the candidates, sitting in chairs we'd dragged onto the stage from various rooms, Mr. Chambliss caught my eye and glared.

What the hell have you gotten me into? his eyes asked. Not just me. It had been my idea, but everyone had pressured him, especially Mom.

Ten candidates. Ten people who had some sort of leadership experience and weren't afraid to face the truth app while millions watched.

Silhouette did the opening. Senator Wasserman had wanted her to read from a teleprompter; Silhouette responded by feigning sticking her finger down her throat. When she was finished explaining how this would work, and how viewers could vote afterward, she invited me to ask the first question.

I stepped up to a candidate at random and looked for his name on the note card I was holding. "Mr. Elling, are there things about you that you wouldn't want anyone to know?"

He nodded. "Yes."

"Can you tell us what those things are, please?"

He raised his eyebrows. "*All* of them?"

"Start with the worst. Ms. Lark will signal when your time is up."

As the congressman from North Carolina began confessing to a career built on doing favors for people with money, I checked Mr. Chambliss, who looked like he was getting ready to swallow a mouthful of bugs. He was right to be afraid. I wanted him to be chosen, but we'd go just as hard on him as we planned to on everyone else.

Even assuming enough people are foolish enough to vote for an unemployed science teacher for president, why in the world would I want to be president of the United States of Titanic? he'd asked when I told him we wanted him to be one of the candidates.

I understand you don't want to do it, I'd shot back. *That's one of the reasons you'd be perfect.*

In the end, Mom had been the one who persuaded him.

————

I stepped up to Mr. Chambliss. "You know the drill. Give us your worst."

Mr. Chambliss raised his eyebrows. "For starters, I was complicit in a scheme to rob veterans' graves for parts." He folded his arms across his chest. "I can probably stop there. That alone makes me unfit for this position."

"Maybe it does, and maybe it doesn't. Go on."

Mr. Chambliss glared up at me through bushy white eyebrows. "You're enjoying the hell out of this, aren't you?"

"No." I wasn't enjoying watching Mr. Chambliss squirm. I trusted him—I honestly thought he was the best chance we had. I waited.

"Fine. Remember that picture I showed you, of me with my unit? They're all dead. All my friends died, including my first wife. None of them made it home. Not one."

"I'm sorry, but I don't understand. Why is that second on your list? Why is that something you don't want people to know?"

Mr. Chambliss gave me a familiar look, one he used in class when he thought I was being particularly dense. "It's why I didn't want to help you in the first place, and—until I fell in love with your mom—why I contemplated walking away every day. I don't want to get too close to anyone."

"Because you don't want to lose anyone else."

Mr. Chambliss nodded tightly.

I felt like I had to say something to break the silence, so I said, "Thank you," and took my seat.

Even when he had been our teacher, there was always

that tension there, that push and pull. He didn't want to hear about our personal lives, didn't want us to bother him after hours, yet it was obvious he cared about us.

Rebe stepped up to Mr. Chambliss. "Why do you want to be interim president?"

"I *don't*."

People erupted in laughter. He was telling the absolute truth.

"Let me put it another way, then," Rebe said. "Why did you agree to do this?"

"Because people asked me to. People I care about."

"*Lie*," Boob called from his seat. Basquiat, Molly, and I burst out laughing. No one else got the inside joke. All they knew was, Mr. Chambliss had just goosed the needle.

Mr. Chambliss looked baffled. "If that's not the truth, then I have no idea why I agreed to do this."

"*Lie*," Boob called again.

Mr. Chambliss looked downright uncomfortable. He swallowed a few times, blinking rapidly. "Let me think about this."

"Take your time," Rebe said gently.

Mr. Chambliss looked around, glancing at me, at Boob, at Molly, his gaze finally settling on Mom. "Maybe it's because I fell in love with a woman—a strong woman, a warrior. I'm afraid I'm too weak for her. Maybe I'm doing this to prove to her, and to myself, that I'm worthy of her love."

I was biased, and I got only one vote like everyone else, but he was my pick.

Basquiat was up next. "Mr. Chambliss, what should we do with all the people who got away with crimes before the truth app appeared?"

Mr. Chambliss uncrossed his legs, recrossed them the other way. "I would draw a line between violent crimes and others. Murder, felonious assault, rape—the people who commit such crimes go to prison." He raised his voice. "Along with all the asshats out there taking justice into their own hands. Everyone else gets a mulligan."

"A *mulligan?*" Basquiat said. "I'm sorry, I'm not familiar with the term."

"A do-over."

"We just let them all off the hook?" Basquiat sounded surprised. "Thieves? Blackmailers?"

"They're not off the hook. In this new world they'll always be at a disadvantage, whether it's finding a job or meeting a new love interest. But if we're going to survive, we have to look toward the future, not build more prisons." He turned toward the other candidates. "Whoever ends up in charge, I hope you'll consider this. Allow people to come clean. Start the clock fresh. Fifty years ago, Nelson Mandela did it successfully in South Africa when apartheid was vanquished. If we can pull out of this tailspin, we won't have much of a crime problem going forward."

People had thirty minutes to vote, but as the returns came in on a virtual screen, the outcome was clear after five.

"Oh, hell," Mr. Chambliss groaned. "Seriously? You're going to pick the guy who's only doing this to impress a woman?"

Sitting in the first row, assault rifle pinched between her knees, Mom had tears in her eyes. She seemed duly impressed.

52

I wasn't prepared for the elation I felt as we rolled off the Parkway exit ramp. It was good to be home, if only for a visit. Yes, the lawns were still waist-high with weeds, and the shoulders of New Hempstead Road were still caked with years of accumulated trash, but they were familiar weeds and trash.

And who knew? Maybe one day the lawns would be green oases again, the roads clean. Anything seemed possible.

We stopped to pick up Boob, then headed to my house to see if there was anything left. It was burned to the ground, charred shingles, bits of furniture, wood, and unidentifiable burnt things strewn a hundred feet from the littered foundation.

As we made our way through the debris, Boob bent, picked something up. It was a sock.

"Hey, see? It's not a total loss." He tossed the sock in

my direction. It was good to see Boob's sense of humor returning.

"You stupid bastards." A middle-aged guy in a New York Mets sweatshirt was standing in the road, fists on his hips, glaring at us.

Mom eyed the guy, her rifle pointed at the ground.

"Excuse me?" Basquiat said.

"You ruined me." He threw his hands in the air. "I have no way to make a living now, even if we recover from this mess you made."

"How did you make a living before we ruined everything?" Basquiat asked.

The guy folded his arms. "I'm a criminal defense attorney."

We burst out laughing.

"You think that's funny? I have kids to feed."

I took a few steps toward him, still chuckling. "I'm sorry about a lot of things, mister, but making it easy to convict criminals isn't one of them. If you need a job, Rebe here is starting up a truth app factory. Stop by once it's up and running. I'm sure she'll give you a job if you pass the interview."

"Sure, no problem," Rebe said.

The lawyer shook his head, stuffed his hands in his pockets. "Manual labor. That's what I'm reduced to."

Clearly, he would make a valuable addition to Rebe and Mott's workforce.

"Come on. You and your mom can stay with me while you're here," Basquiat said.

"I was going to make the same offer," Molly added.

"You know what?" Basquiat put one arm across my shoulders, the other across Molly's, and turned us both toward the van. "That's an even better idea. Stay at Molly's." He caught my eye and winked.

Rebe let go of Boob's hand to answer her phone. After a brief conversation, she lifted her head. "Mott's looking at a factory in Spring Valley. Can we go look at it so I can get your opinions?"

"Suddenly you're a couple of legit businesswomen," I said. "I don't know, you're going to lose your outlaw mystique."

"And you're going to lose a lot of money," she shot back.

That was very true. After sharing the truth app plans with the world and donating my share of Rebe and Mott's enterprise to Beltane and Basquiat's effort to help hungry and orphaned kids, I wasn't going to be rich the way I'd dreamed when all this started. The truth was, my dreams had changed. I wanted to be with Mr. Chambliss and Mom in DC, helping to get the government running and the country back on its feet. Instead of becoming a rich tycoon, I thought I might run for office someday.

On Germond Road, we passed a couple of cops on bicycles. I glanced back at them. "Those are the guys! The cops who made me run laps around the supermarket."

"Stop the van," Mom said.

"Can I do it? Please let me do it," Beltane said.

Mom broke into a smile. "If it'll make your day, go on."

Beltane hopped out of the van on the passenger side. The cops slowed.

"You want to move out of the way?" my pal the red-faced cop said. This felt a little like Christmas morning when I was a kid.

"No, I don't," Beltane said.

The cops rolled to a stop. Red Face reached for his revolver.

"Ah-ah. Drop it." Mom poked the muzzle of her assault rifle out the window.

"This is perfect. I wonder if they'll remember me." I stepped out of the van.

Both cops' eyes went wide.

"You're the lie detector guy," Blondie said.

"No, I'm the guy you shook down behind Pathmark. You took my money and made me run laps. Remember?"

Blondie shook his head. "No."

Laughter erupted from the van.

"*Lie!*" Boob shouted out the window.

Beltane held out one hand. "Give me those damned uniforms. It hurts my eyes to see you in them. You're a disgrace." When the cops just stood there, mouths hanging open, she added, "Now. *Move.*"

Red Face looked at Blondie.

"*Move.*"

They stripped off their uniforms, dropping them into Beltane's outstretched hand. Red Face pulled his wallet from his back pocket before turning over his pants. He was wearing lime-green briefs.

"You owe me six dollars," I said.

He opened his wallet, pulled out the cash, and handed it to Beltane.

"You also owe me twenty-four laps."

"Around what?" Red Face asked.

"The van."

I climbed back into the van and closed the door.

"You heard him. Get going." Beltane pointed.

As they started jogging, Beltane got in as well.

"One!" I shouted as they finished their first lap.

"Two!" everyone in the van shouted as they completed their second. They were trying to act cool, like it was no big thing, like they didn't feel the least bit self-conscious jogging in the road in their underwear.

Mom turned in her seat. "We really don't have time to wait while they do twenty-four laps."

"Let's just stay until it stops being funny," Rebe said.

"It's never going to stop being funny," Basquiat said.

"Seven!" everyone shouted.

They were not in very good shape for police officers. By lap nine, Blondie was bent like he already had a stitch.

"Ten!"

"All right." I was laughing so hard tears were running down my cheeks. "I'm feeling a sense of closure for this particular emotional wound."

Mom put the van in gear, and we drove off.

———

It was strange to sit facing a thick copse of trees and not worry that a sniper was centering a laser target on my forehead. I guess it was still possible that one of the many people who hated what we'd done could be in those woods training a rifle on me (that lawyer, for one, came to mind), but with Vitnik in prison, and Xavier Leaf not only in prison but potentially unable to ever walk again, the odds seemed lower.

I took a deep breath of the cool evening air, felt the familiar stab of pain in my right side. It wasn't as bad as a few weeks ago, at least, and most of the contusions from the other shots had healed.

The door opened. Molly stepped onto the porch, dragged a lawn chair over, and set it beside me.

"It's looking like maybe eighty percent of the active military and National Guard are willing to accept Mr. Chambliss as the legitimate commander in chief, with Austin backing him."

"Which means more civil war. Either that or President Chambliss has a country with a bunch of holes in it that are controlled by warlords."

"He knows that won't work," Molly said. "General Austin's drawing up battle plans. But on the bright side, President Chambliss has already organized what's left of Congress to start planning new elections, so that doesn't suck."

I let that sink in for a minute. Good news. Maybe we'd hit bottom and were headed in the other direction.

"We did good, didn't we?" I asked. "I mean, a lot of people have died, but in the long run?"

"We did good."

"I keep thinking of Claire Mika, that twelve-year-old girl with the colostomy bag."

"I know," Molly said.

"Secrets aren't the same as lies. The truth app doesn't know that."

Molly nodded. "It's way messier than we thought it would be."

"I miss Theo." I don't know what that had to do with what we were talking about. It just came out.

"Yeah."

We listened to the crickets. The wind kicked up, rustled the leaves in the darkness.

"So, my dad is coming home," Molly said.

"Oh my God. That's great!" The whole condom wrapper thing meant nothing now. Molly didn't have to feel guilty anymore.

"Mom said after I was almost killed about four times, it gave her some perspective on the whole thing. And there's more: we're thinking of moving to DC."

I raised my fists in the air. "That would be unbelievable. We could work together for Mr. Chambliss."

"That's what I was thinking." Molly scooted her chair so she was angled toward me. "Which is why I think we need to talk. I've been trying to steer a conversation toward this topic, but I'm getting no reaction, so I figured I'd just clear the air."

"I haven't noticed any steering."

"It was subtle. And you're not all that socially astute."

"No, I'm not."

Molly was looking at her hands. "With all that's happened, I've honestly lost track of what's going on between us. Are we together and we just haven't had time to notice? Are we best friends? What the hell is going on?"

"I . . . don't know. It's been a while since I've had time to think about it."

"Same here." She looked up. "Have you noticed that even when we're not using the truth app, we pause for just an instant before speaking now, to make sure what we're going to say is true?"

I paused for an instant before answering. "Yes."

Molly made a popping sound with her lips. "I'm probably making this more awkward than it has to be, but I guess I'm getting used to dragging things out into the open. I have feelings for you, but, I don't know, it's like . . ." She cast about, trying to put her finger on what it was like.

I looked into her eyes—really looked into them like I'd never looked into anyone's eyes before. What I found was, you really can't look into someone's eyes. The best you can do is look into one eye or the other, or flick back and forth between them.

I leaned in. We missed each other's lips slightly and had to readjust, but like Rebe said, it's not something you do right or wrong, it's something you do. The key was who you were doing it with.

As we kissed, I realized I was doing it with my best

friend, who, before everything had happened, I was convinced I loved madly.

I remembered feeling those feelings, and I remembered being the Sam who had felt them. There hadn't been a drop of blood on his squeaky-clean hands.

That Sam was long gone.

We separated, leaning back into our respective seats.

"Is it like, what you feel for me is a memory of a feeling?" I asked.

Molly gave me a melancholy smile. "You're not socially astute, but you're very wise. There's nothing left of that girl you had a crush on. The boy who had the crush is long gone, too."

"Truth," I said.

Molly leaned forward, looking a little surprised, maybe a little disappointed. "You have your truth app activated?"

"Nah."

"Oh." She relaxed back into her chair. "Good."

Molly straightened her lawn chair so it was facing the yard again.

"You know what would be amazing?" I asked.

"What?"

"If there comes a day when people are so used to telling the truth that we don't even need truth apps anymore, and all these rings end up in landfills."

"Now, *that* would be the best day ever."

"Wouldn't it?"

We gazed off into the trees in comfortable silence, listening to the crickets chirp.

ACKNOWLEDGMENTS

I'm grateful to Joy Marchand Davis and Ian Creasey, whose feedback on the first draft of this book (and many others before it) was invaluable.

To James Pugh, who was once again just a phone call away with some fantastic suggestion whenever I got stuck. Thanks, Jim!

To Kenneth Tagher, who provided crucial guidance on how a bunch of very smart kids might go about creating a portable lie detector. Whether I'm asking about genetics, electrical engineering, quantum physics, or neuropsychology, Kenneth can always provide a detailed scenario about how the science might actually work.

Thank you to my agent, Seth Fishman, who got me started writing YA, and who always has my back.

Sincere thanks to my editor, Kate Sullivan, who fixed the ending, and many things prior to it, and championed my unusual choice of title.

And, as always, thanks to my wife, Alison Scott, for her support and encouragement, and to the twins for understanding that sometimes Dad has to write, even though he'd rather discuss *Monster High* or *Five Nights at Freddy's*.

Turn the page for an excerpt from Will McIntosh's first thrilling YA novel, *Burning Midnight*!

CHAPTER 1

Sully pulled the thin wad of bills from his pocket and counted. Thirteen bucks. He'd hauled his butt out of bed at six a.m. on a Saturday to make thirteen bucks in seven hours. He couldn't work out how much that was per hour, but he knew Dom made more stacking yogurt and cream cheese at Price Chopper.

The flea market was depressingly empty. Most of the other vendors were parked on lawn chairs, their feet propped on tables. Sully spent enough time sitting in school, so he was standing, arms folded.

The timing of this epically bad payday couldn't be worse. It would have given his mom a lift, for Sully to hand her a hundred bucks to put toward the rent or groceries.

He still couldn't believe Exile Music had closed. Nine and a half years, Mom had worked there. By the end she'd been their manager, their accountant, their everything. But she had no accounting degree; she didn't even have a high school diploma. Where was she going to find another job that paid half of what she'd been making?

Sully took a deep, sighing breath and stared down the long aisle.

A girl around Sully's age turned the corner and headed in his direction. He watched her walk, head down, beat-up backpack slung over one shoulder. There was a swagger to her walk, a little attitude. Or maybe the combat boots, the black gloves with the fingertips cut off, the mass of dark braids bouncing off her back like coils of rope provided the attitude.

As she drew closer, Sully looked at his phone instead of staring. It was hard not to stare.

To Sully's surprise, she slowed when she reached his stall. She eyed the orbs he kept locked under glass, running her tongue over her teeth. She was wearing loose-fitting cargo pants and zero makeup. Her brown angular face was striking, her take-no-shit scowl a little intimidating. Not your usual flea market customer.

He cleared his throat. "Anything I can help you with?"

She studied him, squinted, as if he was slightly out of focus. She unslung the bag on her shoulder and knelt out of sight in front of his table.

When she reappeared she was clutching a sphere—a Forest Green. Enhanced sense of smell. Sully didn't have to consult the book to know it scored a three out of ten on the rarity chart. Retail, he could easily get six hundred for it.

"How much?" she asked, holding it up.

His heart was hammering. This one deal could make his whole weekend. "Wow. You find that in the wild?" She didn't strike him as a collector or an investor.

She nodded. "It was caked in mud. I thought it was an

Army Green." Which was a big fat one on the rarity chart. Resistance to the common cold. Sixty bucks.

"Man, you must have died when you cleaned it off."

"How much?" she repeated, with the slightest of nods to acknowledge his comment.

Sully tried to remember how much cash he had on him. Two fifty? Maybe two seventy. Usually that was more than enough, because who brought a Forest Green to a flea market?

His gaze flicked between the Forest Green and the girl's face. "Two fifty?" His voice rose at the last minute, making it sound more like a question.

The girl chuckled, bent to pick up her pack. "I can get three twenty-five from Holliday's."

Sully flinched when she said "Holliday's," but to her credit, she said it like it hurt her mouth.

"Hang on. I can go to three fifty, but I can't get you the last hundred till tomorrow." He'd have to borrow it from Dom.

The girl put a hand on her hip. "I'm sorry. Did I give you the impression I thought three twenty-five was a fair price? Let me rephrase: even the bastards over at Holliday's would give me three twenty-five."

Sully laughed in spite of himself. They *were* bastards. The brand-new store they'd opened in Yonkers was a big part of why Sully's earnings had taken a nosedive. And Alex Holliday himself was more than a bastard. Sully squelched any thought of Holliday before that particular train of thought could start running down the track.

He did some quick calculations. This girl could list the Forest Green on eBay and get at least four fifty. Minus eBay's cut, that would leave her with about four hundred.

"Okay. Four twenty-five." Two hundred dollars profit. He could definitely dance to that tune.

The girl scowled, opened her mouth to counter. Sully raised his hand. "Don't even try to tell me that's not a fair offer." He looked her in the eye. "We both know it is."

She held her scowl a second longer, then broke into a smile. It was a terrific smile, complete with dimples. "You got me. Four twenty-five."

He pulled the cash from his pocket, started counting it out. "Like I said, I can give you two fifty now, the rest next Saturday."

The girl's eyebrows came together. "I hope you're not thinking I'm going to give you this marble now. If you'll have the cash next week, I'll come back with the marble then."

Sully licked his lips, which were dry as hell. If she left, there was always a chance she wouldn't come back. It had happened before; it was never a good idea to give people time to find a better offer.

"Look, I'll give you a receipt. I'm good for it; I'm here every weekend." Sully spotted Neal across the aisle, unpacking used DVDs from a cardboard box. "Neal!"

Neal lifted his head. He was wearing Ron Jon sunglasses despite being indoors, in a cavernous room that was not particularly well lit.

"Can she trust me?" Sully asked, holding his palms out.

Neal stabbed a finger in Sully's direction. "You can trust that man with your life."

From the next booth over, Samantha shouted, "And that's the truth!" and crossed herself. Samantha was Neal's wife, so her testimonial was somewhat redundant, but the girl with the Forest Green didn't need to know that.

Sully turned back to the girl. She folded her arms. "I wouldn't trust my *grandma* with that kind of money."

"Hey, Sully?" Sully hadn't noticed the kid hovering at the corner of his booth. He was twelve or thirteen, Indian, holding a replica sphere—a Cherry Red. "Would you sign this?"

"Sure." Sully reached for the replica and a Sharpie the kid offered, feeling a flush of pleasure that the girl was there to witness this.

"You sure you can trust me with this?" Sully asked as he signed.

The kid laughed.

Sully blew the ink dry, tossed the kid the Cherry Red, said, "Thanks, man. Thanks for asking."

"What was that about?" the girl asked, motioning toward the kid, who was disappearing around a corner.

Sully held out his hand. "David Sullivan." When the girl only looked at his hand, he added, "I'm the guy who found the Cherry Red."

"I know who David Sullivan is." She sounded annoyed. "A millionaire for ten minutes, until Alex Holliday's lawyers stopped payment on the check. Tiny Tim ripped off by New York's favorite billionaire."

The words stung like hot sauce on a wound, but Sully couldn't deny she was just stating the facts without any sugarcoating.

She held the Forest Green by her ear like a shot-putter. "Moving on. We got a deal? I'll see you Saturday?"

"Tell you what." Still trying to shake off her words, Sully took out his key ring, unlocked the display case, and pulled out his two most valuable spheres—a Lemon Yellow (grow an inch) and a Slate Gray (singing ability). Both were rarity level two; together they were worth about two sixty. "Take these as collateral. They're worth way more than one seventy-five. I'll trust *you*."

She considered, looking down at the spheres, then back up at Sully. She scooped the spheres out of his hand and stashed them in her pack. After exchanging numbers in case one of them couldn't make it next week, Sully counted the cash out on the table. She stuffed it in her back pocket and, finally, pressed the cool Forest Green sphere into his slightly sweaty palm.

"See you next Saturday," she said, and turned away.

Sully watched her go, her wrists flicking as she walked.

"Hey," he called after her.

She turned.

"What's your name?"

She smiled. "Hunter."

"As in, marble hunter?"

She pointed at him. "You got it."

"Maybe we'll do more business in the future, then?"

Hunter nodded. "Works for me if your offers are straight."

Sully nodded. "See you Saturday."

When Hunter was out of sight, he held the Forest Green up, rotated it, admiring.

"She's a beauty," Neal called over. His buzz cut always seemed wrong to Sully; his bright, open face just cried out for long, surfer-dude hair.

"I nearly choked when she pulled it out. I've never had a Forest Green before."

"I wasn't talking about the marble," Neal said, laughing.

Sully grinned but said nothing. She was fine, no doubt about it, but not his type. Too serious. Sully liked to laugh.

"I met my first wife at a flea market." Neal put his hand on top of his head. "She was . . . dazzling. Long auburn hair, freckles dusted across her cheeks."

"You do know I can hear you, right?" Samantha called from behind her table, which was covered in tarot cards, crystals, incense.

Neal acted like he'd been jolted out of a trance. "Sorry." He grinned at Sully. "Did I say dazzling? I meant frumpy. Face like a Mack truck. Anyway, back then I was selling Grateful Dead memorabilia—"

"And pirated concert tapes," Samantha interjected.

Sully laughed. "The Grateful *who*?"

Neal didn't take the bait. He knew Sully knew who the Grateful Dead were, because he'd lent Sully one of their CDs. He also knew they put Sully to sleep.

Samantha crossed the aisle and, without a word, set a sandwich wrapped in tinfoil on Sully's table. She always made an extra for him.

"Thanks, Samantha." She patted Sully's shoulder as she passed.

Sully munched on a homemade meat loaf hero as Neal went on with his story. Sully wouldn't want to trade places with Neal, but he had to admit, the guy had led an interesting life. Well into his sixties, he'd never had a real job with a steady paycheck. He and Samantha lived in a little camper that Sully knew well from the many times they'd invited him to hang out after the flea market closed.

After ten years of sharing an apartment with his mom, Sully'd had more than enough of living in cramped spaces. As of last Tuesday, they were in danger of losing even that. If something didn't give, by summer they'd be living in the basement of his weird uncle Ian's house in Pittsburgh. That couldn't happen. It just couldn't. Sully's friends were in Yonkers; his life was in Yonkers.

He tossed the Forest Green in the air and caught it, relishing the hard, perfect smoothness as the sphere slapped his palm. It was a start. Later, he'd call a few of his regular customers and see if anyone was interested in it. If not, he'd put it in the display case. It wouldn't be hard to sell. The values on the rarer spheres just kept rising, and Sully kept his prices ten or fifteen percent below the big retailers'.

They'd get through this; they'd keep the apartment. In two years he'd graduate from Yonkers High with Dom by his side.

ABOUT THE AUTHOR

Will McIntosh is the author of several adult speculative fiction novels and a frequent short-story writer. He has received a Hugo Award for Best Short Story and been named to the RUSA Reading List for Science Fiction, and his first young adult novel, *Burning Midnight*, was a Locus Award finalist and an ALA-YALSA Teens' Top Ten nominee. In addition, Will wrote *Watchdog* for middle-grade readers. Will lives with his wife and twin children in Williamsburg, Virginia. *The Future Will Be BS-Free* is his second novel for young adults. Visit him online at willmcintosh.net and follow @WillMcIntoshSF on Twitter.